USA TODAY bestselling aut━━━━━━━━━━━━━━━
is read in multiple language━━━━━━━━━━━━━━
her sweet romances writing ━━━━━━━━━━━
steamy romances as Emily E K Murdoch. Emily's
had a varied career to date, from examining medieval
manuscripts to designing museum exhibitions,
working as a researcher for the BBC to working for
the National Trust. Her books' settings range from
England 1050 to Texas 1848, and she can't wait for
you to fall in love with her heroes and heroines!

Also by Emily E K Murdoch

The Wallflower Academy miniseries

Least Likely to Win a Duke
More Than a Match for the Earl

Discover more at millsandboon.co.uk.

THE DUCHESS CHARADE

Emily E K Murdoch

MILLS & BOON

First published in Great Britain 2025
by Mills & Boon, an imprint of HarperCollins*Publishers* Ltd,
1 London Bridge Street, London, SE1 9GF

www.harpercollins.co.uk

HarperCollins*Publishers*, Macken House, 39/40 Mayor Street Upper, Dublin 1, D01 C9W8, Ireland

The Duchess Charade © 2025 Emily E K Murdoch

ISBN: 978-0-263-34508-7

02/25

This book contains FSC™ certified paper and other controlled sources to ensure responsible forest management.

For more information visit www.harpercollins.co.uk/green.

Printed and Bound in the UK using 100% Renewable Electricity at CPI Group (UK) Ltd, Croydon, CR0 4YY

For Becky Kramer. Thanks, pal.
And to PB, PB, BB and BB.

Chapter One

Sylvia Bryant hadn't expected there to be anyone actually in the carriage.

'Whoops!' she said in a rush, skirts flying, bonnet clinging to her head for dear life. 'My apologies—did I whack you very hard?'

The gentleman—for gentleman he certainly was, one could tell by the exquisite cut of his coat and the astonished look in his eye—merely spluttered, 'But—but you can't—'

'I am afraid I am commandeering this carriage for an escape,' Sylvia said blithely, trying to ignore her heart racing most uncomfortably in her chest. 'You don't mind, do you?'

It was all she could do to catch her breath.

She hadn't had much time to prepare. Oh, she was always looking for an opportunity to run away, had been for a year or so now, but it wasn't as easy as that...as she had discovered.

The hot summer air had been stifling outside on

the gravel drive, but inside this coach it was thick like honey. The day had so far drifted by in a haze of discomfiting expectations, as it always did at the Wallflower Academy.

A lesson on the correct way to enquire as to a gentleman's marital status, then Miss Pike had demanded that she examine their walks. Up and down, up and down, the wallflowers currently in residence were forced to demonstrate their elegance along the terrace beside the orangery. Eventually, Sylvia had pleaded a headache, and been instructed to go upstairs and fetch a bonnet.

And then return to the terrace.

Miss Pike really was a menace. But then, Sylvia rather supposed she should thank her. If she had not been sent upstairs, she would not have peered out of her bedchamber window…and she would not have seen the carriage. The livery…it was clearly a ducal crest, whose she could not quite remember, having fallen asleep during that particular class.

It had looked tiny from up there. Now Sylvia was seated inside, she could see it was in fact quite spacious.

And in that space was a man.

'Who on earth are you?' the gentleman asked.

Well, Sylvia thought with a wry smile, it wasn't every day that a woman burst into his carriage, she supposed.

'I am Miss Sylvia Bryant,' she said, by way of explanation.

No, that probably wasn't sufficient. The gentleman, at any rate, did not appear calmed.

'And I am Theodore Featherstonehaugh—'

'Goodness, what a mouthful,' Sylvia said conversationally, rapping on the top of the carriage roof. 'Can we be away?'

'We absolutely cannot. Please leave this carriage at once.'

The man's outrage barely registered. *Oh, they were always outraged*, she thought ruefully. Always surprised that she wanted to leave the Wallflower Academy—but then, they never had to live there. Had never been subjected to Miss Pike's ire. Never had to sit there like a dressed-up doll, waiting for the pitying people of the *ton* to turn up and stare.

'Waiting for a friend?' Sylvia said aloud. 'He can find his own way back, I'm sure—I'd like to be away immediately.'

Before Miss Pike realises I'm gone...

That had been the trouble with her last—what, five attempts to leave the Wallflower Academy—not getting away quickly enough. It was all very well to decide to run away, but if one didn't move sharply, the Pike had a terrible habit of noticing that she wasn't there.

The silence probably did it.

Sylvia laughed quietly to herself and saw the confused eyes of the man—Mr Featherstonehaugh—widen in curiosity.

'Look, it's very simple,' Sylvia said calmly, folding her hands on her lap as she had been taught, then immediately frowning and placing them underneath her legs. 'I am a wallflower—well, not really, but I've been stuck here for years, and I've decided I've had enough. Folding napkins and embroidering cushions and smirking at gentlemen and conversation lessons—I cannot take any more! You see, I'm escaping. At least, I will be once I can get this carriage moving.'

She turned, finding to her irritation that the little window behind the coachman was jammed.

'You are running away, and you believe I should assist you?'

The man's voice sounded incredulous, and Sylvia turned to him with her own surprise. Honestly, she was only asking for the tiniest bit of assistance. He was a gentleman, wasn't he? Wasn't a gentleman supposed to assist a woman in distress?

'Yes.' Honestly, was the man dense? 'I won't be a bother.'

Now she was looking at him, Sylvia took in the man's appearance, something she had given absolutely no thought to when she'd wrenched open the door and happily helped herself to a seat. And she saw…

Well. He was a pleasant surprise. She could have accosted anyone, really, and yet here was a man who was impressively handsome in the face. A sharp jaw, an imperious look, but a kindness around the eyes one rarely saw in any man wealthy enough to keep a chaise and four. A slight mark by his left eyebrow—a birthmark, perhaps—in the shape of a swallow in flight that was paler than his complexion. He was tall too, if the cramped way he was sitting was any indication.

Sylvia grinned. It seemed like a small reward for being so bold. Her adventure was going to begin with the most charming of companions.

And then her smile faltered.

Her gaze had been admiring—and as she was no true wallflower, whatever Miss Pike tried to tell her, she had been happily blatant in her appreciation.

Mr Featherstonehaugh, however, was staring with quite a different expression. His startling green eyes, now Sylvia came to look at them, were carefully skating over her skin. All her skin. The thin inch between her spencer and her hands, still hidden under her skirts, the skimming white lace in sharp contrast to the dark brown of her skin, revealed by her décolletage. The darkness of her throat, rising to burning pink cheeks.

Sylvia swallowed.

It was only when people stared like that did she remember just how different she must look. It was her skin, and her world. She belonged in both.

Until someone stared.

Rallying herself for the questions she knew would come, preparing the trite answers she trotted out for strangers whenever they enquired, Sylvia readied herself for—

'I must ask you to leave this carriage,' Mr Featherstonehaugh said, entirely ignoring the colour of her skin for, it appeared, a more pressing matter.

Sylvia's lips parted in curious astonishment. *Well, he was a singular man indeed.* 'Waiting for someone?'

Her enquiry garnered only a slight nod in response.

She had to frown. 'I cannot think who you could be waiting for—there is no one visiting the Wallflower Academy today, and you aren't courting anyone here. I'd know about it.'

She always found out. That was the trouble with being abandoned at a finishing school for ladies who were shy, quiet and retiring. When one was the complete opposite of those things, one had to go in search of conversation.

Goodness, the things that you were told when you truly listened to a shy person...

Mr Featherstonehaugh was staring—and Sylvia had to admit the expression only increased the man's natural charms.

Goodness, she would have enjoyed Miss Pike's last dinner far more if this Mr Featherstonehaugh had been in attendance. The man was worth looking at, even if his conversation was lacking.

'Look, I just want to be taken to London,' Sylvia said brightly, rearranging her skirts as though that would somehow encourage the man to tell the coachman to depart.

Sylvia glanced up, taking in the slightly furrowed brow that brought a crease between the man's eyes... his green eyes.

Something lurched most unaccountably in her stomach.

There was no harm in disclosing her escape plan to her accomplice, was there?

'I have heard there are a great number of opportunities in London. I have made it there twice, though once I was discovered by the Pike—'

'A pike?' Mr Featherstonehaugh looked bewildered. 'You were accosted by a large fish?'

Sylvia couldn't help but laugh as she leaned back into the comfortable soft furnishing of the carriage. The man had to be wealthy, certainly, with a luxurious carriage like this. What on earth was he doing here?

'Miss Pike,' she explained ruefully. 'I suppose it was indecorous to call her the Pike, but honestly, the way she swims about the Wallflower Academy looking for prey, it does suit her. The fact that she happened to be in London that day was most unfortunate. The second time—'

'Do you make a habit of running away?' Mr Featherstonehaugh spoke with a sardonic air, an eyebrow raised and brow unfurrowed.

He appeared to have relaxed. Which was all to the good, Sylvia thought. It would be a most awkward journey to London if he was going to fret all the way.

'It is not so much a habit as an indictment of my success.' She sighed. 'Though I have faith in you.'

'In me?' Mr Featherstonehaugh looked taken aback.

Sylvia nodded with a grin. 'Yes, you are by far the most pleasant person I have attempted to rope into an attempt. Now, are we to be off?'

Once again, the man glanced at the door. 'No. We certainly are not.'

'Gentlemen have far more resources than us poor ladies,' Sylvia said, deciding to attempt to tug on the man's heartstrings. Honestly, could he not see she was in distress?

Perhaps not. That was the trouble with being so forthright, she supposed. She should ape Daphne, and ensure her eyes were red-ringed before she ever endeavoured anything like this.

Well, she could try.

'I just… I just want to escape,' she said, ensuring her voice quivered ever so slightly.

Mr Featherstonehaugh's raised eyebrow did not lower.

Sylvia gave it up immediately. Falsifying her temperament never had been her style. 'Being semi-imprisoned in a marriage factory is all well and good for those who wish to be married, but as I have no desire in that direction, I'm getting out.'

'You do not wish to be married?'

No, and she wasn't going to explain why to a stranger in a carriage until it was on the road. Sylvia fixed him with a glare. 'Look, man, are you going to help me or not?'

A snatch of conversation floated into the carriage. The day was stifling, and if Sylvia had known they would waste so much time just sitting on the drive, she would not have closed the door.

As it was, the voices crept through, regardless.

'When will he leave?'

'—a duke!—'

Sylvia's eyes widened as she turned back to Mr Featherstonehaugh.

At least, that was what she had assumed. Theodore Featherstonehaugh. That was his name, but she had interrupted him, had she not? Prevented him from giving his full title.

Now, this was far more interesting.

'You are a duke—how delightful,' she said cheerfully. 'I shall add you to my collection.'

He stared with wide eyes. 'No, I'm Featherstonehaugh—'

'The Duke of Featherstonehaugh—a mouthful indeed. Of course, you are not the first duke I have met,' Sylvia continued conversationally. 'My friend Gwen married one. Rilla married an earl, though I'm not quite sure what she sees in him. Now, if I was going to choose a husband—'

'I must insist that you leave,' said the Duke firmly.

Sylvia just as firmly ignored him. '—then I am not certain that I would wish to marry an earl. Oh, it's all very well and good, I suppose—'

'Please, get out of the carriage,' the Duke said in a tone that suggested retribution if disobeyed.

Sylvia tried her best to ignore him, but it was a challenge when a gentleman was clearly desperate not to have her in his carriage. 'I wouldn't want to become a countess. What a dry title.'

The Duke fixed her with a serious look, one of concern and slight irritation. 'Miss Bryant. Please. I cannot take you to London. The impropriety—impossible. You must return to the Wallflower Academy.'

'Oh, must I?' Sylvia shot back, the frustration she had forced down finally spiking in her tone.

But the man did not appear to be cowed by her sharpness. His gaze held hers unflinchingly, and when he spoke it was with a calmness quite at odds with her fiery determination. 'You must.'

It was all very disappointing. But there was nothing to be done about it, and if Sylvia was anything, she was a pragmatist.

Most of the time. She would allow herself, later this evening, to daydream about a completely different outcome to this adventure. Where the Duke and herself were on the road…and had arrived at an inn because London was simply too far away…and there was only one room available, and—

'You really should go,' the Duke said.

Sylvia sighed. 'I suppose I should, as you aren't actually leaving.'

How discouraging. But it had been impulse only which had led her here, not careful planning. She would have to ensure that her next attempt was better orchestrated.

'It was very pleasant to make your acquaintance, Your Grace,' she said cheerfully.

The Duke flushed such a dark red, Sylvia was almost certain she could feel the heat from his cheeks. 'Ah. Good.'

His manners were a tad lacking, to be sure, but it was a rather unusual situation, even Sylvia could admit that. Well, she would simply have to creep back into the Wallflower Academy and hope the Pike was still putting the wallflowers through their paces on the terrace. She could…could say she had taken a short nap. Yes, that would work. And she had her bonnet, which she had been sent upstairs for.

No one would be any the wiser.

'Good day, Your Grace,' Sylvia said, inclining her head.

The Duke inclined his own head, bringing his face scandalously close to her own as Sylvia rose from her seat and attempted to step past him to the opposite carriage door.

It was downright mischievous of her. There was no need for it; the door through which she had entered was perfectly suitable, and if she had a mite of the wallflower reticence and shyness that the rest of the Wallflower Academy inhabitants had been born with, she never would have considered it.

But Sylvia was determined. Why should she depart the carriage in which she had intended to make a dramatic escape with no tale to tell?

She knew it had been a mistake the moment her knee touched his.

Knees were not supposed to feel like that—as if water

rippled under the surface. The merest contact, her knee through her underskirts and gown to his breeches and knee—it was ridiculous.

Yet the sudden rush of heat unsettled Sylvia, made her leg quiver just as she raised the other to reach the door.

The Duke gasped and moved.

Why he moved, Sylvia did not know. She would have made it around him, almost certainly, and his sudden jerking movement did more to unbalance her than assist her on her way.

Sylvia's poise tipped. She reached out a hand, grasped at thin air instead of the steadying side of the carriage, and she was falling, falling, sure to bump her head most painfully on the carriage bench as she—

Softness, and strength, and sultry warmth. Strong arms around her and a seat that was far too hot to be a carriage bench, even at this time of year.

Sylvia blinked. She looked up into the astonished gaze of the Duke. One of his hands was placed around her shoulder, holding her steady, and the other—

Well.

Swallowing hard and finding, to her astonishment, that her mouth was dry, Sylvia looked at the Duke's other hand. It was on her knee.

She was in the man's lap. *His lap!*

'Ah…' Sylvia managed.

Why her voice was so thin, she could not tell. But then, she did not appear to be able to tell anything very much. Her mind was whirling, all rational thought absent, and the panting rise and fall of the Duke's chest was doing something most strange to her own.

This...this was new.

Oh, she had met gentlemen before. She had even encountered some attractive ones—who made her body burn and thrum, made her wonder just what it was that wives enjoyed that single ladies like herself had to forego.

But never before had she touched one. Never before had she found herself in such close quarters in a carriage with one.

And she had never thrown herself into one's arms to discover that the warmth emanating from his hands on her shoulder and knee were working strange wonders within her.

Wonders that ached for more. More what, she was not quite sure.

More of whatever this was.

'I do apologise, Miss Bryant,' the Duke whispered.

He was looking down in horror, and delight, and he was not moving to right her. Sylvia stared up at him, head still reeling, and placed a splayed palm against his chest.

The Duke's breath hitched in his throat.

Think. She needed to think, but she had never had to think before with the thoughts of the pressure of a man's lips tingling on hers. Never had to navigate a conversation after falling into the lap of...well.

She had never been kissed. And, unless she was greatly mistaken, that would very soon be rectified. There was no mistaking the look in the Duke's eyes, a heady desire that seemed to spark like lightning between them.

And words were tumbling from her lips, quite beyond her control. 'Well, I... I suppose...if we are already here, then there's no chance of a k—'

The carriage door was wrenched open.

'Sylvia Bryant, I won't have any more attempts to escape the respectable confines of the Wallflower... the Wallflower...'

Ah. Botheration.

Sylvia attempted to sit up, but lounging across the Duke of Featherstonehaugh's lap made that difficult. Her head spun at the sudden rise and stars winked in the corners of her vision.

Think, Sylvia. Think. There has to be a way out of this.

The Duke was speaking rapidly. '—most dreadful misunderstanding—not what it looks like—'

When Sylvia had sufficiently blinked, a most surprising sight came into view.

She was still sprawled across the Duke's lap, and his hand was still delightfully resting on her knee. The carriage door was open and there, standing with her hands resolutely on her hips, her lips so tightly pressed together that they were naught but a thin line...was Miss Pike, her pale skin splattered with scarlet.

Sylvia grinned. 'Oh, dear! What a scandalous situation to have found myself in, Miss Pike. Whatever are we to do about it?'

Chapter Two

Well, this was a disaster.

Theodore tried to take a long, deep breath. It would perhaps have calmed his frantic nerves, prepared him to explain to the shouting woman that nothing, absolutely nothing, untoward had occurred, helped dispel the impression of the beautiful woman nestled in his arms, squirming against his—

He breathed in and coughed at the same time. It sounded as if he was drowning in an inch of mud.

'No amount of spluttering will get you out of this one, young man!' Miss Pike—and he could see now why the wallflower who had attempted to accost the Duke of Warchester's carriage had called her 'the Pike'—glared with such ferocity that Theodore took a step back.

He could not go far.

Miss Pike had insisted he and Miss Bryant be marched up to a small study, perhaps the size of his bedchamber in the lodgings he had taken in town. It was not much of a bedchamber. It was not much of a study.

Within it was a desk, three chairs, a longcase clock that appeared to be stuck chiming, the irate proprietress of the Wallflower Academy, himself...and a woman whose fiery beauty was making it mightily difficult for Theodore to concentrate.

Much to his detriment.

'Are you listening, young man?' Miss Pike snapped.

The honest answer was 'no'. Theodore had not even wanted to come to this Wallflower Academy in the first place. It was his friend, the Duke of Warchester, who had arranged to meet with the stablemaster here for tips on the races. A foolish errand, in Theodore's view, but despite having so much quite literally riding on those next races, Warchester had found himself otherwise engaged. London had been unpleasant, and the man had been such a good friend to him these last few weeks, so Theodore had offered to go in his stead.

He hadn't entered the school itself. Obviously. A place like the Wallflower Academy would not welcome men like himself with no title and no fortune. He was hardly marriage material.

Instead, his carriage had been boarded by a woman with sparkling eyes and a witty tongue, he'd become entangled with her in a way that would absolutely make sleep difficult this evening, and he was now being berated by a woman who, it appeared, would shortly explode.

Theodore swallowed. And she seemed to be under the impression that he was a gentleman! It was always the way, until they discovered his parentage wasn't exactly—

'I said,' Miss Pike went on with a most hearty sniff, 'that I have never encountered anything so scandalous in all my life! The two of you, in a carriage, where anyone could have seen you—'

'The door was shut at the time, Miss Pike,' interrupted Miss Bryant helpfully, a wicked look in her eye. 'If you had not opened the door—'

Miss Pike took a long, deep breath, swelling in apparent fury. 'My point is that you were seen cavorting in a gentleman's lap!'

Theodore watched, transfixed, as the young woman took a sharp intake of breath and replied to the older woman with just as much fury.

'I was not cavorting!'

He was also not a gentleman, though Theodore thought this was hardly the moment to point this out. No, he was just a man who did not know who his father was and who had grown up knowing, to the very pit of his stomach, the value of a hot meal. His school had been very particular about that, pointing out his debts when his allowance had been late. Not quite the upbringing of a duke, though he'd attended with quite a number.

Well, this was all going to get very awkward. He had not exactly lied—he had given his name, his true name, and what more could a man be expected to do?

The precise etiquette of speaking with a woman who

was attempting to commandeer one's friend's carriage was not something covered in any of the instructions he had received as a boy. Now a man of one and thirty, Theodore was still utterly perplexed.

You will laugh about this one day, he told himself firmly as the two women bickered, seeming to forget he was even there. *You will look back on this day and laugh at the tangle you managed to find yourself in.*

The question was, how precisely was he to untangle himself?

'—absolutely nothing else for it,' Miss Pike said sternly, speaking over Miss Bryant and compelling her, eventually, into silence. 'I never thought I would be forced into such an action, but there it is. You leave me with no other choice, Miss Bryant.'

For some reason, the young woman paled. Her smile faded, a look of half astonishment, half disbelief clouding the beauty of her expression.

Theodore swallowed. Not that he had noticed how beautiful she was. Obviously. It was hardly the done thing to be wandering about, noticing how beautiful ladies were. How warm, and supple, and unresisting—

'You cannot be in earnest,' Miss Bryant breathed, half bewildered, half laughing.

Theodore's head jerked from one to the other. Clearly, he had missed a portion of the conversation, for he was at a complete loss. 'In earnest about what?'

Both women firmly ignored him.

'You know the rules, Miss Bryant,' Miss Pike continued decidedly. 'You were instructed on them most closely when you arrived here—'

'Yes, but I never thought—'

'And I am sure the gentleman will agree with me,' Miss Pike said haughtily. 'This is, after all, a matter of honour.'

The way she said 'honour' could have rattled windows.

Theodore tried to smile. This was, when it came down to it, still a misunderstanding. The three of them would be in full agreement at any moment, he was certain. Just as soon as they disentangled—

'He won't agree to it,' Miss Bryant said, glancing at him.

The glance was impressive. Theodore had never seen anything like it. In one swift movement, which could have been missed if one had blinked, the young woman had examined him closely, made an assessment, and confirmed that assessment with a curt nod.

Right, this has gone far enough.

'Look,' Theodore said, trying for a balance of firm and polite. They were ladies, after all. 'It is simple. Miss Bryant accidentally entered—'

'You are quite correct, it is simple,' stated Miss Pike, a determined glint in her eye that should have told him to run. 'Very simple indeed. You will marry Miss Bryant.'

Theodore laughed.

It was the wrong thing to do. His chuckle echoed

awkwardly in the small room. Neither of the ladies echoed his merriment. He ceased laughing almost as quickly as he had started as a heavy weight dropped through his lungs into his stomach.

Marry—marry her?

The woman couldn't be serious. They couldn't actually expect him to…could they?

'This is the Duke of Featherstonehaugh, Miss Pike,' Miss Bryant was saying in a hiss. 'I am sure he would not wish to marry me—'

'The…the Duke of Featherstonehaugh?'

All too late, Theodore saw the gleam in the eye of the woman before him, and his heart sank.

Oh, hell.

He had to say something—had to explain that he wasn't a—

'All the more reason for you two to wed!' Miss Pike said with something like triumph in her expression. 'We can't have a duke's honour besmirched by the suggestion—'

'No one's honour is being besmirched—' Miss Bryant was attempting to speak but she was being overpowered by the older woman.

Theodore merely stared in horror.

Oh, hell's bells and all its—

'Though I admit I do not recall the Duchy of Featherstonehaugh,' Miss Pike was musing, her expert eye casting over Theodore's attire. 'Where precisely is it?'

Think, man. Think! Just tell them the truth, tell them—

'It sounds Irish to me, which is perhaps why we do not know it,' cut in Miss Bryant with a curious eye. 'But a duke is a duke, Miss Pike, no matter where—'

'Yes, and he's a far better match than I could have ever expected for you,' the older woman said sharply, as though Theodore was not standing right before them. 'But marriage it will have to be. No gentleman found in such a scandalous situation, alone with a lady, would expect anything less,' Miss Pike was saying in a voice that sounded very far away. 'Arrangements will have to be made. You can be married from this house, Sylvia. The Rector will be more than happy to oblige, I do not mind the indignity of…'

Plans. Plans were being made. This was a disaster. She still thought he was a duke. Yes, he should have explained in the carriage, but there hadn't been much point. He had never expected to see her again.

Now here she was, standing just a few feet away—how had he not noticed just how close she was, how her hand was a mere foot from his own—thinking that the Duke of Featherstonehaugh was going to marry her.

Hell and all its inhabitants.

He had to say something. Theodore knew this ridiculous charade could not continue, but he could hardly disabuse her of such a ridiculous notion as she stood right beside Miss Pike…

And besides, it was rather pleasant to be treated like a duke. Just for five more minutes.

'—a few weeks is all I will need to put together the arrangements,' the proprietress of the Wallflower Academy was saying. 'Nothing too expensive for you, Miss Bryant, of course—'

'Of course,' Miss Bryant said dryly.

There was just a hint of pain in that voice. Theodore had not noticed it before, but the instant Miss Pike had suggested—well, demanded—that they wed, Miss Bryant had not appeared delighted.

Theodore was hardly a catch. He knew that. But she did not.

It made no sense. Unless she had been lying, Miss Bryant had been most clear to him in the carriage that matrimony was not her desire—though if she believed him a duke, he thought wretchedly, perhaps she had decided that she could override her principles. Yet even in the brief time he had known her, that did not ring true.

Miss Bryant's dark eyes met his own and Theodore's entire stomach clenched. Then something else did, a little further down.

This was ridiculous. Steeling himself for a most unpleasant conversation now the situation had got entirely out of hand, Theodore plastered a smile on his face. 'Will you excuse me for a moment, Miss Pike?'

'Excuse you for… Just what do you think you are doing?'

Grabbing Miss Bryant's hand and pulling her fiercely at the same moment that he opened the door to the corridor, Theodore half dragged, half hauled the young woman out of the Pike's study.

'Won't be a moment,' Theodore said breezily, attempting to smile at the horrified older woman. 'Don't mind us.'

Shutting the door despite her loud remonstrances, Theodore marched down the corridor, still pulling Miss Bryant behind him in his wake. An empty room, that was all he needed.

The first room was a laundry closet. Better not—he had been discovered in one scandalous position already today. Fate did not need to be tempted again.

The second door revealed a music room. A blonde woman shrieked and dropped the music sheets she was holding.

'Hello there, Daphne,' Miss Bryant said cheerfully. 'Practising the concerto again?'

Theodore slammed the door. Was there not a single empty room in this place?

The third door, thankfully, revealed what appeared to be a small sitting room. It was not elegantly attired and was perhaps used as the Pike's—Miss Pike's—private room. It would do.

Thrusting the woman into it and slamming the door behind him, Theodore took a deep breath and looked at Miss Bryant. 'I cannot marry you.'

Right. There. It was said.

Perhaps more baldly than he had intended, but there

was nothing for it. Now, all he had to do was brace himself for tears, and—

'Of course you cannot,' Miss Bryant said blithely. 'What a foolish idea. Don't worry—just trust me.'

Theodore stared.

This day had been a complete fiasco. Unsolved enquiries at the bank, an argument with a man at the Post Office—and now this wild encounter with a woman who did not appear to understand 'no'.

He needed to be more clear.

'Miss Bryant, I am sure you are very—' Theodore began.

Miss Bryant snorted with laughter. 'Oh, you don't need to give me that speech, Your Grace.'

Your Grace. Christ.

'I am not in a position to marry anyone. It is no comment on you or your character or your—'

'Complete poverty, lack of family name or connections and strange and mysterious abandonment at the Wallflower Academy?' Miss Bryant grinned. 'I told you, trust me.'

Trust her? Theodore would trust her just about as far as he could throw her.

The thoughts, unbidden, rushed into his mind. Of his hands clasping her waist, drawing her closer to him… merely so he could throw her further, naturally. And then he was throwing her, and Miss Sylvia Bryant was falling, with her skirts flying, onto a bed. A bed upon which Theodore swiftly descended, covering Miss Bryant's body with his own—

'Your Grace? Your Grace, can you hear me?'

Theodore blinked. Miss Bryant was a mere three inches from him. She was waving a hand before his face and examining him with concern.

Taking a hasty step back from the intoxicating presence of a woman whose rosewater scent surely had something to do with the intriguing vision which had momentarily flashed through his mind, Theodore attempted to collect his thoughts.

Firstly, he could not marry her. What could he offer her? Absolutely nothing, save a mystery he could not solve. Until he found his father, he did not even technically know his own name.

Secondly, he needed to clarify his distinct lack of title at the soonest opportunity. Five minutes ago would have been perfect.

And thirdly, if he did not leave Miss Sylvia Bryant's presence soon, he was liable to forget the first two and do something truly scandalous.

Like kiss her.

'Look, an engagement is not the same as a marriage,' Miss Bryant said confidently, folding her arms as though she had to explain this to men all the time.

Theodore tried to speak, but his throat was tangled up and the sound he uttered was more like a groan of panic than anything coherent. Pretending to be a duke for five minutes was an innocent enough charade, but an engagement—

'You do not have to worry about a thing,' continued Miss Bryant, as though she frequently contracted engagements. 'If you would just listen—'

'If I would just listen— If you would just listen!' burst out Theodore, unable to contain himself. 'Miss Bryant, I say again, I cannot marry you!'

She fixed him with a stern glare. 'And why not?'

For so many reasons, he wanted to say. *Because I am not who you think I am. I am not even who I think I am—I don't know anything about myself. I am not a gentleman, I am not a member of the ton, I have no money, no fortune, just a mystery.*

Because you make me want to kiss you, and worse, and you are a lady—he could see that by the way she held herself, the delicacy of her movements, even as she'd launched herself into his lap.

Theodore's jaw tightened.

'I cannot marry you,' he repeated, taking refuge in the one statement he knew to be irrevocably true. 'Even if I wanted to, I could not.'

The last few words slipped from his lips before he could halt them, true as they were. Because he could see the attractions of Miss Bryant, oh, God, yes. This woman was fire and passion and merriment. Being around Miss Bryant was like stepping into a whirlwind of gold. One came out of it richer, even if one's hair was ruffled and you were no longer sure where your gloves were.

But marrying her? Absolutely not. It was out of the question!

Sylvia grinned. 'But you do want to, a little, don't you?'

Theodore swallowed. He could not marry her.

And yet...she spoke of not wishing to marry, which is not the same as being engaged...

And yet, Theodore couldn't help but admit in the panicked solitude of his mind, being engaged to a young lady and needing to go about London to organise a wedding would be the perfect cover. No one would enquire as to why that man—no one would call him a gentleman—was asking questions, speaking to many people, being curious about things that were arguably none of his concern. He could search for the truth of his father, the truth of where he came from and who he really was, more easily with a prospective bride on his arm.

An engaged man was not a threat. An engaged man did not have to be watched like a hawk. An engaged man could go where bachelors were not permitted.

Theodore's pulse raced in his ears as he tried to think. It would certainly have been a great deal easier if he did not have Miss Sylvia Bryant standing before him, looking...looking like that...her breasts heaving in her gown, thanks to their rush to this room and the heat of the afternoon.

Was this perfect timing? An offer of respectability, just when he needed it?

The door behind him banged open and Miss Bryant winced. Theodore mirrored her the instant the shriek was uttered.

'I have never been so insulted in all my life! You must marry Miss Bryant now—you must surely see the need!' Miss Pike's voice was strained, panicked, desperate.

And he could see her point. Theodore was no gentleman, but he had been raised in the style of one. The right schools, the right etiquette drilled into him, he'd learned the sports of a gentleman and the manners of one. That was part of the problem.

He knew an unchaperoned young lady should not be gallivanting with a man in a carriage, or in a room. When it came to it, an unchaperoned young lady should not be attempting to run away and somehow support herself in a world that was unkind to women. The fact that nothing had actually happened between them in the carriage was both a disappointment and his salvation.

He could walk away from this. Oh, Theodore knew it would be awkward, but for Miss Bryant, not for him. Men simply did not bear the consequences in quite the same way.

But would that be a mistake?

Theodore's gaze raked over Miss Bryant. She was staring with a slight smile, a knowing look in her eyes that suggested there was far more to the woman than a mere wallflower.

Wallflower? Miss Bryant at the Wallflower Academy was poor planting if ever he saw it.

What was she up to? What did she think she could do to prevent this marriage from occurring?

'Look, an engagement is not the same as a marriage...'

Theodore took a deep breath, and immediately wished he had not. The rosewater that he would link for ever to Miss Bryant filled his nostrils, his lungs, his mind—

And then he caught sight of her desperation.

Desperation? Yes, there was a pleading in her eyes he had not noticed, distracted as he had been by the scent of roses. So, she needed this as much as he did—why, he did not yet know.

Time to make a decision.

'Miss Bryant has deigned to accept me,' Theodore said brightly, slipping her hand into the crook of his arm and turning to face Miss Pike. 'Isn't it wonderful? We are engaged to be married!'

Engaged to be married. The words echoed through Theodore's beleaguered mind. What had he done?

Miss Pike trilled, 'Oh, how wonderful! Well done, Miss Bryant—finally. I shall alert the kitchens that we shall need a celebratory tea.' Bustling away, Miss Pike's head reappeared, poking around the doorframe. 'Come on, young man. I cannot leave you alone with your betrothed. In the heat of the moment, who knows what might occur!'

Theodore opened and closed his mouth in panicked denial as Miss Bryant giggled behind him.

Striding forward, Miss Pike grabbed his arm and pulled him away. 'You may depart and we can discuss the details another time. A summer wedding! How delightful. You know, I always thought…'

As the proprietress of the Wallflower Academy continued, Theodore turned and caught a momentary glimpse of Miss Bryant before he was wrenched away.

'I'll visit tomorrow,' he called over his shoulder, his lungs tight and the words only just making it past his lips.

Tomorrow. Tomorrow—when he would have to tell Miss Bryant the truth, and cause a hell of an upset.

Marvellous.

Chapter Three

It was unlike Daphne to drop the sugar tongs into her cup of tea, but then, it was unusual for Sylvia to declare something so unexpected.

'For the last time, Miss Smith, attempt some decorum at breakfast!' Miss Pike called down the table in a ringing voice.

Sylvia shot the Pike a glare, but it did nothing to calm the frazzled nerves of her friend. The delicate wall-flower—perhaps one of the few actual wallflowers in the entirety of the Wallflower Academy—was blushing so darkly pink, Sylvia could almost feel the heat coming from her.

At least she would have done, if the day itself had not already reached a stifling temperature, and the buttered toast on her plate wasn't wafting up its own delicious warmth.

'M-My apologies, Miss Pike,' Daphne murmured.

Sylvia nudged her elbow—an attempt at solidarity

that only ensured her friend dropped the sugar tongs again, this time with a clang against her plate.

'Honestly, Miss Smith!'

Daphne's cheeks grew to a boiling red and Sylvia's glare became a scowl as she looked furiously at the Wallflower Academy's proprietress.

But it made no difference. Miss Pike was already chattering away to another wallflower, completely ignoring Daphne's discomfort.

Which Sylvia had made worse.

Picking up the sugar tongs herself and wiping them on her napkin, Sylvia hastily placed them back in a bowl filled with white cubes and passed it down the table. 'Miss Pike, sugar for your tea?' Then she looked at her friend. 'I am sorry for nudging your elbow.'

''Tis no matter,' said Daphne quietly, a determined smile on her face. 'Please, think nothing of it. What did you say?'

It was perhaps a tad too teasing for her shy friend, but Sylvia could not help it. 'I said that I was sorry for nudging your elb—'

'You know what I meant!' muttered Daphne, lowering her voice before glancing up and down the table.

Sylvia did know what she meant. It was, after all, the statement which had caused the sugar tongs to slip from her friend's fingers in the first place.

'By the way, I am engaged to a duke.'

'I said that I am engaged,' Sylvia said brightly, taking a bite of her hot buttered toast. 'To a duke.'

'Sylvia!'

'It's true!' she said, perhaps too defensively. 'You just wait—he promised to return today to see me.'

To see me. Miss Sylvia Bryant, engaged to be married to prevent a scandal. Or to cause one. Same difference.

'It's going to be wonderful,' she said radiantly, deciding not to include Daphne in her runaway plan this time. The poor woman was shy enough already—who knew what holding a secret of this magnitude would do to her? 'He is remarkably handsome, with an impressive chaise and four. I really am quite delighted with him.'

Daphne's cheeks were still pink as she gawped at her friend. 'Sylvia! You speak as though you have selected him from a catalogue!'

Sylvia giggled. 'Oh, he's one of a kind, I can promise you.'

Yes, no man had ever been so useful. Already she was given greater freedom and autonomy in the Wallflower Academy—and that was only the beginning. Soon, she could start to plan a much more permanent escape. Falmouth was an awfully long way away, but it would only be the first stop on her adventure.

'I'll visit tomorrow...'

Just the memory of his voice, the determination in his words, his absolute conviction that he would not marry her—the medley, in short, of Theodore, Duke of Featherstonehaugh, was enough to spark heat all through her body.

Quite significant heat.

Sylvia swallowed, and was about to tell Daphne just a hint more of the slightly unusual circumstances in which she and the Duke of Featherstonehaugh had found themselves, when she caught a glimpse of Miss Pike out of the corner of her eye.

Time for her to depart.

'I'll tell you all about it later,' Sylvia said impulsively, rising from the table and letting her tea-stained napkin float to the carpet. 'I have to leave. I need to—'

She did not bother completing her sentence. Miss Pike had taken the bowl that Sylvia had sent down the table and popped not two, but three of the exquisitely expensive white sugar lumps into her steaming tea. How the woman could drink tea on a boiling day like this, Sylvia did not know.

What she did know was that she did not want to be in the breakfast room when Miss Pike took her first sip.

She almost made it out of the door. Sylvia's hand was on the handle, turning it and bringing it towards her, when the yelling splutter behind her erupted into the room.

'Eugh—salt! Salt! Ladies, who in heaven put salt in my tea?'

Sylvia had slipped out of the room and left the door ajar before anyone could start looking around the table for a guilty face.

It was not one of her best pranks. In truth, she had little energy for such things in heat like this. She could not remember a summer so stifling, though, in truth, every season was stifling at the Wallflower Academy.

In fact, Sylvia thought as she meandered along the corridor towards the hall, it was a marvel they had not succumbed to swimming in the pond, the heat was so—

'Oh!' she said, stepping into the hall and seeing a tall figure speaking hurriedly to Matthews, the footman. 'There you are!'

The two men turned, one with an expression of severity, one with pink cheeks.

'You were expecting this gentleman, Miss Sylvia?' asked Matthews suspiciously. His face softened as Sylvia pressed a kiss against his cheek, squeezing his arm.

'Now, I know you do an excellent job of safeguarding us from rogues and villains, Matthews,' Sylvia said with a grin she kept purposely for the elderly man who kept watch at the front door. 'But you need not worry. The Duke of Featherstonehaugh and I are engaged.'

'Ah,' said the Duke woodenly. 'Yes, on that note—'

'Engaged! Ah, yours is the celebratory afternoon tea today then, Miss Sylvia,' said Matthews, his face relaxing as he patted her hand. 'Couldn't have happened to a nicer—'

'Miss Bryant?'

Sylvia and the footman looked round at the stiff and slightly stubborn face of the Duke of Featherstonehaugh.

'Yes?' she said sweetly.

He did not reply. At least, not in words. The man

Sylvia had teased with news of their engagement—really, she should have explained all to him yesterday—marched the four steps to the front door, pulled it open and looked pointedly at her.

Sylvia sighed. It was rather unfortunate. Poor man. He hadn't asked her to invade his carriage and demand matrimony…

'Right. Do not mind us, Matthews. We are going for a walk in the garden.'

She marched past the footman without waiting for him to recommend the necessary fripperies: a bonnet, a shawl, lace gloves, to protect her modesty.

Modesty. She was stuck here in the Wallflower Academy, and would be until the end of time if she was always to worry about her modesty.

Sylvia glanced up with a smile at the Duke of Featherstonehaugh as she passed him in the doorframe. There was sufficient space to walk through it while keeping a respectable three inches between them, and only for a moment was she tempted to lean into him, allow a shoulder to brush past his shirt, see if she could feel the boiling heat in him today that she had felt yesterday.

But she did not. Instead, her feet crunched on the burning dry gravel of the drive.

'This path is more shaded,' Sylvia said, not bothering to tilt her head over her shoulder as she spoke. He could hear her.

The Duke of Featherstonehaugh's footsteps matched hers as he walked alongside her, tall and silent. When the gravel gave way to lawn, parched and brown, the crunch was almost precisely the same.

It was only when their path had moved towards the winter garden, overhung with silver birches that rustled in a non-existent wind, did Sylvia speak again. 'I suppose you would like to know my plan.'

The Duke of Featherstonehaugh breathed out heavily. 'Before you tell me what wild adventure you are hoping to experience next, I must tell you—'

'Adventure?' Sylvia interrupted him with a smile as their footsteps slackened, ceasing to be a march and slowing to a meander. 'I suppose I would like an adventure if possible, but, to be quite honest with you, anything that isn't sitting around here learning about the myriad forks used at Court or practising Mozart for hours on end would feel quite adventurous.'

She met his eyes as she finished, and was surprised to find that the green was so much more sparkling than she had remembered. Green eyes. A rarity. But then, he was a rarity, wasn't he? A duke, and unmarried—at least, she presumed he was. Miss Pike had not yet seriously forced her wallflowers to memorise *Debrett's*, but Sylvia wouldn't put it past her.

So, green eyes, and tall, with a jaw so sharp it could cut and a seriousness that made Sylvia's breath catch in her throat.

How was a man like this, with a title to boot, unmarried?

'I am afraid I am not much of an adventure,' the Duke of Featherstonehaugh said softly.

Sylvia grinned. 'Ah, you have no sense of adventure, then?'

'It isn't that—more that, in fact, I—'

'Now, you see, what I am about to propose may not seem like an adventure to you. In fact, I would hazard a wager that it definitely will not,' Sylvia said with a sigh as their path curved around a corner. 'What appears adventurous to a woman entrapped in the Wallflower Academy will undoubtedly seem like a mere excursion to a gentleman like you.'

'Miss Bryant, I—'

'Oh, I think after what the Pike believes we have shared, you can call me Sylvia, don't you?'

She had not intended to speak with such familiarity, but then, it was her way. The niceties and limitations of Society were just so…dull.

The Duke of Featherstonehaugh's eyes widened. 'You would wish for that intimacy, after less than four and twenty hours of acquaintance?'

Sylvia shrugged. 'Why speak of the weather, and the time of year, and the gown adorning the prettiest woman in the room, when there are so many far more interesting things to discuss?'

The man's eyes could not become wider, but his jaw did drop. 'I am hardly familiar with—'

'Why is a starling's wing so beautifully patterned, do you think?' Sylvia said, one of the birds in the tree above catching her eye. 'So dull from a distance and yet blue and purple and green when one is close. Is it to tempt us to edge closer? To still ourselves until the creature trusts us, and only then are we permitted to be indulged with its beauty?'

She had stopped, when she was not sure, to stare up at the bird. It chattered in the silver birch overhead and the brilliant sunlight made it shine. Blues and greens shimmered in the heat of the air.

Sylvia lowered her head and saw the Duke of Featherstonehaugh staring, an expression of pure curiosity on his face. She flushed, heat undoubtedly colouring her cheeks. 'Right. My plan.'

'Miss Bryant—Sylvia, I must protest—'

'No, you don't need to protest, that is what I am trying to tell you,' said Sylvia happily. Really, it was a clever idea, and he would know that if he would just let her explain. 'We will pretend to be engaged—only you and I will know that we have absolutely no intention of actually trotting down the aisle. It will be a complete charade.'

Deafening silence followed her pronouncement.

Well, the silence one could find in a dreamily hot garden in an English summer. Bumblebees drunkenly meandered from blossom to blossom, their hum vibrating stickily through the air. Birdsong floated down from the lusciously verdant trees, starlings' mixed with a blackbird's. The total lack of breeze allowed the sounds to seep into every corner and crevice of the place.

The Duke of Featherstonehaugh was staring. 'You do not wish to wed?'

Sylvia grinned. 'Not in the slightest. The gossip will die down, give it a few weeks, then you can break it off quietly. I have no family to speak of, no one will get upset.'

A raised eyebrow. 'Not the Pike? I mean, Miss Pike?'

'Well, perhaps her,' Sylvia admitted, trying not to chuckle at the Duke of Featherstonehaugh's immediate adoption of the nickname. 'But what can she do? Nothing. I can gad about town with you and plan out a proper escape without anyone being concerned, and you won't find your reputation ruined. It will be an engagement that does not end in marriage—unusual, true, but hardly a rarity.'

'You talk about a proper escape, but where do you intend to go?' The Duke of Featherstonehaugh looked concerned. Concerned for her? 'You are a young woman, Miss Bryant, with no means of support and travelling alone—'

'Women travel alone all the time,' she said dismissively, pushing aside the twist of concern in her stomach. 'I have saved a great deal of pin money, I assure you, and—'

'But what will you do when that runs out?'

Sylvia tried not to glare. They were very good questions—questions she had not wished to consider. 'I have a plan,' she said, as firmly as possible.

The Duke of Featherstonehaugh did not look overly convinced. 'And that plan is—'

'None of your business—we are not actually engaged,' Sylvia pointed out decisively. No emotional tangle required here. 'Look, I just need to visit the docks and purchase a number of—'

'You absolutely will not visit the docks.'

'It's my business,' Sylvia said curtly. 'And a pretend engagement is just the sort of ruse I require to help me move about freely. You will have no other obligation other than to accompany me. Do you see?'

From what she could tell of the man's expression, he did see. Mostly. The slight frown that creased his forehead revealed just how deeply he was thinking, and Sylvia took the chance to examine him a little more closely.

What she saw was impressive.

His clothes. Just like yesterday, the Duke of Featherstonehaugh was wearing a coat of detail and expense. She had silently remarked upon it, been impressed by the choice. But it was more than the clothes; it was the man who filled them. There was a presence, a boldness, a confidence in the width of his shoulders and the expression on his face. There was a knowledge, deep within, that he was worthy of a person's time, and that anyone in his presence should be grateful.

It was…intoxicating, to say the least.

'And what do I gain from this arrangement, Sylvia?'

She swallowed, burning heat scalding up her spine. She had offered the man the opportunity to call her by her name because it felt only fair, considering that she would be using him as a chaperone to help plan her escape. It had never occurred to her that hearing those three syllables in his mouth would feel so…so intimate.

As though they were alone.

Well, they were alone. But not truly alone. Anyone could come upon them here in the Wallflower Academy gardens. But when the Duke of Featherstonehaugh said her name, he spoke it as though he possessed her. As though she belonged to him. As though at any moment he could press her up against that silver birch tree, getting bark all over her gown, and—

Sylvia cleared her throat. 'I suppose you gain the benefit of my company. 'Tis not much, but a duchess charade should pass the time in an entertaining manner, and it is all I have to offer.'

When she lifted her eyes to his green ones, she tried to communicate the unspoken second half of that speech.

Because you are not bedding me, Your Grace, no matter how delectable you are.

She could brook no misunderstanding; this proposition was not *that* sort of proposition.

Not unless—

No, Sylvia thought resolutely. No, this was a means to an end. An engagement of convenience, to quell any hint of scandal, and the chance to go back home, to where she had been happy.

And that was all.

'You seem very certain it will work.'

Sylvia beamed. 'Well, Your Grace, I believe Society will move onto another piece of gossip before long. A few weeks, perhaps a month. Then some scandal will happen, and all eyes will move on.'

The Duke of Featherstonehaugh looked unconvinced, but he had not immediately walked away nor laughed at her suggestion. The mere fact that he was considering it, in fact, was a good sign.

It was perhaps the first time that Sylvia deflated. 'Is it truly so awful,' she asked quietly as the starling above them flew off into the brilliant blue sky, 'the idea of pretending to be engaged to me for a short month?'

The Duke of Featherstonehaugh looked at her closely, stepping forward to close the gap between them, and Sylvia gasped.

There was something…something truly potent in the man's eyes. Goodness, she had never seen anything like it. A boldness and a directness she had never seen in the expression of a gentleman.

A gentleman would not have stared so directly. A gentleman would have maintained a proper distance between them so her breasts did not brush up against his coat. A gentleman would have heard the gasp in her throat, seen the sudden connection they were about to share, and apologised while stepping away from her, far away.

The Duke of Featherstonehaugh did none of these things. He remained there, breathing perhaps a little heavily—because of the heat, surely, Sylvia told herself—his fierce gaze fixed on hers as though attempting to read something within her soul.

It was mesmerising. Sylvia could not have moved an inch if her life had depended on it.

'I will agree to this charade of yours,' the Duke of Featherstonehaugh said softly, 'but first, I must tell you that—'

A crunch on the lawn.

Sylvia whirled around, taking a hasty step away from the gentleman who was far too intoxicating for his own good. 'Miss Pike!'

'Miss Pike indeed,' scowled that lady, scarlet about the face in this heat. 'Now, shall the three of us take a walk around the gardens? We can then discuss the plans for your marriage.'

Sylvia glanced up at the Duke of Featherstonehaugh. Whatever it was he wished to tell her, it could wait… unless he was about to brutally wrench apart her plan and tell Miss Pike that the engagement, such as it was, was off?

For a heart-stopping moment the gentleman squared his shoulders and looked resolutely at the proprietress.

Then he said quietly, 'Let us walk and plan this wedding.'

Chapter Four

'I know how to behave!'

'Do you?' Miss Pike raised an imperious eyebrow. 'Do you, Miss Bryant?'

Sylvia winced as she stepped out of the carriage onto the gravel. There was a very particular tone the proprietress of the Wallflower Academy took whenever she wished to make one of her charges feel small, and years of living in her care had not diminished its efficacy.

'Yes, I do,' she said defiantly, sweeping her shawl over her shoulders and glaring at the Pike. 'And I shall not let you down.'

Or herself, Sylvia thought silently as she stepped forward to allow Miss Pike to descend from the carriage. She had an opportunity, and she was not going to waste it.

'London gets busier every year,' fussed Miss Pike, gazing about Hyde Park with the look of a hungry child seeking cake. 'Do you see him?'

'No,' said Sylvia airily. 'Not yet.'

'But he said he would meet us here,' Miss Pike fretted. 'And it is not like him to be late!'

It was all Sylvia could do not to snort with laughter.

Not like him? The pair of them knew almost nothing about this Duke of Featherstonehaugh, save that he was handsome and willing to enter into a ridiculous charade for her. Which, truth be told, made him far more delightful than half the men she had ever met. But still. Miss Pike had barely been able to contain her excitement at the idea of another one of her charges marrying a duke, twittering about it to anyone who would listen at the breakfast table.

Sylvia's focus raked over the myriad people in Hyde Park, striding about in the summer sun. Gentlemen with tall hats and canes, ladies with bonnets and shawls and spencer jackets. Chatter about the Season, about which modiste to frequent, about a duel that was supposed to be a secret but everyone knew about, all mingled around her as people passed.

She could not help but grin. This was where she belonged—with people. Real people, not the stuffy dullards they sent to the Wallflower Academy.

Daphne excepted, of course. But one friend could not satisfy the longing for real life, the life that others led passionately and freely here in London.

Miss Pike had said she had no idea what real life was, that she had been closeted and protected for too long at the Wallflower Academy. Sylvia had argued with her, pointing out that she had seen far more of the world than

Miss Pike. And besides, her runaway plan did not end in London. It did not even end in England.

A smile crept across her face. Soon she would partake of that vibrancy, that energy, that bustle—

'Ah, there you are.'

A shiver of something hot scurried down Sylvia's spine as she turned to see Miss Pike curtseying low and murmuring something about how delightful it was.

Sylvia did not listen to her. She was too busy looking at the Duke.

It had been a few days since she had seen him, yet she had not misremembered an inch of his fine stature and assertive presence. He stood there, silently letting Miss Pike ramble on, and his gaze caught hers.

A flutter in her stomach. A tightening of her lungs. A tingling in her fingertips.

Then the Duke stepped forward, entirely ignoring Miss Pike, and offered his betrothed his arm. 'Come, Miss Bryant. I am sure Miss Pike understands our need to converse. You will accompany at a distance, Miss Pike.'

Sylvia almost laughed aloud. Why, she had never heard anyone speaking to the Pike like that!

Yet, quite in opposition to the way the proprietress treated Sylvia on a daily basis, Miss Pike was inclining her head and muttering about what an honour it was and how fortunate they were in the weather and all sorts of things that Sylvia would have listened to, if the Duke had not marched her forward.

He did not speak for a few minutes. Sylvia was not exactly panting to keep up with him, but his pace was swifter and his stride longer than hers. Miss Pike was surely falling behind.

It appeared the Duke had a similar thought. Glancing over his shoulder, he nodded to himself. 'She cannot hear us.'

'I am glad you suggested meeting here,' Sylvia said brightly, staring around curiously. 'I've always longed to watch the world go by at Hyde Park. My friend Gwen says the most fascinating people—'

'I am not the Duke of Featherstonehaugh.'

Sylvia halted in her tracks so suddenly that her arm was wrenched painfully by the still moving man.

He halted also, his expression a picture of remorse. 'I know admitting it to you like that was very blunt, but—'

'Not the Duke of Featherstonehaugh,' repeated Sylvia, her pulse throbbing in her ears.

'Not a duke,' corrected the man who Sylvia now did not know how to address. 'I never said I was a—'

'But you…you said…' Sylvia stumbled, her mind racing as she attempted to transport herself back to that day less than a week ago.

'You are a duke—how delightful. I shall add you to my collection.'

Theodore, for that was the only name of his that she could recall, had taken her arm again and was propelling her forward. Almost instinctively, Sylvia glanced over her shoulder. Miss Pike was still far enough away to have reasonably not heard the confession.

But—not a duke?

'You assumed, and I let you assume—for far too long, I know,' Theodore was saying under his breath, his speech so rapid that some of his words ran into each other. 'It seemed easier with the Pike—dammit, Miss Pike, standing there, and you seemed so eager for an engagement—'

'Yes, to a duke,' Sylvia pointed out sharply. 'It's a little hard to plan a duchess charade without a duke.'

Blast, it was all coming undone before it had even begun. How could she go about the place with a—a… what was he?

'Are you a marquess?' she asked hopefully.

Theodore snorted as they turned a corner, the path meandering amongst some trees. 'I don't know who I am.'

This was getting ridiculous. 'But you gave me a name—a most preposterous name, now I come to think of it. Was that a lie, too?'

Sylvia gasped as Theodore cast her a look that was both mortified and outraged.

'I do not lie.'

She swallowed, tasting the discomfort on her tongue. It was a rather startling accusation, to be sure—but then the whole situation was rather startling.

Not a duke. Well, try as she might, she could not precisely recall the man saying he was a duke. What a disappointment. Who did not want to be engaged to a duke, even if one had an agreement with said duke that would prevent one from ever being a duchess?

It was a crying shame, but then, when had her schemes ever been successful?

'My name is Theodore Featherstonehaugh, and that is my mother's surname,' he continued in a low voice. 'I don't know who my father is. Not yet.'

Sylvia's eyes widened. Now, this was getting interesting. 'You seek your father?'

Mr Featherstonehaugh nodded briefly. His serious eyes were shadowed for a moment, a flickering expression of pain and distrust and something else that Sylvia couldn't quite make out.

And then it was gone, and his face was smooth and controlled.

'He must be a gentleman. An allowance was sent every month, even after my mother… Arrangements were made for me to attend an impressive school, where I made excellent friends, some of them titled, and after I turned one and twenty I expected the allowance to cease. It did not. It did cease two months ago. Things are getting…challenging. Oh, I have saved, of course, but my expenditure… My landlord on Kennerleigh Street will not hold back on my rent forever.'

Sylvia stared curiously up at the man spilling these intimacies to her. A man who did not know his father. Well, she could hardly relate. She knew far too much about her father. His unkindness. His lack of care. His disinterest in his own daughter. She had to look at his sharp eyes every time she faced a looking glass.

'So you seek the money?'

Mr Featherstonehaugh laughed darkly and a shimmer of heat flushed through Sylvia. 'I seek the truth. You…you cannot know how unpleasant it is to take you into my confidence.'

'I don't think I'm that bad,' pointed out Sylvia sharply. The cheek!

His laughter this time was warmer, his hand squeezing her own. 'I do apologise. I merely meant… Sylvia, I am an outsider to Society. I have no father's name, nor character, nor position to guide me.'

Outsider.

Sylvia swallowed, glancing at her hand on the man's arm. The sleeve of her gown was long and her gloves were appropriately worn, yet still there was a sliver of her skin visible. Her dark brown skin.

She inhaled slowly. This conversation was not about her—and besides, what was there to say that had not already been said? Unlike Theodore, she could not hide what made her an outsider, what marked her out as different. Impressive clothes, talent on the pianoforte, carriages, titles—nothing could change how others saw her.

It had irked her when she had been a child, and saddened her as she had grown. Now, all she felt was a dull sort of strange acceptance.

Sylvia was who she was, and she was not ashamed.

'If you think to educate me on being an outsider in

Society, sir,' she said quietly, 'I hesitate to suggest that I could teach you a thing or two.'

His eyes met hers. 'I suppose you could.'

Sylvia took a deep breath. This conversation was not about her—and besides, what was there to say that had not already been said? 'So you seek your father—the truth of who he is?'

'Or was,' interjected Mr Featherstonehaugh with a wry shake of his head. 'His death, I presume, occurred two months ago. I have spent my life, Miss Bryant—'

'I think we can dispense with the formalities, now I know your greatest secret,' said Sylvia with what she hoped was an encouraging smile.

Strange. Her smiles were usually teasing or mocking, rarely with malice but always with mischief. But not this one. In this moment she wanted to tell him so much more than words could encapsulate.

That she understood the longing to belong to something. That, though her own father was not someone to seek out, she knew the undeniable tug of family. That this false engagement had not been a mistake.

Perhaps he understood her. Perhaps he did not. Theodore continued. 'All my life, I have wondered if I am the son of a tradesman or a prince. Either could be true, yet the not knowing is weighing on me now as it has never done before. Am I even a gentleman?'

'Surely you must be,' Sylvia said without thinking.

Theodore raised an eyebrow, the sunlight highlighting his swallow-shaped birthmark as they reached the

Serpentine. There were boats upon it this sunny day, and the laughter of the children who dipped their toes in at the edge rang out across the water. 'You think so?'

'I mean, look at you!' Dropping his arm though continuing to walk alongside him, Sylvia looked up and down with a far more discerning eye than she had previously cast over him and saw...

Sylvia swallowed. He truly was the picture of a gentleman. At least, what she had always pictured a true gentleman to be. Tall, with broad shoulders and a proud jaw. His eyes were bright, fiery, with that quiet confidence she had spotted in him the moment they had first met. But there was more—more that was revealed with a greater knowledge of him.

He wore a jacket and breeches, paired with Hessian boots, that a gentleman would wear, yes. He held himself...well, like a duke. Like the dukes she had met.

When her attention returned to his face, Theodore was grinning. 'And do you like what you see?'

Heat splashed across her cheeks. 'I... I was merely—'

'Yes?' he said quietly.

Sylvia swallowed hard. Was he...teasing her? He was so serious most of the time, it was hard to tell.

'You look like a gentleman,' she said aloud, mostly to distract herself from the most odd thoughts rushing through her mind. 'You act, in fact, like a duke! My friend Gwen married one and I must say that your manners and his are much alike.'

Theodore shrugged as they continued to walk around

the Serpentine. 'I went to the right schools, met the right people, wondered once if perhaps my father…but I did not have the right name. I do not have any name.'

'And Featherstonehaugh is not sufficient?' The words had slipped from her lips before she could stop them, and Sylvia tried to smile as he stared curiously. 'Cannot you ask her…surely she—'

'She died.' Theodore's tight jaw told her in no uncertain terms that the topic was not to be continued.

Sylvia swallowed. 'I am sorry for your loss.'

'Thank you.'

Silence fell between them, just for a few moments, and it was a comfortable silence, one Sylvia had never known before.

Then Theodore cleared his throat. 'What were we saying?'

Sylvia inhaled deeply. 'Well, Featherstonehaugh is a respectable enough… I mean, your mother's name… She was the one who raised you, it sounds, she was the one who—'

'Without my father's name I cannot know my place in the world.' Theodore's voice had grown rough, coarse.

Sylvia's jaw tightened. 'Well, as someone with their father's name, I can promise you it does not solve all problems.'

She stared straight ahead as she spoke and could feel Theodore's eyes raking over her face, but did not give into the temptation to meet his gaze. She had said too much already.

'That is why I agreed to this engagement.' His voice was strong, unfaltering, so clearly certain that he was right that there was little to say to disagree with him. 'A man with no name of repute going about London, asking questions? That would elicit suspicion…and if he is still alive—'

'I cannot imagine he would welcome such an intrusion,' Sylvia said bluntly.

Her words had perhaps been too blunt. Theodore halted, his expression one of surprise.

Sylvia tried to smile. 'I am sorry. I… I say what I think, which has its downsides. I meant—'

'I know what you meant. Perhaps you are right,' said Theodore, resuming walking but at a slower pace. 'Perhaps he has remarried, or had a child, a true son. A true heir. That would explain the cessation of funds.'

'Perhaps,' Sylvia said quietly.

It was most strange. Here was a man that a week ago she did not know, and yet now she probably knew him better than anyone. He had poured out his life to her— at least, the headlines—and their engagement of convenience had another intricacy woven into the pattern.

How much more complex could it become?

'So. Your father,' she said bracingly, checking once again that the Pike was out of earshot. 'Where do we begin?'

'We?' He stared blankly.

Sylvia nodded briskly. 'Yes, we—is that not the point? We are engaged to be married. No one will be surprised if we meander across London together. So, where shall we start?'

For some reason, Theodore was staring in what appeared to be amazement. 'You'll help me?'

It was her turn to be confused. 'Why would I not?'

It was perfectly simple, Sylvia reasoned. Theodore was not a duke—a disappointment, to be sure, but as she had never actually expected to marry him, she supposed it was hardly the end of the world.

It was the engagement that mattered. That meant she could come into London…well, not whenever she wanted, but far more often than the Pike would have permitted her before. She had to plan her escape. How often did ships leave Falmouth for Antigua, anyway? Surely someone would know at the docks.

There was so much of the city she had never seen, never explored. If she was permitted to come here at all, it was to walk with the other wallflowers in Hyde Park—dull—or to attend Almack's but not be asked to dance by anyone.

Hardly a riveting affair.

'I love a mystery,' Sylvia said aloud with a grin. 'So, I ask again, where shall we start?'

'I have absolutely no idea,' Theodore replied with a dry laugh. He halted, turning to look over the shimmering Serpentine. Gentlemen and ladies passed them, chattering away or in contemplative silence. 'To be honest, I do not know.'

'I'll have a think, and we can—'

'Look, I do not mean to be rude,' he said, cutting across her with a searching look. 'But you are a lady who has lived in a box, miles from London for…how long?'

Irritation prickled. 'Long enough.'

Theodore inclined his head. 'I am not sure why this is a good idea. Far better for you to break this off and—'

'No,' said Sylvia urgently.

Far more urgently than she had intended. Theodore raised an eyebrow, drawing attention again to his birthmark, and once again heat splattered across her face.

It was most annoying. She was not typically one to be embarrassed, but there was something about this man. Something that made her far more conscious of herself than she remembered.

'I want to be here,' she said quietly. 'I want to explore London, to manage my own schedule, to see the Queen's house and the Tower of London and—'

'You want to go sightseeing.'

There was just a hint of mirth in his voice, and Sylvia did not appreciate it.

'I want freedom. You men, you think nothing of the ability to go where you choose whenever you want. It is nothing for a man to plan a journey to the Caribbean, but should I wish to do so, it is complicated, difficult, impossible even. But I will do it.'

'This whole thing started because the Pike—dash it all, Miss Pike—wanted to save my honour. My honour as a duke,' Theodore said with a wry smile. 'Old

Warchester is happy enough for me to use his carriage for a while—he thinks the whole thing is rather amusing. But what about your reputation?'

'Reputation?' Sylvia repeated.

Reputation? She had never had much of a reputation. Oh, at the Wallflower Academy she had a reputation for mischief and noise, but that was what happened when you lived in a building full of shy, quiet women.

'You'll be a…a spurned woman,' said Theodore, lowering his voice and glancing past her shoulder to, Sylvia assumed, ensure the Pike was still at an appropriate distance. 'Whether or not I am a duke, you will have been engaged—engaged, and then a jilter. Does that not worry you?'

In all honesty, she had not thought that far ahead.

'You wish for me to jilt you?'

'It's far more honourable than a duke abandoning an engagement,' Theodore pointed out. 'Though I am happy to do so. It's not as though "the Duke Featherstonehaugh" has a real reputation to lose.'

'It would be far fairer for me to take the blame—it's my fault you're involved in this at all—' Sylvia thought aloud '—I suppose you could leave me at the altar.'

Become a spurned woman.

Sylvia's heartstrings tugged, just for a moment. A spurned woman. One who could have been married but was set aside by a gentleman.

He was right. If she had any intention to marry, having a chequered past, a failed engagement, would surely be a great detriment to her plans.

Fortunately, she had no such plans.

'I am bored,' Sylvia declared. 'Not of you—I've had more enjoyment with you in the few hours we have spent in each other's company than in the last decade put together.'

Was that red in Theodore's cheeks? Perhaps not. Perhaps it was merely a trick of the light.

'I am bored of my life—tired of the Wallflower Academy, tired of always seeing the same faces and doing the same things and never having the chance to live,' Sylvia said impulsively. She had not intended to be this open, but...but something in this man drew it out of her. 'I am three and twenty and have seen little of the world since I entered the Wallflower Academy six years ago. My father... There was no place for me in his household, I was a mistake he preferred to forget. You have nothing to worry about—I will not fall in love with you, this engagement will definitely end and, in the meantime, I can help you find your father.'

There was a wry smile across Theodore's lips. 'You can say that you won't fall in love with me with that much certainty?'

'Do not be offended. I have no intention of ever falling in love,' Sylvia said, drawing her hands together and sighing as she looked out over the Serpentine. What would it be like to see the sea? Or the Thames? 'Marriage is not my future.'

'And you know what will be?'

'I told you I had a plan, and that…that is to go back.'

'Back?'

Sylvia hesitated, but the man had proven himself to be trustworthy. It was difficult to deny Theodore this knowledge, especially when she wanted him to know. 'I…yes. Back to the Caribbean—Antigua. Marriage would prevent that and, besides, I read. Day after day, the newspapers are full of it—men who mistreat their wives, abandon them, decry them. Women are injured, disgraced, and all because they want their own freedom, their own lives, their own choices. The number of broken engagements! True ones, I mean—the number of men promising marriage and then it all leads to nothing and…no. No, I will not put myself in the power of another. First my father, then Miss Pike—there has always been someone dictating where I go and what I wear and—'

She caught herself just in time. It was all too much, too vulnerable, too painful.

'I will not marry,' Sylvia said quietly.

'I have never met anyone who speaks with such conviction.' His voice was not censorious, but not exactly curious. Somewhere in the middle. 'Is it truly that simple?'

Sylvia swallowed. *Yes*, she wanted to say. *Yes, because I have seen what marriage does for women. It binds and it constricts, and even when you think you can trust a man, he is not quite honest. Not quite true.*

And he has no incentive to be kind to you, and you have no choice but to live under those conditions.

No. No, I will not do it.

She smiled brightly. 'I want to see the world—at least, the portion of it on my doorstep, and London is apparently one of the greatest cities in the world. So, let's make a plan. Where shall we start in the hunt for your father?'

Sylvia watched him hesitate, watched him think carefully, evidently concerned that he could not take her words at face value.

How, precisely, she was supposed to convince him, she did not know.

'Investments have been made over the years that will give me an income, albeit reduced,' Theodore said eventually. 'That's the trouble with long-term investments—I won't see real profit from them for many years. Besides, it's not money I seek from him but answers. If you can help me find him, ascertain who I am…well, I would be most grateful.'

A smile spread across her cheeks as excitement flared in her heart. Not only a fake engagement, but a mystery! Oh, this was far better than embroidering the same cushion over and over again at the Wallflower Academy, or learning how to pair a gold brooch with the right earbobs.

'Excellent,' Sylvia said promptly. 'Where shall we start, Your Grace?'

It had been a teasing expression and she was all the

more delighted to see Theodore scowl. 'Don't call me that.'

'Whatever you say, Your Grace.'

'I mean it.'

Sylvia grinned. 'Yes, Your Grace.'

Chapter Five

'He's here!'

The shout went up across the drawing room and Sylvia rolled her eyes as she carefully licked a finger and turned a page.

'He's here, Sylvia!' Daphne's face was flushed when Sylvia looked up at her friend. 'Aren't you excited? Your duke!'

Ah. Yes.

Though Theodore found the whole thing most odd, he had agreed with Sylvia that it would be best to keep up the charade of his title at the Wallflower Academy.

'I do not approve,' he had said sternly.

'Neither do I,' Sylvia had lied cheerfully. 'But if you want the Pike to continue to make it easy for us to meet—for you to accompany me, without a chaperone—then keeping up the pretence of your dukeness is essential.'

'Dukedom.'

Sylvia had nodded. 'Whatever you say, Your Grace.'

Your Grace. In the drawing room, as wallflowers crowded to the window to gaze at the duke who had captured the heart of the least wallflowery one among them, Sylvia smiled.

It really was so easy to irritate the man. She would have to remember that.

'I'm sure it will be pleasant to see him,' Sylvia said aloud.

Daphne's face was a picture of confusion. 'I would have thought you would be far more delighted to see him, Sylvia. You...you do love him, don't you?'

That was the trouble with Daphne. Shy, hateful of attention and a hopeless romantic. Sylvia trusted her as she did no one else in the Wallflower Academy, though that wasn't saying much, but the less she knew about these particular shenanigans, the better. Daphne had never betrayed her before. But her expressions might just do that.

'I think very highly of Theodore,' Sylvia said honestly.

Her friend's cheeks flushed on her behalf. 'Theodore! How intimate.'

The doorbell jangled and there were murmured yelps as wallflowers attempted to return placidly to their seats in the drawing room. Two of them ran into each other, a third dropped her embroidery and another picked up a book to hide behind. Unfortunately, the book was upside down.

Sighing inwardly, Sylvia tried not to notice. That was

the trouble with wallflowers. They were not being shy intentionally. That was how they were.

'A gentleman visitor to see you, Miss Sylvia,' said Matthews stiffly from the doorway.

Gentleman visitor. Sylvia tried not to smile as she rose as elegantly as she could, dropping the book onto her chair and stepping towards the hallway.

Gentleman. Was he? Theodore had no idea and, in truth, neither did she. He had been raised as one—but had he been born one?

That thought flitted away the moment she saw Theodore standing in the hall, hands behind his back, spine straight. There was a gracefulness and elegance about him that seemed to say gentleman…but could that be taught? Could such refinement be inherited—perhaps a clue to the background of his father?

'Ah, Miss Bryant,' said Theodore stiffly, bowing.

Sylvia dropped into a curtsey as swiftly as possible. 'Your Grace. Matthews, do you have a shawl about you?'

The footman blinked. 'Shawl?'

'Never mind. Come, Theodore,' Sylvia said, seeing the glint in Theodore's eye that said quite plainly that he would not permit a repeat of the irritating moniker. 'Let us find a corner in which to sit and plot.'

'Plot?' repeated Matthews.

Sylvia ignored him. Taking Theodore's arm and ignoring his mutters about not capturing everyone's attention and acting with decorum, she marched him through the front door of the Wallflower Academy and out onto the drive.

The sun was shining, the air was thick with heat and Sylvia smiled. She always felt better when she was outside the Wallflower Academy. It was not precisely a prison; the furnishings and the food were too good, from the little she had read in the newspapers about true finishing schools.

But still. There was something oppressive about the place after six years. Something entirely unsuited to her temperament.

'You look nice.'

Sylvia almost tripped over her own foot. It was only thanks to the swift movement of Theodore that she did not make a greater acquaintance with the gravel of the drive.

His hand on her wrist, his strength through her arm, the world spinning—

Theodore dropped her arm. 'You seem to be in the habit of falling over.'

Sylvia cleared her throat as her mind continued to whirl. 'Yes. Yes. Right.' Sitting down—that was what she needed. Somewhere to sit. 'The rose garden.'

It was too early, sadly, for the rose garden to be out in its full splendour, but the place was beautiful enough. The fresh green of spring had given way to the rich green of impending summer and the air was filled with the scent of the copious lavender that grew at the feet of the rosebushes.

Sylvia dropped gratefully onto the bench that the Pike had ordered to be placed there a few years ago. She couldn't fall if she was sitting.

'I saw a great number of faces peering at me through the windows,' said Theodore quietly as he sat himself down beside her. 'I suppose I am an object of great amusement?'

'Curiosity, I would say,' countered Sylvia, trying not to think of the way Daphne had lurched to the window. 'For all that the Wallflower Academy is designed to marry us off, it does not happen that often, and a duke is a rarity.'

'You said your friend Gwen was married.'

'Yes, and Rilla. But they are the only two who have been married from our ranks for...oh, five years? Six?' Sylvia attempted to speak lightly, but there was a darkness in her voice she could not hide.

Two of her three closest friends had succumbed. Gone off to be married, started new lives. Lives of being bound to one person and one person alone. Losing their names, their autonomy...

Oh, she saw them often. Once a month or so. It was not enough.

'I hope our engagement has not pricked any ears and caused too many questions.'

Sylvia blinked and returned her attention to the man seated beside her. Very close beside her. It was only now she had twisted to look at him that she realised just how close they were.

Why, the man's leg was almost touching hers!

Trying not to think about it, Sylvia nodded. 'Yes, I think Miss Pike is delighted with herself and the other wallflowers are intrigued. No one suspects. At least, I do not think so.'

Theodore was nodding. 'That is all to the good. And how, precisely, are we to end the engage—'

'Your father,' Sylvia said decidedly.

Well, there was no point in fretting about ending an engagement that wasn't even real. They could worry about that later—she was far more interested in tracking down the mysterious Mr Featherstonehaugh.

But not Featherstonehaugh. That was the whole point.

'I have a list of questions prepared,' Sylvia said briskly, pulling out a folded paper from her bodice. 'Firstly… Goodness, are you quite well?'

There was a flush to his face, his eyes were overly bright and…perhaps he was not unwell. Sylvia was not an expert in the male, but…but was that a flash of heated desire?

Then Theodore shook his head and swallowed, hard. Sylvia tried her best not to notice the bob of his Adam's apple but…well. He had a most pleasing throat.

'Do you typically keep things in your bodice?' he said, his voice a little hoarse.

Discomfort flamed through Sylvia's body. Was it so unusual? All the ladies here at the Wallflower Academy did so…but then, wasn't that the problem? She had been so little in the world, it was impossible to know exactly what was appropriate and what was just something they had always done.

Sitting up straighter, she said firmly, 'My list of questions. Are you ready?'

'No one is ready for you, Sylvia Bryant,' he teased with a wry smile. 'No amount of training at the best university would prepare a man for your onslaught. Though, I admit, I am enjoying it.' It was most unfortunate how easily disconcerted she was when he looked at her like that. Theodore nodded vaguely, his expression sharpening only by degrees. 'Yes? Yes.'

He wouldn't get very far in discovering his father with that attitude, Sylvia thought ruefully. Thank goodness she was here to assist him.

'Right,' she said confidently. 'Firstly, what did your mother tell you about your father? Presuming that she told you anything at all, that is.'

Theodore cleared his throat, the disquiet he felt so obvious across his face he might as well have had the word tattooed across his forehead. 'I… She was not forthcoming.'

Sylvia waited. A bee bumbled along, worshipping the lavender. She waited.

'She said he did not want to be known as my father,' Theodore said shortly. 'That was all. I learned quickly to stop asking questions that would not be answered.'

Sylvia nodded, glancing at her paper. 'Secondly, when were you born?'

'I don't know precisely. Some time in August 1782.

My mother fell ill, a long fever after the birth. She was never told the precise date. But—'

'And do you have any other siblings? Your mother, I mean—did she have any more children? Obviously, we do not know about your father, that information will have to come,' said Sylvia as she waved a hand.

To her great confusion, there was a frustrated look on the man's face. 'No. I was her only—'

'When did the money start arriving?' Sylvia interrupted, unable to help herself. Goodness, this was absolutely thrilling! A real mystery, one she could help solve. 'And how much was it? Which school did you go to, and was it one that your mother chose, or did your father—'

'Sylvia,' interrupted Theodore, most rudely in Sylvia's opinion. 'I will not—'

'I don't think we'll get very far if you don't answer me,' she pointed out reasonably. 'After all, without knowing—'

'Dammit, woman, I've never spoken of this before!'

And he was gone, his presence beside her suddenly absent, and Sylvia gasped at the sudden lack of him. How did his presence have such an effect on her? Why did his rising to his feet to turn and glare—most rude, too—leave her feeling so empty?

'This is—' Theodore had lowered his voice but the strength of his tone remained. 'This is my life, not some cheap entertainment on a stage!'

Guilt seared through Sylvia. 'I… I'm sorry—'

'I'm having to face the fact that I was not wanted, that it was preferable to throw money at me than actually meet me, looking for clues I never spotted of a father who clearly did not wish to know me!' Theodore's shoulders were heaving, his breath short. 'I apologise for my directness, but you... I...'

Oh, it had all gone wrong. Her intentions had been good...well, mostly good. Sylvia was not sufficiently ignorant of her own heart to try to convince herself that she was being completely altruistic.

She had hurt him. And somehow, hurting him had injured herself.

'I am sorry, Theodore. I... I should not have been so unthinking,' Sylvia said quietly. 'My father chose to send me away, a mistake from his youth—a Grand Tour consequence he never expected. I know better than to press you.'

Theodore turned away, just for a moment, as he took a deep breath. Then he looked at her. 'You are swift to apologise.'

'When I make mistakes, I own up to them,' she said frankly, trying not to sound too bitter. 'You cannot run from your mistakes, not in a place like this.'

Her mouth was suddenly uncomfortably dry. No, she couldn't run away from her mistakes. But others could. They could run away from her.

Theodore sighed heavily, pulling a hand through his hair. 'Do not misunderstand me, Sylvia. I... I am impressed by you. Springing this engagement on me may not have earned my friendship but your candour has. But I will not be treated like a child and I will not be interrogated like a suspect.'

His steady gaze bored into hers and Sylvia was forced to push aside the observation that Theodore Featherstonehaugh was remarkably handsome when he was fired up.

When he stood there like that, almost vibrating with certainty, laying down the law…

Well. There was something most electrifying about it. It made her tingle all over—tingle in some places more than others.

Sylvia inclined her head, using the small movement to both ground herself and buy herself a few more minutes. 'In that case, Your Grace—'

'I told you not to call me that.'

'—why don't you tell me, in your own words, what you do know?'

For a moment, she thought he was going to decline and leave. Walk away, not just from her, and the Wallflower Academy, but the scheme they had concocted. Go and find his father on his own.

Or not find him, if his sleuthing skills so far were anything to go by.

But after his focus swept over her face, Theodore nodded and slowly returned to the bench. Sylvia absolutely did not move two inches to the right to be closer to him. Most definitely not.

The heat of his leg could be felt even through the

layers of his breeches and her gown and underskirts and Sylvia was absolutely not thinking about it. Definitely not.

'I was born some time in August 1782,' Theodore repeated quietly. The fire had gone from his voice but there was still a sharpness, a strength that caused little tendrils of heat to cascade across Sylvia's chest. She did her best to ignore them, but could not entirely. Instead, she tried to focus on his words.

'My mother was an only child, with no family—a sickness took her parents young, and they were apparently only children themselves. My only living relatives, if they are alive, are on my father's side, and he... My mother always said my father could not be involved with us—*could not*, that was her phrase. I always thought... I mean, I imagined he was already married when they met,' Theodore said with a sigh. 'He would not be the first man to take a mistress, and my mother would not be the first woman to be set aside upon giving birth to a child.'

Sylvia's throat tightened. 'No. No, she would not.'

It was on the tip of her tongue to tell him—to spill out the truth of her own past. But Theodore continued. 'I know he was a little older than my mother, by five years or so. I know he lived in London, that his family was here. That was where he returned after I was born. I know the funds are—were—deposited into my bank on the fifth of every month, though they will not tell me by whom. When she knew she was dying, she wrote a letter—I must have been five, perhaps six years of age. The letter was responded to, and apparently it was decided that I would not go to my father upon my mother's death but to an orphanage. Arrangements, I was told, would be made for my schooling when I was older. And…and that is all.'

Sylvia blinked. 'That is all?'

Theodore turned, smiling, towards her. His hand on the bench shifted, brushing against her own. 'This isn't a play, Sylvia, or a dramatic opera. In real life, mysteries do not come with three or four obvious clues just waiting to be pursued.'

Warmth spread through her, though whether that was because of his words or the intense closeness of his body, she was not so sure. 'I know that. I just…well. It isn't much to go on.'

Theodore's smile was more a grin now. 'Is that not what I said in Hyde Park?'

For a most inconvenient reason, Sylvia's heart was fluttering. It made thinking a challenge, which was annoying because he was sitting there, smiling, waiting for her to respond.

And all she could think was how handsome he was. And how close he was—the closest she had ever been to a man in her life.

Except that first time they'd met, when she'd fallen into his arms…

'You know, we may have to spend a great deal of time

together,' Theodore said slowly. 'Pretending to plan a wedding. Hunting down my father.'

Sylvia waited for the rest of the sentence, but apparently there was no more forthcoming. 'And?'

'Well, I have no wish to make this false engagement…complicated,' he said lightly.

At first, she was not quite sure what he meant. When the reason for his delicacy was suddenly made clear to her, she could not help but laugh.

'I told you,' Sylvia said briskly. 'I won't be doing anything so foolish as falling in love with you.'

'You haven't asked me whether I intend to guard against falling in love with you.' Theodore's words were low, more a murmur, and they thrummed in her bones. Sylvia's breath caught in her throat, the implication transfixing.

But he could not have meant it like that. He could not mean that he liked her—that there was any chance that he could actually fall in love with her.

She smiled brightly—the same smile she plastered on her lips whenever she needed to look happy, despite what was circling in her soul. 'You're not going to fall in love with me.'

'You sound very sure.'

There it was again—a hum of amusement in his voice and yet his tone was low, intimate…seductive.

Sylvia straightened. Not seductive. Not at all. 'Men do not find me attractive.'

'Now, where on earth would you have gained that

idea?' And he was closer to her now—how, she did not know, but most definitely closer. Too close.

It was all she could do not to laugh. 'I'm the abandoned illegitimate daughter of mixed heritage stuck in a house full of wallflowers. I have little to recommend me.'

'You are a very beautiful woman.'

This was not happening.

'It's a fake engagement, Theodore. You…you don't have to—'

'I know I don't have to,' he said quietly, his eyes unwavering as he stared into her own. 'But you are beautiful, and we both know this is going nowhere.'

'Which is a shame.'

She had not intended to blurt out the words, but they had escaped her lips.

Theodore's eyebrow was quizzical. 'It is?'

'It…it's just…' Sylvia hesitated, but what did it matter? 'I was always curious. About…about a kiss?'

Theodore's eyes danced. 'In another world I could show you—teach you. But the rules of propriety… I shouldn't.'

Sylvia swallowed and tried hard not to look at his lips, which were effortlessly inviting. 'I suppose you shouldn't.'

But she wanted him to. Oh, how she wanted him to. She could almost taste the buzz of desire in the air, and—

'But, as this is going nowhere, and we are both abso-

lutely clear that this engagement is naught but a sham,'
Theodore continued in a low murmur, 'why not…enjoy
ourselves?'

Sylvia swallowed, wetting her lips as she tried desperately to think of a reply. 'I… I…'

It did not matter.

It did not matter because her attention was caught by
the curve of his smile. It did not matter because of her
pulse, thundering in her chest.

And, most of all, it did not matter because Theodore
was kissing her.

And oh, what a kiss. Sylvia had never been kissed
before, true, and she had never been touched like this.
Theodore's hand was cupping her cheek, pulling her
closer, and his other hand on the bench made it possible
to lean into his arm. Into his embrace.

Their bodies tilted together, and Sylvia almost slipped
off the bench as Theodore's lips pressed against hers,
earnest and demanding, and she whimpered before she
could stop herself as his tongue claimed entrance.

She let him.

She had not intended to do so. Kissing Theodore
Featherstonehaugh was not part of the plan. But the
pleasure rippling through her, the giddy intensity that
was causing all thoughts in her mind to become nothing but *Theodore… Theodore… Theodore* meant that
she welcomed him in, her hands somehow clutching his
cravat to pull him closer.

His tongue ravished her mouth, causing such delight to thrum through her that Sylvia gasped. 'Theodore...'

The kiss was broken. The moment ended. She looked up into his eyes, cheeks burning, and knew that she absolutely, positively, could not do that again.

Kissing this man...it was addictive. One taste of him and she would never want to stop kissing him.

Theodore cocked his head. 'There. What do you think of your first kiss?'

It was a miracle she was still standing.

'Not...not bad.'

That was it—she could not let him see just how much the moment had affected her. How he had affected her. How his touch had reached something deeper in her than merely her mouth.

'Not bad?'

Bad? Saints preserve her.

'Not bad,' Sylvia repeated, surprised at the momentary strength in her voice. 'Now, can we get back to the mystery at hand?'

Theodore had a far too knowing look on his face as he nodded, shifting away from her on the bench by a painful few inches, but he appeared to decide not to push the subject.

'What do you suggest as our first method of attack?'

She wanted to launch herself into his arms and kiss him so senseless that neither of them could walk. Not that she was about to admit that.

Sylvia plastered a false smile on her lips and quipped, 'I have the perfect place to start. The orphanage.'

His smile immediately departed. 'The orphanage?'

'There is no better place,' said Sylvia, noting the warmth dissipate between them as Theodore's jaw tightened. 'You want answers, don't you? Well, then. It's time for a trip down memory lane.'

Chapter Six

Every step that Theodore took along the street curdled his stomach. His feet rebelled. Everything in him was desperate to halt, to turn around, to not see again the building he had left all those years ago.

'You can't see the records, Theodore. I'm sorry.'

'You're not sorry—you're keeping my past from me... my future. I'm about to go to school and I want to know who I am—'

'Your father was most insistent.'

Theodore's mouth was dry.

Fortunately, Sylvia had enough conversation for the pair of them.

'—not been down here before, and what beautiful buildings! The white stone, truly beautiful in the sunlight...'

It wasn't that he wasn't listening. He was listening, in a way. It was comforting, having the sound of Sylvia's thoughts filling his mind instead of his own. But Theodore could not ignore them completely. Not as memories of traipsing down this very street as a child kept forcefully resurfacing.

Think of something else. Think of the debts piling up. Think of the pile of post by the bed, letters unopened in fear of what you could find there. Think of—

'And I never knew…oh. Is that it?'

Theodore steeled himself for the moment he would have to see it. His jaw was tight, a pulse throbbing in his wrist, his lungs rigid.

He looked up.

There it was. Strange—part of him had wondered whether it would be precisely the same. The same crack in the window on the second floor. The same dusty brown paint on the door. The same sense of menace oozing from it.

But it wasn't. From what he could tell, standing here on the pavement and looking up, St Kilda's Orphanage for Waifs and Strays looked completely different. For a start, there were more doors.

'I… I think it's a private home now.' Sylvia spoke softly, that gentleness Theodore was coming to expect from her at the most unexpected times returning. 'Or many homes. Did it look like that when you were here?'

Theodore shook his head without speaking.

No. No, it did not. These homes looked cared for, loved. As though those who resided here did so by choice. There were planters on the windowsills filled with flowers. The windows were clean, the roof mended, and there was smoke coming out of all the chimneys.

He could not recall a time when all the fires had been lit. Movement. Warmth. Contact.

Theodore looked down. Sylvia had slipped her hand into his. It comforted him in a way he had not expected—like a punch to his gut, a physical reminder that he was not alone.

He was not alone.

'Come on,' said Sylvia brightly, though there was a brittleness to that smile he was starting to recognise. 'Let's begin our enquiries.'

Theodore immediately tried to resist her tug. 'No, I—'

'We'll never find out anything if we don't ask,' she said briskly. 'Come on.'

It was impossible to resist her.

No, that was not quite right. Theodore had managed to resist kissing her from the instant her carriage had deposited her at the Lancaster Gate of Hyde Park, as agreed, for which he rather thought he deserved a medal.

'You can say that you won't fall in love with me with that much certainty?'

It had been a foolish thing to say.

The kiss had been a mistake—one he'd indulged in, one he'd enjoyed far too much. One he would not permit himself to repeat.

The temptation of kissing Sylvia had been far too great.

Theodore had always been careful in his dalliances

with women—opera singers or a young widow in need of release. Never someone like—

Sylvia was rapping on the first door before he could stop her.

'Sylvia, wait, I don't—'

'Good afternoon,' Sylvia said cheerfully as the door was opened and a maid peered out at them suspiciously. 'I wondered, when did you move in here?'

Theodore groaned as the maid's eyes widened. Honestly, she didn't have much subtlety. Or nuance.

'I mean, you and your master and mistress and whoever,' continued Sylvia. 'I'm trying to find out when this place became a house, not an orphanage.'

This had gone on long enough. Theodore stepped forward and smiled at the maid. 'We are investigating my past, miss, and hoped you would be able to help us. Any information you could give us would be most useful.'

Readying himself for a rebuke, Theodore wondered—not for the first time—whether he might have had greater success in this endeavour if he had kept Sylvia out of it. After all, it wasn't as though the maid was just going to—

'Oh, it was about two years ago,' the maid said nonchalantly, leaning one hip against the doorframe and grinning at Sylvia. 'I thought it was a bit suspect, moving into an old orphanage, but they say half the buildings in London used to be something else, so why not, I suppose. Were you an orphan here?'

'Not in the slightest,' said Sylvia with a beaming smile. 'Thank you.'

Theodore tried not to laugh as the maid grinned and shut the door.

Sylvia turned to him with a smile—a smile that faded as she took in his expression. 'What is it?'

'You!' Theodore had not intended to speak quite so plainly, so he was not surprised when Sylvia stepped back to the pavement with pinking cheeks.

'I am sure I don't know what you mean,' she said, her voice firm as ever.

But he was not fooled. Bold Sylvia might be, absolutely determined to have her own way at every juncture, yes…but there was something more delicate about her than she wanted to let on.

Theodore swallowed down the myriad questions he wanted to ask—*what made you so determined? Why do you hate people's attention? Why do you always smile like that when you think a smile is demanded?*—and stepped back to stare up at the building.

True, it had felt deeply uncomfortable right under his skin when Sylvia had knocked on that door…but he could not deny that they had gained their answer. An answer to a question he would not have had the gall to ask.

She was…artless. No, not quite. But as Theodore studied her face and took in the beautiful contours of her cheeks, the curve of her lips, the determination in her jaw, he knew there was no malice in her.

They were very different people.

'Two years ago, then, at least,' he said aloud. 'Strange to think that all traces of the place I knew are probably gone.'

'I don't suppose the records would have been kept, now the place is closed down,' said Sylvia with a sigh. 'I am sorry. It seemed like the best place to start.'

'It was,' Theodore said with a slow nod. 'And…in a strange way, it has been good to come back here.'

She looked at him questioningly at that remark. 'It has?'

In a way he could not quite describe, though he would try. 'When I left here, it…it wasn't on the best of terms. I was about to go to school and I was desperate to know who I was, where I sat in the social order I was about to join. There was an argument. They had details of my father in their records but I was forbidden from seeing them. When I broke into the office—'

'I'm sorry—you broke in?'

Theodore smiled. 'It sounds worse than it was. Still, it did not go down well. It was quite bad, to tell the truth. When you said you lived in a semi-prison, I felt that deep within me.'

'You did?' Sylvia looked surprised. 'I mean, I have dreamt for years of escaping the stifling lessons at the Wallflower Academy, dreading the sort of future Miss Pike painted for me, for all of us. The very idea of living that stiff, stilted life, married to a stuffy Englishman who doesn't care to laugh, following all the rules. That's my idea of a prison. But you—you're a man, Theodore. You can do…well, almost anything.'

'Except be wanted.' He had not intended to speak so directly, but it was said now and he could not take it back. 'My father could have taken me in but he would rather I lived in an orphanage, at school, at university…'

Theodore's throat closed and he was unable to continue.

He had said too much. He couldn't look at Sylvia, didn't want to see the pity that always spread across a person's features the moment they discovered just how tragic his childhood had been.

She would suggest they return to the carriage and make a swift departure—

'Let's walk,' Sylvia said decidedly.

Theodore blinked as he looked up. 'Walk?'

'I always feel better when walking,' she said decisively, slipping her arm through his. The movement was becoming so natural now, Theodore was starting to wonder how it had ever started.

And so they walked. Not in any particular direction, not with any great sense of purpose. As far as he could tell, Sylvia was steering him, for he put no conscious effort into deciding left or right or straight on at each junction.

Within minutes, they were streets away from the orphanage and Theodore's chest was lighter. A burden he had not noticed he was carrying had been lifted from his shoulders. The air was fresher. Birdsong sweeter.

'I know what you mean.'

Theodore glanced at Sylvia. She had not looked at him as she spoke, and the false smile—or at least, the smile he was almost certain was false—was back. But there was an edge to her tone that he had never heard before. 'Mean?'

'Living in a place you are not wanted,' said Sylvia vibrantly. Too vibrantly. 'It's not just the Wallflower Academy that has been that place for me. I… I lived with my own father for only a short time.'

Swallowing, Theodore decided not to speak. The woman beside him was talking as though she had never said these words before, as though she were dredging them up from a place so deep within her that she had never thought to go there.

Their steps echoed on the empty pavement.

'My father was not a titled man, but he was a rich one,' Sylvia said quietly. 'Rich enough to travel. He didn't want to see the cathedrals of France or the rivers of Italy. He wanted to see parts of the world that few others in London would have seen. He went to the Caribbean. Antigua.'

Well, that answered a few questions. Theodore nodded, but remained silent.

Sylvia glanced up with a wry smile. 'It may have escaped your notice, but I am of mixed heritage.'

'It hasn't entirely escaped my notice,' Theodore said admiringly, his eyes raking over her dark skin and brilliant eyes. Not much of Sylvia's body had escaped his notice, though he was hardly going to admit to as much.

She smiled, and it was a genuine one, a smile of warmth, and there she was. His Sylvia.

His Sylvia? Where the devil had that thought come from?

'She fell in love, of course. My mother, I mean,' Sylvia added with a wry smile. 'She adored my father, she believed every good thing about him. She believed in him. She gave over her heart and would have done anything he wanted—and he asked for everything.'

Ah. Theodore knew the end of this tale, had encountered it through his friends a few times over the last twelvemonth. It never ended well.

'My father promised marriage and clearly persuaded my mother that there was no reason to wait to consummate the passion she felt,' Sylvia continued, in the most expressionless tone Theodore had ever heard. 'I am the result.'

Theodore nodded. It was most odd; she spoke lightly of a topic that in polite Society would be considered outrageous, yet there was no shame in her voice. Nothing that suggested she wept over her origins. Nothing leading him to think she regretted her birth.

'And of course, he abandoned her.'

His neck stiffened. Ah, there it was—the edge was back.

'He left without telling my mother, the day after she told him they would be welcoming their first child,'

Sylvia continued. There was a grit in her tone as they crossed the street that made Theodore wince. 'They were engaged to be married, at least as far as she was concerned, and that was when he told her that he had a bride waiting for him, in England. The right family, the right name—my mother was a distraction, he said. He had bought his ticket to Saint Kitts and onward, and he saw no reason to change his plans. I'm told he felt guilty years later, when he married and had a child of his own. A son, far more important, but apparently, he realised just how devastating his abandonment had been. And so he came for me.'

She could attempt to speak lightly as much as she wished, but Theodore was not fooled. As they passed under cherry blossom then oak trees, leaves spreading out and shading them from the sun, he could see the pain flickering across her face as the dappled shade moved.

There was hurt there, real hurt. And a clear distrust of men.

'But...your mother?' Theodore said quietly.

Just when he thought Sylvia's expression could not be more stormy, it flickered into deep pain. Then she said quietly, 'I don't know where she is.'

Theodore's foot almost slipped off the edge of the pavement. 'You don't—'

'I don't know,' Sylvia repeated, anger barely contained under the surface of her words.

It didn't make sense. She spoke with such vehemence

about her father, her mother with much tenderness…but she did not know where her mother was?

Evidently his confusion was showing. Sylvia slipped her arm from his and clasped her hands before her. She'd done that before, Theodore could not recall when, but she had been distressed at the time.

'You don't have to tell me,' he said quietly. 'Lord knows, I can understand the desire to keep some things to yourself.'

Sylvia's steps had slowed until they were barely moving. She halted under a wide spreading oak tree and the shade belied the anger dancing in her eyes.

'Why would you want to know?' she said belligerently. 'You have your own troubles. I am nothing to you—a kiss here and there perhaps to keep you entertained, but your search is independent of me.'

Theodore swallowed.

A kiss here and there to keep you entertained. Well, if he had ever wondered what she thought of him, he had a good idea now.

The trouble was, he wouldn't say no to another kiss. An intimacy of that kind with Sylvia was enough to spark fires in any man.

But he would not be that man. He would not prove to her, as though she required any proof, that all men were simply ready to take what they could get.

'I want to know because…because it's a part of you. Your story,' Theodore said slowly, looking ahead of his sentences for any potential pitfalls. 'And you don't have to tell me. But this fake engagement would be a lot easier, and more enjoyable, if we felt we could trust each other. Wouldn't it?'

Quite inexplicably, his breathing had become short.

Why did this matter? He could not explain it, even to himself. That it was important was clear. There was a desperate need within him to win this woman's trust, come what may.

Sylvia was examining him closely, her eyes narrowed as she considered. And then—

'I was taken,' she said curtly. 'Taken from my mother when I was eight years old.'

Theodore's eyes widened. 'You weren't—'

'My father wished for me to be raised in England. He had a fit of conscience, I suppose, much against his wife's will. She did not wish to have a reminder of his debauchery around her and her son,' said Sylvia with a shadowy laugh. 'As though every Englishwoman doesn't stare at me when I enter a room.'

Theodore bit his tongue.

'I wrote to my mother over the years. Every month,' Sylvia continued softly, her eyes full of emotion. 'Every month I wrote to her and she never wrote back. I started to hate her, and then I worried about her—had something happened? Had a storm come? Had she grown ill?'

She understood, then. The wondering, the questioning. There was a parent out there he did not know, and she knew what it was to seek for such—

'I found the letters, all of them, years of them, when I turned eighteen,' Sylvia said quietly. The edge was back, and it was sharpened. 'Opened, but unsent. In my father's bureau.'

Theodore cursed under his breath.

'My father walked in and…well. My temper isn't a new character trait.' Sylvia tried to smile. 'It had all been for my own good. He had wanted me to settle in England, to stop thinking of the warm waters that beckoned, the brilliance of the hibiscus, the heady scent of the frangipani. I didn't like the dull English summers, the even duller English winters. I argued back, and my stepmother entered and…and it was decided. I would be sent to the Wallflower Academy to learn how to be ladylike…and here we are,' said Sylvia, spreading out her hands as she gestured around them before starting to walk again, more slowly this time. 'I have written again. To my mother, I mean, to tell her that I will be coming to her, but I have no idea if the address is even correct. She might have moved. She might have sailed elsewhere. She might have died. I suppose I will find out when I arrive there. I… I hope I still have some family there. Someone that looks like me.'

Her voice was melancholy. *Someone that looks like me.* Sylvia had evidently spent years at the Wallflower Academy and never encountered another person like her—the same tightly curled hair, the same dark complexion, the same ability to stand out in a crowd.

'You must have encountered someone—'

'Oh, a few times I met the gaze of someone in London, a rarity that always led me to stride forward, yet I never had the boldness to converse.' A little strength returned to her voice. 'To walk down a street, to enter a shop, to sit at the opera and be surrounded by people who look like you,' Sylvia said wistfully. 'Or at least, more like you. I suppose as I was just a child there must have been people who stared at me, my skin lighter than theirs, another sign that I did not truly belong. But my mother... I have her nose, her eyes. I belonged when I was by her side. It is why I wish to go back to Antigua. The...the only place I have ever truly felt at home.'

'Antigua is a long way away.' Theodore was not entirely sure what made him say it, but now the words had slipped from his lips, he had to continue. 'You would be in danger every mile, Sylvia. Are you not concerned?'

She was, he could see it in her eyes, but she had not wished to face it. 'No.'

'This pin money you've saved, is it sufficient to reach Antigua?' They were intrusive, these questions, but he had to know. He...he worried for her. 'Could you afford to hire a companion, someone to go with you?'

'Who would want to come with me?' Sylvia laughed.

Theodore managed to bite down on the response that was impossible. *Me. I'll go with you.* 'I would be willing to contribute, financially, I mean, to pay for a compan—'

'I don't need your money.' The ferocity in her voice

was quite something, but her tone softened as she continued. 'I… I would rather pay my own way. When I reach Antigua, I wish to be beholden to no person. I will begin my life there anew.'

Try as he might, Theodore could not help but respect her answer, even though it tore at his conscience to even think of her attempting to do this on her own.

But perhaps there was something he could do. Didn't Warchester's great-uncle live in Antigua? Could he ask a favour, put the news out that he was looking for—?

'But you didn't ask for my miserable tale,' Sylvia said briskly. 'And you've listened very patiently.'

'I…thank you.'

Sylvia frowned as they turned a corner onto a bustling street, people pouring in and out of shops. His instinct to reach for her, to attempt to comfort her in some way, was forced down.

'Thank you? Why are you—'

'You didn't have to tell me all that,' Theodore said with a smile. 'Thank you.'

And she was laughing again, the portcullis was down, and the delicate and vulnerable Sylvia was gone.

'Oh, it's the same old sob story, I suppose. You should hear my friend Daphne's past—now, that's a story to make you cry yourself to sleep at night,' she said conversationally, as though they were discussing the weather and not one's abandonment by one's parents.

'But you speak…well, forgive me…' said Theodore, knowing there was no right way to say this and saying it anyway. '…you speak very casually of being born out of wedlock.'

The look she gave him was not one he had expected. It was…teasing?

'And why not?' she shot back, picking at a leaf from the hedge they were walking along. 'I mean, so were you, weren't you? At least, that is what you presume.'

It was not a thought Theodore had ever given much time to, and so his physical instinctive reaction was far more violent than he could have imagined.

Take that back.

That was what he wanted to snarl: to force Sylvia to take back those words.

'And why not? I mean, so were you, weren't you?'

It was ridiculous, but as the flash of anger subsided, it was pain and hurt that was left. The two of them had never known loving parents, loving homes. They had been housed, yes. But that was not the same.

'Perhaps I used to be ashamed,' Sylvia was saying, utterly unaware of the sudden rush of anger that had swept through him. 'It is not as though I can hide my background, however. Anyone looking at me knows that my family situation is complicated, and it does not take the Pike long to reveal the truth to any who ask.'

A flash of returning anger. 'She has no right to—'

'Miss Pike believes she has the right to do whatever she wants and, in a way, she is right,' said Sylvia, picking apart the leaf with her fingers and allowing the green shards to fall to the pavement. 'The Wall-flower Academy is her domain. She can do what she likes there.'

Only now was Theodore starting to gain an idea of what it was like to live in such a place. To have one's personal history, one's private family dramas picked over by the proprietress—for her to share that with any-one who asked!

No wonder Sylvia wished to escape.

'So yes, I was ashamed, but I am no longer,' Sylvia said cheerfully, dropping the remnants of the leaf and looking up at him. 'I cannot help how I was made. All I can do is shape the person I am today.'

He could not help but smile at that. 'You are right. Thank you, again.'

'No need to thank me. I fully intend to make you pay for it,' she shot back. 'You owe me.'

There she was again—the playful, teasing Sylvia. But as Theodore watched her, he could see that the vul-nerable, pained Sylvia and the mischievous, flirtatious Sylvia were very much one and the same.

Only a trusted few would be granted visibility of both.

'I owe you?' he said with a smile, attempting to match her jollity. 'Tell me, how do you intend to redeem this debt of honour?'

Her smile was far too broad. That should have been his first clue. The second clue that he was not going to like this outcome was the way she laughed: joyful and uncaring that heads turned along the street to stare.

'You and I,' Sylvia said, grinning, 'are going dancing.'

Chapter Seven

'And I still think it's an extravagance,' complained Miss Pike as she handed Sylvia into the carriage—not, Sylvia couldn't help but think, with much grace.

That was perhaps why she made sure to smile extra sweetly as the door was closed by Matthews. 'And that is why I am going, Miss Pike. Good evening.'

It was fortunate indeed that the coachman decided to drive the horses forward in that moment. Sylvia was not sure what her next retort to Miss Pike's complaints of overindulgence would be, and she was far too excited to argue.

She was going to the ball.

The ball, of course, was the Staromchor ball. Rilla had said that it was one of the most important dates in Society's calendar, and Sylvia had not been about to argue with her. Not after her invitation, alongside one for Daphne, had arrived a week ago.

'A ball!' Sylvia crowed, wiggling in her seat with excitement. 'Aren't you ready to dance with a thousand gentlemen and make them all fall in love with you, Daphne?'

Even though they were alone in the carriage, Daphne shrank back with a look of terror. 'A thousand?'

'Well, perhaps only a few hundred,' amended Sylvia, trying not to grin. 'I'm happy to take the lion's share of the dancing.'

'And the conversation.' Daphne looked out of the window and did not turn back to her friend as she continued to speak. 'I would much rather have stayed home, you know.'

Sylvia bit her lip and prevented herself from replying. *Home.*

Her friend was perhaps the only wallflower who considered the red brick Tudor mansion of the Wallflower Academy to be home. How long had it been since Daphne had arrived? Over a decade, from what she could make out. Daphne was never very communicative about such things.

Home—not a word Sylvia would use. It was moments like this when she felt most at home: in a carriage, flying along the road, the wind whistling through the window and the night beckoning, ripe with possibilities.

Sylvia's stomach lurched. And Theodore.

He had not been particularly excited about this evening.

'Why exactly must we attend?' had been his constant refrain.

Her lips curled into a smile as she clutched her fan

in the rattling carriage. Because, as she had told him two days ago, they had to give Society and the *ton* and, above all, Miss Pike the impression that they truly were engaged. Because they had been invited by the Earl of Staromchor and, most importantly, his wife, her friend Rilla.

And because Sylvia longed for a dance and it had been eons since she had attended one.

'Eons?' Theodore had repeated, raising an eyebrow.

And Sylvia had laughed as the carriage drew away, the smile remaining on her lips for the entirety of the journey back to the Wallflower Academy.

That smile had returned. As their carriage slowed and Daphne's hands started to twist in her lap, Sylvia leaned her nose as close to the window as she dared. Who knew what the Pike would do if she found nose smudges on the glass?

'Here we are,' breathed Daphne, as though they had just reached the gallows.

'Here we are,' murmured Sylvia, excitement flickering through her as the carriage pulled up outside a truly impressive townhouse.

'Here we are,' grunted the coachman, pulling open the door. 'I'm to wait for you. You won't be long, will you?'

'Absolutely not—'

'Hours and hours, I'm afraid,' Sylvia said cheerfully, cutting across Daphne with a severe look. 'If you want to find… I don't know, a tavern or some such place, wait in the warm…'

The expression on the coachman's face made it clear that he was delighted with the suggestion. 'Oh, thank you very much, miss! I'm sure Miss Pike—'

'I'm sure the Pike doesn't need to know about your evening's entertainment,' Sylvia said hastily as she smoothed down her gown.

No, that was probably not a conversation anyone would enjoy.

The coachman gave her a wink, which made Sylvia snort with laughter and Daphne gasp in horror. 'Right y'are, miss. I'll be back at midnight, then?'

Sylvia did not need to look to her left to hear Daphne's little whimper of distress. Oh, hang it all, but she was a good person, even if she made a terrible wallflower. 'Better make it eleven,' she said reluctantly.

The coachman nodded sagely. 'Right y'are.'

As he turned away, Sylvia nudged her friend and said awkwardly, 'I am sorry, Daphne. I…well, I would like to stay here as long as possible, but I know you—'

'Don't apologise,' interjected Daphne with a rare smile in a public place. 'No, no, 'tis fine. I am sure I can find a little nook to…to sit in.'

To hide in, thought Sylvia privately as the two ladies ascended the stairs into the wide atrium, where a footman divested them of pelisses and directed them along a corridor towards the ballroom.

She should have thought of this. It was unlike her

not to take Daphne's morbid hatred of any sort of company into account—but then, she had been eager to see Theodore.

Most strange.

The ballroom was exquisite. Rilla had good taste, Sylvia knew, and it was clear that the old adage was true: style was good taste when it met money. And Rilla had plenty of that now.

The chandeliers glittered, the flowers smelled beautiful, and the sheer number of footmen effortlessly gliding around was dazzling. There were perhaps a hundred people already in attendance—ladies with fans on their wrists and feathers in their hair, gentlemen with canes and ruffles at their sleeves, and there was a murmuring chatter around the room, interspersed with the musicians in one corner tuning their instruments.

A thrum of delight vibrated through Sylvia. A ball. The opportunity to dance!

'There you two are!'

A woman flew at them, embracing both Sylvia and Daphne around their necks with a heavy hug. When she righted herself, Sylvia grinned to see the Duchess of Knaresby, bright-eyed with flushed cheeks quite in contrast to her pale complexion.

'You should be lounging on a chaise,' Sylvia teased, looking her up and down. 'When do you go into your confinement?'

'Never!' declared Gwen with a laugh. 'The last thing

I want to do is be cooped up, though Percy is continuing to threaten me with it.'

'You should be careful, you're getting rather impressive,' said Sylvia, taking in the swell of her friend's stomach. That was no overeating.

Her throat tightened, just for a moment. A child. Oh, to think that Gwen would in a few short months be a mother.

'Thank you for responding to Rilla's invitation,' Gwen said, her smile faltering for only a moment. 'I… well, it's so difficult to make friends in the *ton*, you have no idea—'

'I most definitely do not,' quipped Sylvia with a snort.

'—and I so desperately wanted you and Daphne to… oh…' Gwen blinked, glancing about them. 'Where did she go?'

Sylvia's eyes widened as she mirrored Gwen's attempts to spot Daphne, who appeared to have melted into thin air. 'I never know how she does that.'

'Well, as long as she's comfortable. She never was one for balls, but I thought she simply had to get out of that Wallflower Academy,' said Gwen with a shudder.

Sylvia grinned as a few more gentlemen entered the ballroom. Gwen had not been much of a wallflower either. Suspected murderess, yes. But not a wallflower.

She was prevented from saying any of this, however, by the sharp nudge Gwen prodded into her arm. 'And what's all this I hear about an engagement between you and—'

'Don't talk about the engagement yet!' came the words of their hostess.

It was all Sylvia could do not to smile as she saw Rilla sweep towards them on the arm of her husband. She truly was a magnificent woman, and becoming the Countess of Staromchor had only added to her charms. Her white skin was paired with white, unseeing eyes that nonetheless did not prevent her sharp observations and even sharper wit.

'I suppose Daphne has run off somewhere, as I don't hear her voice,' said Rilla with a sardonic smile, patting her husband's arm. 'You can go away now.'

'Rilla!'

'Oh, I don't mind. I know you three will have a great deal to catch up on,' said the Earl of Staromchor with a laugh. 'Just try not to get my wife into too much trouble, will you?'

'I make absolutely no promises,' said Sylvia solemnly.

Rilla giggled as her husband kissed her cheek and departed, shaking her head ruefully. 'Sometimes I don't know how I manage to keep that man.'

She and Gwen laughed as Sylvia attempted to join in with their merriment.

Her heart softened as she looked at them. Her two friends, who had found such happiness. Without them, she would have struggled to believe it was even possible. Even now, seeing them here, so happy and full of life—Gwen quite literally—Sylvia was willing to bet there were parts of their lives that were not so carefree.

Being married bound you, Sylvia reminded herself. Just because they were happy now, that did not mean they would be happy for ever. It was only a matter of time before something happened and you looked around and realised it was just another cage.

'Now, tell me all about this engagement of yours, and why I haven't been invited to your wedding,' Rilla said severely, her expression becoming serious. 'What does he look like?'

'He...' Sylvia swallowed. She was quite accustomed to describing people in an amusing way for Rilla; her visual impairment meant she saw naught but a little light or dark.

But describing Theodore?

'Theodore is... He...' Why on earth was this so dashed difficult?

And then there he was. Her gaze had meandered to the door and Theodore had stepped through it, his posture tall and his expression defiant.

A smile crept over Sylvia's face. He felt just as out of step here as she did. How strangely pleasant, to find another like her.

'Is that him?'

Sylvia was almost knocked over as the large Gwen— and child—lurched forward.

'You are going to describe him for me, aren't you, Sylvia?' asked Rilla sternly. 'I don't know, you host a ball and rescue your friend from the Wallflower Academy for the evening, and all you ask in return is—'

'Fine, fine, I'll tell you!' Sylvia laughed, cheeks burning though she could not fathom why. What on earth did she have to be embarrassed about? 'Let's see. He's tall.'

'Tall.' Rilla did not sound impressed. 'Is that it?'

'About half a head taller than you, and with a devastatingly handsome face,' Sylvia added, feeling the pressure to be more descriptive. The trouble was, how often did one have to describe a man to whom one was supposed to be engaged? 'He's…he's kind. Aloof sometimes, though I think that's more because he's…not shy, exactly. Uninterested in trying to impress.'

For some reason, her stomach was churning in a most odd way. Not unpleasant. Just…churning. It was drifting lower too, a sense of discomfort that was flickering with heat.

'He is charming when he doesn't intend to be and irritating when he intends to charm,' said Sylvia without thinking.

Gwen laughed. 'He sounds perfect for you.'

'He really does,' said Rilla, a raised eyebrow displaying her surprise. 'Where on earth did you find him, Sylvia?'

Sylvia was too hot now. Because the ballroom was filling up, she told herself. It was nothing to do with Theodore. Nothing at all.

It was all an act—a con, really, a way to give her the freedom to focus on her permanent escape. She was a useful cover for him, and he was a convenient excuse for her.

That was all.

It wasn't as though Theodore could offer her anything. It wasn't as though she even wanted to be married.

'My question,' murmured Gwen, a teasing smile on her face, 'is whether the two of you have—'

'Ah, Theodore,' called out Sylvia loudly, drowning out her friend's most scandalous query. 'Come and meet my friends.'

Heads turned, and not just Theodore's. All too late, Sylvia remembered that ladies did not call out across ballrooms, private or public, to order a gentleman to her side. It was a good thing Miss Pike had not been invited, for she would have been most cutting about it.

As it was, Theodore's brow was raised as he reached them. 'You called?'

Sylvia winced. Well, he did not know what outrageous thing Gwen had been about to say. 'You promised me a dance.'

Her spirits dropped only a tad when he sighed and offered his hand in what could not be described as the best grace. 'Best to get it over with, then.'

'Aren't you going to introduce us to—'

'No, I'm not,' said Sylvia hastily, grabbing Theodore's arm and pulling him to the set that was lining up in the centre of the room, the musicians indicating they were ready.

Her pulse was most inexplicably thundering. What on earth could have got into it?

'And why,' Theodore asked genially, as though the answer was of no great import, 'are we running away from your friends?'

'Because once I have to introduce you to them, I have to lie,' Sylvia said quietly, her gaze faltering just for a moment. 'It's been difficult enough with Daphne, and Rilla is far more inquisitive. I won't lie to them unless I absolutely have to.'

When she met his eyes once more, it was to see not censure, but a strange sort of commendation.

'I had not thought of that.'

Try as she might, it was a challenge to shrug nonchalantly. 'I am not… I have many faults; I dare say you have already noticed a few. But I will not lie, not if I don't have to.'

'Even if it means marching me across a dance floor?'

Sylvia saw the teasing smile a heartbeat after he spoke, and relief washed through her. 'Especially then.'

Theodore opened his mouth to reply but in that moment the musicians started up and the dance began. A Scotch reel. Excellent. She knew that dance well and would not be required to think much. All she had to do was—

Sylvia's lips parted in astonishment the first instant that she stepped forward and raised a hand to touch Theodore's. Something had happened. Something most unexpected and inexplicable. There was…heat. In her hand.

Their hands parted and the heat was gone. Sylvia

half expected to see a burn mark where their fingers had touched, even through their gloves, but there was no visible sign of anything untoward.

Her eyes met his and she saw an answering look. Had he felt it too?

Perhaps he had. Sylvia had never seen Theodore so closed off, so unwilling to meet her gaze. But as the dance progressed and she stepped forward to take his hands, Sylvia could not help but gasp.

The moment was over in a breath yet the repercussions lingered on her skin, even through her gloves.

It was…unsettling. Unbalancing. Theodore's presence had never had that impact on her before—at least, not to such an extent. Why here, under the shining lights of Rilla's ballroom, did such proximity unsettle her?

Sylvia raked her curious gaze over Theodore as he waited for the pair next to them to complete their movement. He was handsome. That was the one descriptor she had been unwilling to use aloud for Rilla's benefit, yet in the privacy of her mind she could not deny it. It had been one of the first things she had noticed about him when she had barrelled her way into his carriage.

Handsome. And charming. And lost, in a world that required everyone to be categorised and labelled and understood by their parentage.

Who was this man?

'You're very quiet,' Sylvia said, unable to remain in silence any longer. 'What are you thinking about?'

Theodore's smile was too knowing. 'That is rather a dangerous question, do not you think?'

They stepped together, and apart, and every inch closer increased her temperature and every step away cooled it.

'I am not so sure of that,' Sylvia quipped, attempting to keep her racing heartbeat under control. 'We know so little of each other, after all. I am always intrigued to learn more.'

Theodore's steady expression did not waver. 'You know more about me than anyone else on this planet.'

Sylvia shivered as they clasped hands once more—for the dance, no other reason. She would surely not have done so unless the dance had required it.

So was it the sudden intimacy, the masculine scent she breathed in as Theodore's side was pressed against hers, or the revelation that she was the world's leading expert in Theodore Featherstonehaugh that had made her quiver?

'I am honoured,' she managed to say as their hands parted.

Theodore's smile was tight. 'You should be. Yet still you ask what I am thinking.'

'I… I…' Why wasn't her mind working?

'I was thinking of our kiss.'

Sylvia almost tripped over her own skirts.

The sentence had been calmly said, in a low voice so that no one else, likely as not, had heard.

But she had. And Theodore knew she had; she could see it in the seriousness of his eyes.

'Our kiss,' she breathed.

'Yes, we've only shared one,' Theodore said easily, no colour tinging his cheeks. 'That is what I was thinking about. Well, you did ask.'

She had, and now Sylvia was wondering what could have possessed her. She had to put a stop to this—end the ridiculous notions that were swirling around her mind, tempting her to taste him again.

'Which obviously cannot happen again,' she said firmly, her voice a mite stronger this time. 'This is all an act, isn't it? All pretend.'

Sylvia turned on the spot and when she came back to face Theodore it was to see a completely blank expression, as though her words had not affected him at all.

Which was all to the good, she tried to remind herself as the two of them held hands and started to parade down the set.

Do not think about how good he smells. Do not think about his hands around yours, strong and steady. Do not think about how hot you feel.

Sylvia was determined, she would not raise his hopes. Or hers. Matrimony was entirely out of the question for her, falling in love not on the cards, and that kiss...

Well, if anything could shatter her resolve, it was that kiss.

So she could not, would not, allow him to think that something could come of it. Ensuring that her expression remained as resolutely blank as his own, Sylvia waited until they were at the end of the set. Their hands parted. They stepped back. They waited for the next pair in the set to promenade.

'We understand each other, don't we?' Sylvia could not help but say it. She had to know, had to ensure that there was no possibility of misunderstanding.

She would not fall in love.

Theodore appeared to hesitate, but only for a moment. 'Of course,' he said lightly. 'Love is not the plan.'

Chapter Eight

The doorbell jangled and when Matthews appeared he did not look any happier to see Theodore than the last time.

'You again,' he grunted.

Theodore attempted to smile. 'Good afternoon, Matthews. I have an appointment with—'

'Miss Sylvia, yes,' muttered the footman, looking most displeased that one of his charges would be leaving his purview again. 'She's waiting for you in the—'

'Thank goodness you're here, we need to leave immediately!' In a rush of silk she grabbed Theodore's hand.

Giving out a groan as he lurched backwards down the steps of the Wallflower Academy, Theodore attempted to steady himself as Sylvia rushed to the carriage.

What the—?

'Ah, Your Grace!' trilled a voice that was most unwelcome.

Ah. That would explain it.

Sylvia was groaning, dropping her head into her

hands, and Theodore turned with great trepidation to look at the woman who had elicited such a response.

Miss Pike beamed. 'So pleasant to see you again, Your Grace.' She lowered herself into a most obsequious curtsey.

Theodore's chest tightened as he returned the pleasantry. Really, it was too much. No woman had ever curtseyed to him like that before, and though another man might have enjoyed the compliment, he could not.

How could he? The Pike—dammit, Miss Pike—was only giving him the due she presumed a duke would expect. Perhaps a duke would.

As he was not a duke, he could not say.

'Miss Bryant tells me you are venturing into London again. Three times this month so far—how very…exuberant,' said Miss Pike carefully, as though the final word in her sentence was distasteful.

Right. He was a duke. How was a duke supposed to behave?

Imperious, and derisive, and rude. Perhaps less of the rude. More of the imperious.

'London has a great number of calls on my time at present,' said Theodore as magnificently as he could manage.

And he would have been able to hold the pose if Sylvia had not snorted with laughter as she clambered into the open-topped carriage behind him.

'Indeed,' said Miss Pike, her smile faltering slightly. 'And may I presume that all these calls on your time are related to preparations for the wedding? I have held out on informing Miss Bryant's father of—'

'And so you should. You know I wish to be the one to inform him; that was our agreement,' Sylvia's irate voice shot out behind Theodore. 'Honestly, Miss Pike, I told you before. When I am ready to tell him—'

'It's gathering chatter in the *ton*, my dear,' cut in Miss Pike with a steely glare Theodore was not quite able to escape. 'An Irish duke no one has ever heard of, engaged to a woman never formally launched in Society... If you ask me, he will hear about it from another's lips soon. It may be best to—'

'It is my life, I will tell my father what I choose,' snapped Sylvia, opening the door beside her. 'Come, Theodore.'

It was not in Theodore's nature to be ordered about, but there was a note in Sylvia's voice that made it impossible to disobey. Besides, he hardly had much of an excuse for the Pike. Blast, Miss Pike. He had not been organising a wedding, and he had no intention of doing so.

Bowing quickly to Miss Pike and clambering into the carriage before she could say anything, Theodore instructed the coachman to drive on.

'So I am to understand that the wedding is being planned, Your Grace?' Miss Pike had somehow clasped the side of the carriage and was looking up at Theodore with a most severe expression.

Panic flooded his veins. He was not a liar. He was

many things—and some of those things he did not know, was hoping to discover—but deceit was not in his nature.

He stared down at the sharp eyes of the proprietress of the Wallflower Academy and knew he had to say something... something...anything—

'All in good time, Miss Pike,' Sylvia said smartly. 'Shall we go?'

Theodore's mouth was dry, painfully so, but he managed to nod and garble something about 'forward'. Miss Pike released the carriage just in time to prevent herself being swept off by it, and the wheels crunched into the gravel as the horses eased into a trot.

Only after the gravel drive of the Wallflower Academy gave way to the road did Theodore lean back in relief. 'That was close.'

'Imagine living with her.' Sylvia shuddered. 'The woman does not know how to cease a line of questioning.'

He could well imagine. Each time Theodore attempted to imagine what it was to live in the Wallflower Academy, to be one of its inhabitants—he knew Sylvia well enough now to know she would describe herself as a prisoner—his mind was unable to comprehend living under the power of one such as Miss Pike.

She could have given the director of St Kilda's Orphanage for Waifs and Strays a run for his money.

'We need to start thinking of a plan to break off our engagement.'

Theodore blinked in the dazzling sunlight as the hedges rushed past them and stared at his companion.

Sylvia was carefully removing her gloves and stuffing them in her reticule as though nothing could please her more than feeling the rush of air across her palms. She looked thoroughly unconcerned, as though this was a perfectly normal topic of conversation.

Theodore swallowed. And perhaps it was. They both knew this was just a scheme, a plot, a ploy. A scheme that had to end at some time.

Still. That knowledge did not explain the rush of disappointment that pooled in his stomach and made it hard to concentrate. He was being ridiculous. He had known that the moment Sylvia had made it perfectly clear she saw him as nothing more than a means to an end.

Her pronouncement had been far harder to hear than he had expected.

Theodore cleared his throat, hoping the action would similarly clear his mind. This was the agreement, and he was not going to break it now. He needed her just as much as she needed him. Perhaps more.

'How go your plans to permanently escape the Wallflower Academy?' he asked aloud. 'I presume that you are working on them.'

'Oh, I have a great number of ideas, and I must say that venturing into London more often has proved very helpful,' said Sylvia brightly, twisting in her seat to better face him. 'Do you know just how many coaching inns there are within a three-square-mile radius?

Of course, not all of them go all the way to Falmouth.
I may have to change...'

Theodore stifled a smile. And there it was. Sylvia
might be the more talkative of the two of them, the more
comfortable marching into a room and demanding its
attention, but there was so much of the world she did
not know. So much she was unprepared for.

A twinge of pain seared him. Would she be safe on
this escape of hers? She must take his advice and hire
a chaperone.

He pushed the thought away as sternly as he could.
Sylvia Bryant was not his responsibility. He had his
own problems.

'I suppose you intend to take whichever ship will take
you to Antigua soonest,' he said aloud.

He was going to lose her.

Theodore started at the thought. Lose her? He did
not have her. But of course, Sylvia was clearly not planning on returning to England. When she left, he would
never see her again.

He swallowed down the pain that rose at the idea.
No Sylvia for the rest of his life. It was a terrible future to face.

'I cannot decide whether to explore other islands in
the Caribbean before I arrive at Antigua,' Sylvia said
blithely, as though she were choosing between two pas-
tries in a patisserie.

Theodore's eyebrows rose. 'Why—'

'Why not?' She shrugged, leaning back and closing

her eyes in the dazzling sunlight. 'I may never be able to afford to travel again. Home or adventure? I may have to let chance decide.'

It was perhaps unsporting of him, but then, Theodore was not necessarily a gentleman. He did not have to abide by the *ton's* rules if he were not a member. And so, most unchivalrously, he took advantage of the moment that Sylvia had her eyes shut and allowed himself to luxuriate in just looking at her.

Damn, but she was beautiful. Those eyelashes, long and dark. The swell of her breasts, the curve of her buttocks pressed into the carriage seat. Just to behold her was to admire her. It was a wonder really that no man had—

Sylvia opened her eyes. 'Where are we going, then? I know it's not to… I don't know, order wedding invitations or select a bridal cake. It's not, is it?'

The concern on her face made Theodore smile, though he did so mainly to prevent any suspicion that he had already been smiling.

Just a little. Not that she needed to know that.

'We will not be selecting a bridal cake today, no,' he conceded. 'No, I thought of somewhere we could go that might help with finding my father. They have… records, I suppose you would call them.'

Sylvia's expression was not suspicious, more curious. As the carriage rumbled around a corner and the city of London came into view, she asked, 'And what makes you think this particular place, and do not think I have not noticed how mysteriously you speak of it, will have records of your father? I mean, why him?'

Theodore swallowed. Why, indeed?

It was more of a gut instinct. Something told him his father had to be someone great—something important. Why else would his mother have made him promise? Why had the money always come, enough for him to receive a gentleman's education?

Was it possible—and he barely liked to think of it, in case the opposite were true—was it conceivable his father had been important? In government, perhaps?

'I... Before my mother died, she instructed me to make her a promise.'

The words had slipped out before he could stop them. His cheeks burned to speak of her again, the woman who had given him life and who he only had vague memories of. Truth be told, only in the dark of night when he really tried could he conjure up his mother's face.

Guilt gnawed at him, like a dog worrying a bone, scraping against the inside of his ribs.

'A promise.' Sylvia spoke quietly. Peculiar, how she could move from wild and exuberant to kind and gentle in a breath. 'You never mentioned this before.'

Theodore inhaled deeply. 'I never thought I would tell anyone. I knew—at least, I thought I knew—that my father was unable to be with us. Precisely why, I do not think I ever articulated to myself. I must have been but five or six years old. I knew others had mothers and fathers and I had only one, but it was only when my mother…when she suspected how ill she was…'

He was not going to cry. It was not an attempt to keep the emotion down, more a statement of fact. Try as he might, the tears had not come. Not for years.

'Consumption. She disappeared slowly, like a painting fading in sunlight. There were times when I thought… but she knew, far better than I, that her days were coming to an end. And so she made me promise that when she was gone…that I would not seek out my father.'

His breath had caught in his throat as he spoke, but that was nothing to the sudden lurch in his lungs as Sylvia reached out and took his hand in hers.

The contact was striking. No gloves, skin on skin, and though it burned with a fiery tension that he could not understand, Theodore could also not ignore just how she squeezed his fingers and how comfort washed through him.

'I am betraying her,' Theodore said thickly, his voice heavy with emotion as the carriage slowed, attempting to make its way along a busy street. 'I promised her not to do the very thing I…that we—'

'You were a child, and she exacted that promise from a child for your own good,' Sylvia said softly. 'Never having met her, I can see enough gentleness in you to know that she meant it as a kindness.'

A kindness?

Theodore blinked through blurring vision. He would not cry.

Focus, man. Kindness. Yes, perhaps Sylvia was right.

'I don't know. I thought for a time that I would honour her request for the rest of my days. She must have had a purpose in keeping me from him.'

'Or him from you.' There was a worried look on Sylvia's face now, something clouding the brilliance of her eyes. 'Did it ever occur to you that he could be dangerous? That she was, in fact, hiding a vulnerable child from a threatening man?'

Theodore's eyes widened. It had not occurred to him. How astonishing; all these years of wondering, and that possibility had never struck him.

'You are a man now, with none of those vulnerabilities that one would find in a child,' Sylvia continued, as though she had not rewritten his past. 'The man who could have hurt you when young cannot touch you now—especially if he is dead, as you believe.'

'Perhaps,' Theodore said ruefully, tightening his grip around Sylvia's hand and relishing how her fingers wove between his own. 'But she was the only woman who has ever loved me. Going against her wishes… She would be so ashamed of me, I think, but I have to know. I… I have to know. A part of me feels incomplete without that knowledge.'

'Well, speaking as someone who has a parent living who quite abandoned them in the womb, plucked them from happiness and then sent them away when life got complicated, I can tell you that it's not the end of the world,' said Sylvia, that edge Theodore knew so well now returning to her voice.

He looked up. Sylvia's chin jutted in defiance of a man who was not here, and he could not help but notice the smile, that false one that crept onto her face when she had no other recourse, had returned.

'I am sure he is not—'

'You do not know my father,' Sylvia said dryly. 'I am evidence of a mistake in his eyes. Proof of his past that he has no wish to recall. Good intentions may have existed at the beginning, but he had not the strength of character to choose me over his wife.'

Theodore's stomach lurched. Was that what he would be? A sudden reminder of a dalliance his father would have preferred to forget?

'He has said in letters since that he hopes my time at the Wallflower Academy will make me see how he is righting old wrongs by providing me with such an opportunity.' Sylvia laughed, and there was no mirth in the sound. 'As though I could forget that I had been sent there as a punishment for my mere existence. As though I could see past his marriage and pretend that his affair with my mother—a woman who loved him, a woman he abandoned—could be forgiven.'

'I am sure he is not—'

'You do not know him.' Sylvia's words cut across his and though there was no malice in his direction, Theodore could hear the anger deep within each syllable.

He swallowed. 'No. No, I do not.'

'If he had ever bothered to speak to me for more than a minute, if he had spent any time with me...' she said quietly as the carriage slowed, trundling along the London streets at no more than a walking pace. 'I have never been so lonely as when I lived in that house with him. No companion, no governess, no nursemaid. Just day after day of attempting to amuse myself, knowing any noise I made that carried beyond the room I was within would gain naught but censure.'

Theodore's heart twisted. How was it possible to have the thoughts he himself had experienced years ago, spoken to him by a woman who was so very different from him?

The loneliness. The isolation. The boredom.

It was as though she had been alongside him in the orphanage. If she had been, then perhaps the two of them would have been a little less lonely.

'If he had truly wished to get to know me, he would have seen I did not belong in the Wallflower Academy,' Sylvia said dryly, smiling, but with a sadness that tore at Theodore's heart. 'But there it is.'

There was a coldness to her last sentence that surprised him. The emotion must have shown on his face, for his companion squeezed his hand once more and then withdrew her fingers.

'If someone cuts me out of their life, I cut them out of mine,' Sylvia said quietly. 'And it is for ever. I offer little forgiveness, not after I have received so little.'

A throb of his pulse lurched in Theodore's temple.

Cut out of their life. Was that what had happened with his father? He could hardly fathom how a man who clearly had no interest in his by-blow would welcome the sudden arrival of a long-lost son.

Was this a mistake? Should he turn back now, prevent himself from making the final mistake?

'He won't want to see me.' Theodore breathed the words slowly, half afraid that they would skitter away from his tongue, so tenuous was his grip on them. 'Even if there's a chance he's alive, he won't see me.'

'If he doesn't, it's because he's a fool and doesn't know you,' said Sylvia fiercely—far more fiercely than he had expected. 'Anyone who knows you as I do would know that you are worth knowing.'

There was a flush in her cheeks as she spoke and she would not quite meet his gaze, which only made heat flood through Theodore.

'Well, that was a compliment—and from Sylvia Bryant, no less!' Theodore attempted a light and jovial tone, hoping that by teasing the woman beside him they could both ignore the sudden rush of attraction that had sparked between them.

At least, it had sparked through him. Surely she had felt it too? He could not be alone in that…could he?

'It was not a compliment.'

The glare that Sylvia gave him made Theodore smile more naturally now. 'It was! You said—'

'I know what I said, and it was fact, not a compliment,' she said warningly. 'Don't you start getting a large head—'

'I'm just saying, that is the nicest thing you have ever said to me,' Theodore teased.

Sylvia's glare did not diminish. 'Oh, hush.'

'But if you wish to compliment me again—'

'Anything you say, Your Grace,' Sylvia shot back sweetly.

A twist in his stomach. It really was starting to get most irritating when she called him that. 'You are purposely trying to antagonise me.'

'And is it working?'

God, there was nothing like flirting with Sylvia.

No, not flirting, Theodore thought hastily. Jesting. Joking. That was all. It was the sort of banter he would enjoy with anyone—like his friends from his university days, like Warchester or Stafford. Probably. There was a strange sort of heat in his loins that was remarkably different.

'No, it is not working,' said Theodore decidedly, grinning. 'In fact, it's starting to grow on me.'

Sylvia's outraged expression meant she was about to say something, he was sure, but at that moment the carriage drew to a halt and the pair of them looked around, slightly startled at the fact that they were no longer moving.

Theodore braced himself. 'We are here.'

Chapter Nine

'*We are here.*'

And here appeared to be…a print shop.

'Reynolds Printing Emporium…' Sylvia said slowly as Theodore descended from the carriage on the other side. 'And we are here because…?'

'Because,' Theodore replied as he stepped around and opened her carriage door, 'they have printed newspapers in London for over fifty years.'

A newspaper, Sylvia thought as she rearranged her skirts after sitting for so long, then gazed about her. Was Theodore expecting to find a scandalous reference to his father here? Perhaps a gossip column, mentioning a man who had abandoned a woman and their child?

But…well, she was no expert, but she had seen enough of the world to know this was not a unique occurrence. Why, the pair of them had both experienced something similar.

So why were they here?

Theodore sighed. 'You'll have to trust me on this—

my instincts tell me there's something here. You, of course, think it's a foolish idea.'

Shock curled around Sylvia's heart. 'I didn't say that!'

'You did not need to. I can see the thought plastered all over your face,' he said with a smile. 'I'm not an idiot.'

'I did not say you were! It's just…of all the people in the world, how will you know—'

'I don't know, not exactly,' said Theodore wistfully. 'But I feel that once I read about him I'll just…know. I suppose that is ridiculous, but I have always trusted my gut on such matters.' He gave a languid shrug, reminding Sylvia of just how tall the man was. And broad. So broad.

Sylvia blinked. He'd kept on talking and she had completely stopped listening. Now he was looking at her as though expecting a reply.

Bother.

'Let's go inside,' she said firmly.

A line appeared between Theodore's brows, highlighting his birthmark, as he frowned. 'That is just what I…never mind. In we go.'

The print shop appeared to be almost abandoned. When they stepped inside and a bell rang over the door, a great amount of dust floated down, coating them with a fine grey shroud. There was dust and cobwebs everywhere. The small space featured a counter and a bell, both thick with dust, a few cabinets that appeared to have never been opened and a door which presumably led to something more impressive. There was a thud, thud, thud occurring some way off. A printer's press, Sylvia presumed, but why anyone would—

'Right,' said Theodore steadily. 'Let's begin.'

It was difficult not to admire the man as he strode forward, rang the bell and stood upright with an expectant look on his face.

Here was someone who knew, perhaps, in his heart of hearts that the information he sought was more likely to bring pain than pleasure. There was surely no good news in the secrets of Theodore Featherstonehaugh's past, yet he pursued it.

Why?

Because he needed to know who he was.

Sylvia smiled wistfully as she stepped past him to look through the stained and dirty windows. It was not something she could entirely understand. She had known precisely who she was for as long as she could remember.

Perhaps that came from always being the most obvious person to look at in a room. Sylvia could never have been accused of being uncertain, not ever, but it was a careful construct built over many years. She would never show weakness if she could help it, her skin marking her as someone who could easily be a target—be singled out. But if this was what Theodore needed—

'Ah, there you are,' said Theodore smartly as the inner door opened and a man with ink-stained fingers and a slightly dazed look appeared. 'I have an appointment. Mr Featherstonehaugh.'

'Now, that is a name my typesetters would wish to avoid.' The man revealed a toothy smile with several gaps, as though he had painted ink upon a select number of teeth. 'Records, was it?'

Theodore nodded smartly and a flicker of admiration fluttered through Sylvia.

There was something so…so powerful about him. Gentleman or not, and perhaps they would soon find out, Theodore exuded a power quite unlike that of other gentlemen she had met.

Perhaps she had not encountered many fine gentlemen. Those who attended the Wallflower Academy dinners or afternoon teas typically came for one of three reasons. Either they came to gawp at those less fortunate or they came to find a pliable wife but left disappointed because they didn't want the reality of a wallflower, or they were forced there by well-meaning, charitable mothers.

Even the Duke of Knaresby and the Earl of Staromchor, who had been so disagreeable as to marry her friends, were not like Theodore.

Theodore was…

Sylvia tried to focus on her footsteps as she and Theodore were ushered into another room. There was a pride in him, a presence that compelled those around him to take notice. To acquiesce. To help. He had little wealth, no title, and yet he…he shone. Before the printer knew what he was doing, he was bringing them cups of tea—with very inky stains around the handles—and even offering a tin of biscuits. By the evidence of his own expression, he could hardly believe it.

'Happy to oblige, sir,' Mr Reynolds was saying, waving his own cup of tea as the printer behind him churned out what appeared to be a playbill. 'Don't get many people looking for them there newspapers.'

Sylvia glanced at Theodore, waiting for him to respond. He took his time in doing so, clearly weighing up each word carefully before committing to it.

She stifled a smile. Well, true gentleman or not, Theodore had certainly gone to the right schools. If you put him in with a gaggle of blue-blooded toffs you wouldn't be able to pick him out.

And the place was distracting. Almost a warehouse, its ceiling was high and the walls far apart, with trestle tables and boxes and cabinets and drying racks and two printing presses, one of which was in motion. A trio of men were moving around it, delicately adding oil here or pushing a lever there, and the whole thing continued to churn away. The noise was loud, though not deafening and, unlike the front of the shop, the place was spotless. Other than the ink splatters.

'That is most kind of you, Mr Reynolds,' Theodore said slowly. 'I would also appreciate looking at some of the more recent editions. Those from the last few months, say.'

His serious eyes met Sylvia's and a jolt of understanding passed between them.

'You think there will be news of your father from two months ago,' Sylvia said in an undertone as the printer bustled away to retrieve the requested newspapers, 'when your allowance halted. You mentioned it before.'

Theodore nodded, a wry smile on his face. 'Well, it would make sense, wouldn't it? Births, marriages, deaths—that's the sort of thing we should be looking for.'

'Either your father died,' Sylvia said, ticking off on her fingers and almost dropping the slippery teacup, 'or he got married—'

'Or his wife has born him an heir.' The daylight in the print shop was greyed by the cobwebs over the windows, or else Sylvia could have sworn that a shadow had passed over Theodore's face. 'It's not about the money, though I admit I feel the loss of my allowance, but I have friends who can help. It's about finding my history. Finding the other half of my family.'

'Here y'go,' panted Mr Reynolds as he returned with a heavy stack of newspapers in his arms. He dropped them heavily on a trestle table just to their right. 'You stay as long as you want, though we're out of biscuits.'

'I am sure I can make your generosity worthwhile, Mr Reynolds,' Theodore said hastily, patting his pockets and pulling out something shiny.

The clink of coins moving from one hand to another was done without any further comment.

'You read as long as you like.' Mr Reynolds beamed. Evidently, the coins had been of sufficient value and number to keep him very happy indeed. 'Always happy to help a gentleman and lady.'

With much bowing, now money had changed hands, the printer moved to the other side of the room, a good fifteen feet away, and started shouting at one of his workers for allowing the ink to run low on a particular part of the machine.

Sylvia watched Theodore's attention flicker, as though unwillingly, to the pile of newspapers. Then he looked away.

In that pile could be the secret of who he was. Where he came from. What legacy, if any, he was to inherit. A name, a reputation…anything.

Her mouth going dry, Sylvia desperately tried to think of something to say. How did one comfort a grown man who still did not know where to place himself in the world?

Hesitantly, she stepped forward and touched Theodore's arm. He jumped, evidently so lost in his thoughts that he had not noticed her move, but his face softened into a smile as he met her eyes.

'This whole false engagement was my idea,' she said quietly, though the noise of the printing press undoubtedly drowned out most of their conversation anyway.

'You wanted to find your father, and you've been distracted from that by balls, and dancing, and—'

'Not kissing you again,' Theodore said with a wry smile.

He was jesting, that was all, Sylvia told herself as her whole body warmed at the memory. That was absolutely not a real suggestion that he wanted to…that they should…

'You don't have to be here, you know. Helping me, I mean,' said Theodore, his smile fading. 'You probably want to go to the coaching inns, ask when the mail coaches come, investigate ships leaving Falmouth for the Caribbean, purchase a suitable trunk, that sort of thing.'

Yes, that sort of thing. The sort of things that Sylvia had always told herself she would do if she ever had the chance to come to London without the Pike circling around her.

Now she was here, with Theodore, they did not seem to be quite so urgent.

'Two pairs of eyes will work quicker,' Sylvia said, jerking her head to the trestle table upon which sat the copious newspapers. 'The sooner we unravel the mystery of your father, the sooner you can help me plan my escape.'

A teasing smile was playing on Theodore's face again. 'You drive a hard bargain, Sylvia.'

'It's the only way I know how to live,' she quipped,

forcefully ignoring the quivering butterflies that had just erupted in her stomach. 'So. Where shall we start?'

When they approached the trestle table, it was to see that morning's newspaper on the top of the pile. The headline overtook almost everything else, printed in a huge font that screamed out:

SOLICITORS SEEK HEIR OF THE DUKE OF CAMROSE

'You never know,' jested Sylvia with a grin. 'You could be the son of a duke!'

Theodore rolled his eyes. 'Can you imagine—me, a future duke? If that had been my lot in life, I would have been sent to Eton, not the local grammar school. I'd be dripping in diamonds, or whatever it is that dukes drip in.'

Sylvia snorted as she brushed her fingers over the type. 'You'd think a duke would know where his son had gone gallivanting!'

'You would think so,' said Theodore with a laugh. 'So we want the newspapers from two, perhaps two and a half months ago...'

Soon the trestle table was absolutely covered in newspapers. There did not appear to be any particular rhyme or reason to the way Theodore moved through them, so Sylvia did not attempt to replicate his approach but instead created her own.

First, look at the headline on the front. After discounting the preposterous idea that Theodore could be the missing son of the Duke of Camrose, who, from the brief article, appeared to be a distant cousin, anything interesting was pointed out to Theodore: a great nobleman who had scandalously asked for a divorce, his wife who had scandalously refused, a terrible shipping accident—

Theodore had faltered on a story about a minor baron who had gambled with his investments and lost a great deal, but then put it aside after reading that the man was barely a decade older than himself.

'Fine, let's look at the time you were born,' Sylvia said, pushing back a stray curl of hair and sighing heavily. 'August 1782, you said. Can you be any more accurate?'

Theodore shook his head. There was a thumbprint of ink near his chin, the warmth of his hands obviously picking up the print from the newspapers. 'August, that's all she ever told me.'

And on and on they read. Hours slipped by, fresh cups of tea being brought by Mr Reynolds and left silently at one end of the trestle table, and still the pile of curious news stories that Theodore considered worthy of further investigation remained perilously low.

Sylvia's real problem was that she was finding it difficult to concentrate.

Not because the newspapers were not interesting. Her education had been minimal at best, grossly abandoned at worst, and Miss Pike had been more interested in educating her ladies in the polite way to enquire as to a man's income than the news of the world.

And it was all here. Gossip and scandal, yes, but also politics and economics, great discoveries in science and—

'Oh, my apologies,' said Theodore hastily as he brushed his arm against her breast as he leaned forward to help himself to another cup of tea.

Sylvia opened her mouth to say something jovial and light-hearted…and found to her horror that she could not.

Instead, her cheeks were burning and her heart had skipped a beat. What on earth was wrong with her?

Another twenty minutes swiftly answered that question, and not in a way that she appreciated. It happened again when Theodore lunged to prevent a newspaper from slipping to the floor—a lunge that brought him intensely close to her, his breath on her neck, his arm around her waist.

It was over in a moment, but that moment was long enough. Sylvia swallowed hard, and attempted to push down all emotions that told her the truth. That she liked Theodore.

Liked him, as a man.

It was a route that would only end in tears, she told herself sternly as she turned a page and scanned the smaller headlines now that she was halfway through the edition for August the sixteenth from the year 1782.

His tears. Her tears. It did not matter.

'You know, I am thankful,' came Theodore's low murmur, far too close to her ear.

Sylvia started so rapidly that she almost whacked him. 'My apologies, I—'

'No, I should have been more careful, I should not have startled you,' he said with a wry smile, turning to lean back against the trestle table as he exhaled slowly. 'It feels as though we have been here no time at all. I could spend a great deal of time with you quite happily, Sylvia.'

She was not going to read more into that than there was, she told herself firmly, utterly ignoring the fact that her body was leaning closer to him, as though she was a magnet and he the North Star.

It was merely a politeness. He did not mean—

'Thank you, Sylvia,' Theodore said slowly, his eyes darting to her lips before returning, as though he had not intended to allow the slip, to her eyes. 'You are something very special. There are few wallflowers who would—'

'I am not a wallflower,' Sylvia breathed. Oh, no, she was leaning closer to him. She had one hand on the table right by his hip, and she was leaning closer to—

'No, you're not.' His focus was fiery, his presence just as potent as it always was, and he did not move away. 'Not in the slightest.'

It was out of her control now. Her eyelashes were flickering, she was leaning, leaning in and leaning up, offering up her lips and—

'Did y'find anything?' called out Mr Reynolds from the other side of the room.

Sylvia jerked away and stepped around the trestle table, putting as much polite space between her and the man she had almost kissed as possible.

What on earth had she been thinking?

'Yes, thank you, Mr Reynolds!' yelled back Theodore to the well-meaning printer. He grinned at Sylvia, no shyness in his face, no indication that they had almost done precisely what they had agreed they most certainly would not do. 'Did you spot it?'

'Spot it?' repeated Sylvia weakly.

Perhaps she had misunderstood. Perhaps they had not been about to kiss, and she had just built it all up in her head, and—

'Here. At least, I think it's me. I believe it must be, though it brings me no pleasure to claim it for my own,' he said quietly. 'Take a look.'

He pushed a newspaper over to her. It was open at page seventeen and near the bottom was a small square entitled 'Local woman refuses to name father of her child'.

Sylvia looked up, lips parted. 'Oh, Theodore.'

His smile was a tad forced, but she could not blame him for that. 'Go on. Read it.'

Half wondering whether she should be reading something so personal, Sylvia looked down and read the short paragraph.

Miss Molly Featherstonehaugh, eighteen, gave birth to a boy named Teddy Featherstonehaugh exactly a month ago but still refuses to name the father. When pressed by the Reverend Raglan in the absence of any family to own up to the name of the man who had got her in such a condition, Miss Featherstonehaugh declared that the father had no wish to be known and she would not wish to impose.

Sylvia swallowed, her heart breaking for the girl. Eighteen. Not too young to be a mother, but one alone, without family, perhaps without friends, pressed at all sides to declare a name she would not…

When she looked up, Theodore was smiling. 'I had forgotten that she called me Teddy. I wish there was someone in my life to do it again.'

'I don't mind volunteering,' Sylvia said before she could stop herself.

It wasn't her imagination this time; Theodore Featherstonehaugh's cheeks were definitely reddening. 'You don't have to—'

'Well, why not? We're friends, aren't we?' she said as briskly as she could manage. 'And look, you weren't born in August.'

'I wasn't?' Before she could stop him, Teddy had stridden around the trestle table, bringing his intoxicating presence back to her side, and stared. 'Oh, dear God.'

The date of that edition of the newspaper was clear to see at the very top of the page. The twelfth of August.

'I wasn't born in August?' whispered Teddy, an astonished look on his face. 'I was born a month before.'

'Probably on the twelfth of July, based on the way that sentence is phrased,' Sylvia pointed out, doing her utmost not to lean back into the man's strong chest again. 'You'll have to change your birthday.'

He breathed a laugh, a gasping, astonished laugh that ended in an exhale.

'Now, when you do marry—for real, I mean—you will be able to tell your future wife that you were born on the twelfth of July 1782, and your mother was a strong woman who did not put up with any nonsense from a vicar,' Sylvia said, grinning inanely through the sudden pain of thinking of a wife for Teddy.

Teddy snorted. 'Marry for real? Oh, Sylvia. You know I will never marry.'

'What? You will surely—'

'I am hardly a catch, am I?' he pointed out with a shrug that did something most strange to Sylvia's throat. 'Not gentleman enough to offer her a comfortable home, with no profession to make my own way in the world…no way to earn money. Reliant on his friends for crumbs, staying with them as an unwanted guest when his money runs out. That's no way to build a life. That's no life to offer a woman. But for people without… One cannot build a marriage without something substantial. Something more.'

Sylvia stared up into his serious expression and wished, for the first time, that she had something more to offer.

It was foolish. Embarrassing, even.

'I do not want to marry,' she found herself saying aloud. 'I will not escape one cage and place myself into another.'

The Wallflower Academy had taught her that much. Being sent there as punishment, unable to control her own life, choose her own meals, practice her own hobbies, go to London when she wanted, speak when she pleased…

Sylvia glanced sideways at her companion. But this man…he was different, wasn't he? Different from every other man she had encountered. Surely he—

'And will your future wife be wanting another cup of tea, sir?' asked Mr Reynolds, appearing at the end of the trestle table with a tray. He was evidently doing another tea run for his men.

A heat, a joy, a certainty that everything was right with the world settled across Sylvia before she reminded herself that it was a lie.

She was not going to marry Teddy Featherstone-haugh. It was all a lie.

'My future wife? Oh, she will,' said Teddy quietly and a shiver ran up Sylvia's spine.

She was not going to marry Teddy Featherstone-haugh.

Chapter Ten

'This is a foolish—'

'It is the best idea I have ever had—'

'It is not,' Teddy said fiercely, attempting to keep up with the rapid footsteps of the woman who was fast becoming the only person he wanted to see in a day. 'And after gaining such a lead two days ago at the printers, I don't think we should—'

'Ah, Madame Delphine,' Sylvia said with a charming smile that made his stomach swoop, the bell over the door ringing as the two of them careered into it. 'I hope we are not late.'

Teddy would have been out of breath if his strides had not exceeded Sylvia's, but still, he was beyond irritation and starting to reach indignation as the patisserie door closed behind him.

'This was not part of the plan,' he hissed in the woman's ear, trying to ignore how this vantage point gave him a most delectable view of her décolletage.

For goodness' sake, man, concentrate!

'And I told you, if we are going to convince the *ton* that I am engaged to be married to an actual man, who actually exists,' said Sylvia serenely, her lips barely moving, 'then I have to be seen in public with an actual man, who actually exists, actually wedding planning!'

Wedding planning.

That was surely the source of the jolt to Teddy's stomach. Not the letter he had sent that morning, filled with many crossing-outs and rewrites, folded haphazardly and then paid for extortionately to reach Antigua. Not the fact that he was standing in an incredibly small shop that was filled not only with the scent of sugar and flour and all kinds of confection, but the temptation of Sylvia Bryant.

Try as he might, he could not quite ignore the rosewater. How did she always exude such a delicate scent?

'Besides, testing out the flavours of a bridal cake is not much of a hardship,' Sylvia pointed out, in what she evidently thought was a reasonable voice. 'You cannot tell me you would mind an hour of eating cake with me?'

Parts of Teddy that were not supposed to stiffen in public started to become most inflexible. 'I didn't say—'

'Excellent,' Sylvia said smartly, grinning and placing a hand on his arm, just for a moment. 'I knew you'd come around to my way of thinking.'

It was the swoop of the stomach that did it. Though her fingers left his sleeve almost the moment they touched it, Teddy could not ignore the sensation that he had missed a step while descending a staircase.

It wasn't unpleasant. No, that wasn't the word—it was unexpected. Unusual. Uncontrollable.

'Where is Madame—ah, Madame Delphine, I do hope you received my note.'

Sylvia stepped over to the counter, where an impressive woman in an apron had appeared with a curious expression. Teddy remained where he was—not, he told himself, because he had an excellent view of the way Sylvia's hips moved when she walked, but because there was hardly sufficient room at the counter for the two ladies. He would only get in the way.

'…something light…anything too dense will be quite unsuitable in this heat…'

Teddy smiled as he watched her charm the patisserie owner. There was something very artless about Sylvia. It wasn't that there was no guile in her; she certainly attempted guile whenever she thought it would benefit her. But it was delightful, watching her. Seeing how she was purely herself, never altering her character for anyone they encountered. The printer, the patisserie owner, the boot boy on the side of the road or the coachman who was evidently delighted to be given the excuse to spend some hours in a tavern. They were all greeted and treated by Sylvia as…as people.

He couldn't explain it any other way—they were people to her, individuals, not just a means to an end.

And the way she smiled…

Teddy started as Madame Delphine looked over Sylvia's shoulder, caught his eye and smiled. The smile was too knowing for his liking. His chest tightened awkwardly as Madame Delphine said something in a low voice to Sylvia, who turned to look at him. The two women chuckled and then continued their conversation.

His expression wooden and his hands now stiff by his sides, Teddy wondered whether there was anything to be gained by enquiring as to what that was all about.

Probably not.

Just a few minutes later, Sylvia was returning to his side. 'Madame Delphine is going to bring out three options for us to—'

'What was all that about?' Teddy asked before he could stop himself.

Damnation. Those were unwise words.

Sylvia was raising a sardonic eyebrow. 'What do you mean?'

He sighed, fixing her with a direct look. 'You know what I mean.'

'Oh, the look and the laughter?' She grinned. 'Wouldn't you like to know.'

'That is why I asked,' Teddy said, more sharply.

Well, honestly! It had been a direct enough question, and he didn't see why she…but then, it truly was none of his business, was it? A private conversation between two ladies; it could have been about anything…

Sylvia's expression had softened. As Madame Delphine started to bring over small trays covered in cake samples that she laid out on the counter, Sylvia murmured, 'She asked me about you. In a way.'

Teddy's attention snapped away from the deliciouslooking cake to the admittedly delicious woman standing before him. 'In a way?'

Her smile was friendly, though there was a shyness there he had never seen in Sylvia before. 'She said how clear our mutual affection is. That you adore me. That she has never seen quite such an adoring man in all her time here.'

Sylvia's gaze did not waver.

Teddy swallowed as heat rose, thankfully hidden at his neck by his cravat.

'That you adore me. That she has never seen quite such an adoring man in all her time here.'

Adoring. Well, he'd never thought to put a name to what he felt for Sylvia. It did not matter anyway, did it? He could hardly offer marriage, and she was a woman for whom matrimony seemed to hold no allure.

'I have a great amount of respect for you,' he said aloud, perhaps more tautly than he had intended.

Sylvia's knowing smile did not fade. 'Yes, that is what I thought you'd say.'

Teddy's shoulders slumped. 'And I like you. You… you're a very nice person.'

Nice person? Nice person?

There was something in him roaring to get out and it was currently screaming that 'nice' was the sort of thing one said to elderly aunts—not that he'd had one— or about mediocre cups of tea.

Not about women who sparked desires in him he had never felt and seemed to trespass most inconsiderately on so many of his dreams.

But he couldn't say that. This was all an act, Teddy reminded himself. A plan the two of them had concocted. Well, mostly Sylvia. But it benefited them both and they would gain nothing by changing it now.

Not that he could change it now.

'Thank you,' Sylvia said solemnly. 'I like being a very nice person. Would you like to try some very nice cake?'

Teddy shook his head ruefully as they stepped forward together. 'You're teasing me, you know.'

'Goodness, am I, Your Grace?' And there was that mischievous smile, and the awkward moment was over. 'Heavens. I suppose I shall just have to attempt to cease such a terrible thing. Vanilla and raspberry sponge cake?'

Madame Delphine muttered something about closing the shop to give His Grace privacy.

Ah. Right. He was supposed to be a duke.

As it was, she had left five different cakes upon the counter. The one on the very right, nearest Sylvia, looked very much like a vanilla and raspberry sponge.

'You know, I am starting to think that people enjoy planning weddings more than they enjoy having them,' Teddy said with a laugh, picking up a pair of cake forks and offering one to Sylvia. 'I mean, how often does one have the excuse to go cake-tasting?'

'Not nearly often enough, to my mind,' said Sylvia, spearing a sliver of the sponge and eating it with a look of rapture on her face.

He couldn't help but laugh. 'It can't be that good.'

'I'm sorry, I'm in the middle of a private conversation with this cake,' Sylvia said in a whisper, closing her eyes. 'And you're not invited.'

Teddy snorted, but the moment the sponge and raspberry medley hit his tongue an inadvertent groan left his lips. 'Oh, my goodness.'

'That's what I said. Or thought. I think I temporarily lost the power of speech,' said Sylvia with a laugh, opening her eyes and looking at the second. 'And what do we have here?'

Only then did he notice that before each plate of cake was a small piece of card, folded lengthways, upon which a very French script had been written.

He peered at the card by the cake second to the right. 'Coconut and blackberry. Hmm. It doesn't sound particularly appetising.'

'Then you are at perfect liberty to leave me to consume the entire—'

'Hold off there. I didn't say I didn't want any!' Teddy laughed, their forks clashing as they both attempted to take a large chunk of the cake.

Silence settled in the patisserie. Teddy had to admit that, despite the unexpected combination of flavours, the second cake was almost as good as the first—and that was a high bar.

'It makes you wonder how we are ever going to choose,' he said ruefully. 'I wouldn't mind one of each of these. Why stop at one?'

Sylvia's eyes glittered as she beheld him silently for a moment, before saying softly, 'For our pretend wedding?'

There was that jolt again. 'Oh. Oh, yes, of course,' Teddy said hastily, hating how swiftly he had been able to lose himself in the dream of what this pretend future could be. 'I suppose I should just enjoy the tasting, without expecting a greater feast at the end.'

Could he say anything more suggestive? It did not help that his gaze took in the delicate way that a blob of cream had settled in the corner of Sylvia's mouth, her lips inattentive to it.

Teddy swallowed.

This was getting out of hand. He was not marrying Sylvia. He was not marrying anyone! He was hardly in a position to offer such a thing to anyone.

Sylvia turned back to the counter. 'How else do you deny yourself, with the hope of a greater reward?'

Teddy tried to smile, but his concentration was lax and when he spoke it was without the typical self-censure he practised so often. Which, in hindsight, was a mistake.

'Well, I decided to sink all of my saved allowance into an investment that won't mature for a decade, leaving me no money for rent now, in the hope that I will one day own my own home. You seek adventure and I seek security,' he said with a shrug. 'Your life in a cage makes you wish to fly free and my life without a home makes me want one. That's what my investment is for.'

She was looking at him now with wide eyes. 'A home?'

'Not somewhere like the orphanage, or school, or university, or my lodgings,' continued Teddy, feeling a little exposed at revealing this deep wish. 'Nothing like the Wallflower Academy either,' he added with a smile. 'Just a place I can call mine, that will always be welcoming. Always warm. And where one day, if…if I choose to marry…'

He swallowed. Somehow this was getting too…too personal. Too intimate.

'I hardly frittered it away. I spent it on education and living, is my point,' Teddy said firmly, and quite fairly in his opinion. 'And I have invested. But until it matures, giving me the income I seek, I feel…rootless. Untethered. Maybe I will travel—maybe I will accompany you to Antigua.'

Precisely what had compelled him to say such a thing, he did not know. He did know that Sylvia was looking at him and he wanted to be with her. Not just here, eating cake, delightful as it was. No, he wanted to be with her in the mail coach to Falmouth. He wanted to eat with her in coaching inns and laugh with her as they guessed the stories of the other passengers. He wanted to step onto a ship with her, breathe in the ocean air, stand by her at the railing and look on the horizon for signs of land.

'Accompany me?' Sylvia said softly.

'We could take the duchess charade with us. It would give you greater protection, greater certainty of arriving safely,' Teddy said, hardly knowing where the words were coming from. 'You… I… I do not want anything to happen to you, Sylvia.'

There was a slightly pink tinge to Sylvia's face as she gestured to the fourth cake. 'Fruit cake?'

A question arose in his mind that tripped off his tongue before he could stop it. 'So what will you choose? Will you accept me as your travel companion, or will you choose another? Perhaps you'll choose to remain at the Wallflower Academy and not attempt such a dangerous route.'

Sylvia was laughing again, and there was a look of sympathy on her face—not for herself, but for him. 'You think I have any choice? Teddy, I'll be at the Wallflower Academy for the rest of my life if I don't escape. Why do you think that I'm trying so desperately to get out of there? Besides, ladies like me don't have choices. Most women don't,' said Sylvia quietly, her laughter receding. 'Look at your mother.'

And pain struck Teddy with such force that he thought for a moment Sylvia had lost her temper and decided to stick him with her fork.

Look at his mother.

What choices had she had? Almost none. Heavy with child, given to her by a man who would not own her or the babe, she had done what she could to care for him, before illness had taken her.

There had been no good decisions before her. The orphanage had not been a pleasant place to live, but Teddy could see now it was far better than the streets.

He swallowed, his throat dry. Somehow, Sylvia had both unearthed and resolved a tension he had buried with his mother, all in a moment.

'Now, are you going to try the final cake with me, and make a decision for our wedding?' Sylvia asked with a raised eyebrow.

Heat spread through Teddy's lungs as he smiled. 'And what flavour is this one?'

'You tell me,' she said softly.

It was happening before he knew it. Before he could say anything, before he could reach forward with his own fork, Sylvia had speared a mouthful of the delicious-looking cake and lifted it to his lips.

Teddy was transfixed. His gaze locked on hers, her dark eyes full of something he did not recognise, he did the only thing he could. His lips parted.

The sharp tang and the subtle sweetness of the lemon cake melted on his tongue, but those sensations were nothing to the giddiness in his head and the lurch of his loins as he shared this moment with Sylvia.

'Now, are you going to try the final cake with me, and make a decision for our wedding?'

He could do it. He could ask Sylvia to marry him—make this false engagement real. Why not? Why not spend the rest of his life with this impossible, impetuous, intelligent woman? The life he had invested for, the home he had always dreamed he would buy…how could he live there, content, without Sylvia by his side? Without her laughter filling it? Without her nonsense?

She was completely impossible to ignore, she brought joy into every room, and Teddy wanted her. God, he wanted her as he had wanted nothing else. But until he knew his past, what sort of honourable or dishonourable family she was wedding into, he could not ask her. He would have to wait.

And then Sylvia laughed. 'Is it really that good?'

Teddy swallowed the mouthful of cake carefully, attempting to give himself as much time as possible before having to speak. Swallowing down the cake was nowhere near as difficult as swallowing down the instinct to ask Sylvia if she could ever love him.

Love him? What a foolish thing to think.

She was far beyond anything he could have hoped for—that smile, and that wit, and the way her curves—

Focus, man!

'It's the best of the five,' Teddy said aloud. 'If… I mean, obviously we're not—'

'I think we should order it,' Sylvia said decidedly.

Teddy dropped his fork.

'After all, we've got to keep up the pretence, don't we?' she continued blithely, as though she ordered bridal cakes all the time. 'And there's nothing to stop us eating it even if we don't get married, is there?'

Teddy smiled as convivially as he could manage as Madame Delphine, unerring in her guess that they were finished, bustled out of the kitchen. 'Nothing to stop us at all.'

Chapter Eleven

That was the thing, Sylvia thought as she attempted to stifle her giggles behind a cushion. If Miss Pike did not make the whole thing so enjoyable, she wouldn't do it.

'This is not a laughing matter, Miss Bryant!' the Pike snapped, pulling a sofa cushion up and glaring underneath it before replacing it.

'I think you will find that it is, Miss Pike,' Sylvia said sweetly through her giggles, the cushion entirely unable to muffle the sound of her merriment.

Daphne was wringing her hands by the doorway. 'You really should tell her, Sylvia. It isn't—'

'I order you to tell me at once, Miss Bryant, and that is an order!' Miss Pike's brow was red and her irritation was growing.

Sylvia beamed.

Well, there were almost no amusements at the Wallflower Academy, something she had been quite vocal about the last few months. If the Pike truly wasn't going to update the library or give them a set of boules they could play on the lawn, she was simply going to have to make her own fun.

It was sheer coincidence that the Pike was the victim in all this.

No, not the victim, Sylvia amended in the privacy of her mind as the Pike started to look behind the ornaments on the mantelpiece, muttering something about timewasting as she did so.

Miss Pike was not the victim. An unwilling participant, perhaps.

'This is not a game, Miss Bryant!'

The Pike's tone was stiff and unyielding, and Sylvia tried not to smile. 'I think you'll find it is a game, Miss Pike.'

'Sylvia Bryant, I order you to—'

'Where is her glove, Sylvia?' Daphne's whisper was only just loud enough to be heard over Miss Pike's mutterings, and there was a tension in her voice Sylvia knew all too well.

Poor Daphne. Everything was stressful for her, nothing was easy.

Which was why it was down to people like her, Sylvia, to ensure the Pike did not get too big for her boots.

'And my book!' Miss Pike's hair was starting to look a little unkempt, its owner had raked her fingers through it so many times. 'My book and my left glove, Miss Bryant—both are missing and I have a strong suspicion you know precisely where they are!'

'Perhaps I do, perhaps I do not,' Sylvia said vaguely,

leaning back in her armchair and finding, quite to her surprise, that the enjoyment of the prank was already over.

Strange. She was accustomed to finding mirth in such a thing for hours at a time. When had this become not quite enough to entertain her?

'It makes you wonder how we are ever going to choose. I wouldn't mind one of each of these. Why stop at one?'

'For our pretend wedding?'

Her smile shifted at the memory of his voice. Strong and determined, and yet soft and gentle and—

'Sylvia Bryant!'

Sylvia jumped. She had momentarily become lost in her thoughts, but that single moment had been time enough for the Pike to stride forward and place her hands on the armchair, leaning far too close to Sylvia for comfort.

There was a glare in the Pike's eyes Sylvia had never seen before.

'I am going to ask you one final time, and I expect to be given a reasonable answer,' said Miss Pike, a vein throbbing on her forehead. 'Where is my left glove, and where is my book?'

Sylvia grinned. 'I have hidden two of your belongings in two different places, but I would not fret, Miss Pike. You'll find them soon enough.'

The shriek of frustration the Pike let out was truly astounding. Sylvia had never heard her make such a noise. Without giving her another look, the proprietress of the Wallflower Academy strode out of the drawing room and into the hallway. She did not close the door. Through it emerged the sounds of the two large trunks being opened and their contents flung about the room.

'You really have gone too far this time,' Daphne said quietly, moving over to Sylvia's armchair and dropping onto the sofa nearest her.

'Yes, I seem to have done,' said Sylvia thoughtfully, with just a tinge of regret.

She had not intended it to go this far—nor to give actual distress. But now she had hidden the items so well, she was loath to give the game away.

'Especially,' she added, lowering her voice on the off-chance that the Pike could detect her words even through the doorway, 'as I have hidden three of the Pike's belongings.'

There was a crashing sound from the hallway and hurried footsteps as someone departed at speed.

Daphne sighed. 'You really are a troublemaker, you know that?'

'I am not!' Sylvia was more than a tad outraged. 'I just wish to make things more amusing, that's all. It is not as though we have much in the way of entertainment here, after all. You know that better than all of us. You've been here for ever.'

The words had been spoken before Sylvia could call them back. She watched in horror as her friend's lip trembled, her eyes grew downcast, the colour rose up her neck.

'I am sorry.' Sylvia spoke quietly, knowing a rush of words would overwhelm her friend. 'I did not mean it.'

'But it is true, I cannot deny it,' said Daphne quietly. 'I have been here for ever. At this rate, I will remain here for ever.'

Sylvia swallowed, wondering if there was any choice of words which could bring comfort to her friend. Daphne had the burden, or the benefit, of a father who still visited her occasionally. Sylvia could escape, disappear into the world and no one would truly care. But Daphne… Daphne had to remain here, where her father had put her.

The two of them shared the same cage, but with very different jailors.

'You could come with me, you know,' Sylvia said softly.

Daphne's laugh was dark and bitter, and totally unexpected from the gentle woman. 'Oh, Sylvia. You don't honestly think you're going to get out of here, do you?'

'There you are,' said a third voice. 'Why is your Pike forcibly turning out the pockets of every footman's breeches?'

Sylvia's stomach lurched and she rose so swiftly that stars appeared in the corners of her vision. When they slowly melted away, her eyes rested on the tall and unexpected form of Teddy Featherstonehaugh.

'What on earth are you doing here?' she said without thinking.

His grin was sardonic. 'Is that the way to welcome your betrothed?'

Her betrothed?

It was strange to think of herself as Teddy's betrothed—though she had arguably spent far too much time thinking about him, not as a suitor, but as a man. A man she admired. A man she was, truth be told, deeply attracted to.

Which was precisely why she must never think of herself as Teddy's betrothed. She would not risk her heart being broken—she would not allow it. She had to protect her heart.

'I do apologise. How wonderful to see you, Your Grace,' she said aloud, curtseying low.

When she straightened, it was to see Teddy staring at her breasts. Only when she cleared her throat did he look up, a wicked gleam in his eyes.

'You truly are ridiculous. Now, how swiftly can you be ready for an ostentatious dinner?'

Sylvia did not need to look at Daphne to guess her expression, so her friend's audible gasp came as no surprise, unlike Teddy's words. 'Ostentatious dinner?'

'Yes, my friends are hosting one and I have invited you,' Teddy said with a shrug. 'I... I thought it was about time I introduced you to them. We are engaged to be married, after all. It is expected.'

It is expected.

Yes, he was right. The subtlety of his comment was not lost on her. They had ordered a bridal cake and gone to a jeweller to look at wedding rings, though Teddy had drawn the line at actually ordering one. They had visited the city records to look for his mother's death certificate and the town registry to find out what had happened to the orphanage, and they had created a very careful notebook of all the mail coach times and days, and when ships typically left Falmouth for the Caribbean and how much their fares would cost, and reviewed different-sized trunks that Sylvia could use as part of her escape.

They had done a great deal, Sylvia thought with a wry smile. A great deal to look for Teddy's father, a great deal to plan for her escape, and quite a lot to trick the world into looking at them and seeing a happy couple preparing for matrimony.

But she hadn't met his friends. And that would be expected.

'I am delighted to receive a verbal invitation,' she said aloud.

'My friends aren't the type to commission a calligrapher for a mere Thursday night meal,' Teddy said carefully. 'But they are the type who dress for dinner. Do you have a gown suitable?'

A suitable gown—something the Pike always ensured all her wallflowers had. A twinge of guilt seared Sylvia. She might not be the most cordial person to live with, but there was no real harm in the Pike. And she had teased her beyond—

'Where is my glove?' came a wail from the hall.

Sylvia took a deep breath. 'I will return in a suitable gown in ten minutes. You don't mind waiting?'

'Not in the slightest,' Teddy said with a smile. 'Just don't take too long. I'll miss you.'

I'll miss you. Three words that could have been said by a friend without much thought, a sentiment that tripped off the tongue to anyone you cared about.

And he had said it without any hint of artifice.

Sylvia only just managed to halt her racing mind. It was all part of the act, wasn't it? Yes, that had to be it. She had told Teddy quite firmly that she wasn't going to tell Daphne or anyone else at the Wallflower Academy about their fake engagement. Not that she didn't trust them. It would be easier that way.

'Right,' she said aloud, highly conscious her cheeks were burning. 'Gown.'

When she stepped into the hall, it was to see a scene of absolute chaos. Miss Pike was sitting on the floor in the middle of what appeared to be a nest of cloaks, pelisses and scarfs. There were reticules open in a scattered ring around her and she was sitting there in complete silence.

The guilt was complete. Sylvia strode over to the doormat, lifted it up and retrieved a left glove. Hidden behind the logs in the fire—a fire that would not be lit on such a warm day—was the missing book. The brooch that the Pike preferred with her green woollen pelisse was retrieved from behind the mantel clock.

'I am sorry, Miss Pike,' Sylvia said demurely as she handed the three items back to their owner.

The proprietress of the Wallflower Academy looked up with defeated eyes. 'Sometimes I don't understand you, Miss Bryant.'

A twist of her stomach, a knot no one could undo. 'No one does.'

Except Teddy, Sylvia could not help but think as she rushed upstairs to her bedchamber. Sometimes he seemed to understand her better than he understood himself.

By the time she descended the staircase—slowly, because this blue silk gown was longer than she remembered—Sylvia was relieved to see that the Pike had gone and the hall was mostly back to normal. Except—

'And that should be the last of it,' said Teddy, clapping Matthews on the back.

'Thank you,' the footman said gruffly. 'Would have taken me an age to put all that away.'

It would have done. Sylvia knew how difficult his back had been this last winter. Something twisted, warm and joyful, in her heart as she saw how Teddy had helped the older man.

'Clearing up my messes?' she said as lightly as she could manage.

Matthews had shuffled off somewhere but Teddy turned to look up at her, halfway down the staircase, and an expression in his eyes that she couldn't interpret flickered heat across her collarbone.

'Is that what you're wearing?'

Tension sparked up Sylvia's spine as she froze, one foot hovering in the air, about to descend to the bottom step.

Was what she had chosen wrong? She had thought— well, the blue silk gown was not dreadfully formal, but it was quite clearly an evening choice rather than a day gown. He didn't like it?

Why did it matter so much if Teddy didn't like it?

'I mean…you look beautiful,' Teddy amended.

Sylvia unfroze. At least, she managed to put her foot down on the step and continue walking, though there was something still cold within her. That was probably why she said, 'You don't have to tell me I'm beautiful if you don't like the gown.'

'I don't dislike the gown,' he said immediately.

Was that a tinge of pink in his cheeks?

Sylvia looked down at herself as she halted before Teddy. It was a high-waisted cut, the latest fashion, according to Miss Pike, who admittedly, was sometimes behind the times. The embroidery at the capped sleeves and the hem of her skirt was simple, a darker blue thread, but then Sylvia had never liked an ostentatious design. And that was it.

When she looked back up at Teddy, his cheeks were most definitely pink. 'You hate it.'

'I love it,' he said swiftly.

Sylvia tried not to smile. 'You don't have to pretend.'

'There's nothing wrong with that gown and we are going to be late,' Teddy said, offering his arm as though that closed the matter.

It most definitely did not close the matter, and Sylvia could not help but say as they stepped out of the Wall-flower Academy and towards the carriage his friend had once again loaned him, 'Well, perhaps you aren't a gentleman after all, with manners like that.'

The teasing air in her tone seemed to chill the moment the words were said and, for the second time that afternoon, Sylvia wondered whether she had gone too far.

What was it about her teasing that rang a little harsh today?

Teddy shook his head slowly as he opened the carriage door. 'You may be right.'

He spoke lightly and there was no change in the strength of his hand as he helped her into the carriage. Still. Something nagged at the back of her mind, and by the time Teddy had stepped around the carriage and into it from the other side, she knew she had to say it.

'I am sorry,' Sylvia said quietly.

Teddy did not look at her at first. When he did, it was with a smile she knew well, one that caused her pulse to most unaccountably skip a beat. 'It doesn't matter.'

'It matters to you,' she said as the carriage lurched forward. 'And so it matters. I apologise.'

Teddy did not reply. At least, he did not reply in

words. Instead, he nodded, reached out for her hand and entwined his fingers with hers, and inhaled deeply.

And so they sat there. The journey was not long, around twenty minutes as ever, but for the entirety of the trip they sat holding hands, Teddy's strong fingers gently caressing her own.

Sylvia did not know what to say. What words were there for such an intimacy? No promises given, no expectations offered, no demands made. Just a closeness, a need to be touching. At no point did they speak.

When the carriage slowed and drew up outside a London townhouse that had seen better days, Teddy withdrew his hand from hers slowly. 'We're here.'

It was not a street she recognised. Sylvia had never heard of it, but as she had come to London so infrequently before inadvertently falsifying an engagement with a man she had thought at the time was a duke, that was hardly surprising.

'And your friends are?' Sylvia asked quietly as she stepped onto the pavement, an unsettling and unusual sense of nerves flooding through her.

Well. She could not recall the last time she'd dined out. Out of the Wallflower Academy, that was. In fact, now she came to think about it, had she ever dined out?

Goodness—were the Pike's innumerable lessons to finally be put to the test?

'The Lyndons,' Teddy said as they stepped forward and knocked on the door. 'He attended the same school as me until his father's shipping business collapsed. Some others I know well; some are friends of friends.'

Sylvia nodded, suddenly unsure what to say. 'And… and they think… I mean, do they know about us?'

Us. She wasn't sure if she had ever vocalised that word before. Perhaps Teddy noticed it too, because he seemed unusually tongue-tied.

'I mean…they know I care about you. They know we are engaged. That is all.'

Sylvia tried not to smile, but it was difficult not to when a man as charming as Teddy spoke of caring about her.

Then her reason caught up with her. He liked her, yes, but that was no indication of—a man could like a woman without wanting to—

'There you are—we were beginning to give up hope!'

The door had been flung open and on the other side was an exuberant man with an impeccably cut jacket and a grin.

'Warchester, you old devil, I told you I had to retrieve Miss Bryant,' Teddy replied, loosening up immediately as he clasped the man's hand. 'Miss Bryant—Warchester.'

'Not the real Duke of Warchester?' Sylvia grinned as she and Teddy were ushered into the hall—a very narrow one in which it was impossible for the three of them to stand abreast. 'I hear Teddy has been using your carriage to—'

'Teddy?' The Duke of Warchester raised an eyebrow.

Heat suffused Sylvia's skin violently. Oh, bother, she had—she should never have—

'Don't you dare start using it, you insufferable man…' Teddy laughed with a shake of his head as the three of them moved towards a door. 'Here you go, come and meet the rabble.'

It was astonishing. Sylvia had never seen him so… so relaxed, yet with such bravado. She could see him putting on the act as though he was putting on a coat. It was him, his own, but it was a version of him she had never seen before.

The drawing room was small, well-lit with candles and absolutely packed.

'Here are our hosts, the Lyndons, and Mrs Lyndon's sister and her husband, the Maynards.' Teddy's arm was gesturing all over the place and Sylvia was certain she would not be able to keep track of everyone. 'No one wanted to invite my oldest friend Warchester—'

'Steady on there!' the man he had pointed out said, laughing.

Sylvia laughed too as Teddy added, 'You know what I mean, my friend for the longest time! And here's Mr Stafford, and—'

'My God, I didn't think you'd stoop so low,' came a cold voice from the other side of the room. 'Couldn't find an English girl to tickle your fancy?'

The entire place stilled.

Sylvia could feel every iota of air in her lungs. She

inhaled slowly, relishing the lifegiving oxygen, then turned slowly on the spot.

A man was lounging on a chaise, with a heavy brow and a disgruntled expression. He had the dark hair and pale skin which Sylvia had considered most unusual when she had first arrived in England, but now knew was common—far more common than her own. His mocking gaze did not shy away from hers, staring with no compunction.

No one made a sound.

Then there were footsteps. Just two, heavy and decided, as Teddy stepped between Sylvia and the insolent man.

'How dare you?' Teddy said quietly.

Not a movement from the other guests.

The man shrugged lazily. 'All I said was— Christ, get off me!'

Sylvia gasped, one of the women screamed, and there were calls of 'Steady on there' and 'Quite right too' from the men. Teddy had lunged forward and grasped the man's collar, propelling him upwards in a manner that looked most uncomfortable. Then the two men were moving towards the door, Teddy dragging the protesting brute.

Teddy appeared to ignore all cries from the man and the sounds dimmed as they entered the hall. The sound of a door opening, a thunk that sounded like a fist against a wall, and then the door slammed.

Sylvia remembered to breathe. Desperately needed

air rushed into her lungs as she gasped for breath, a hand clutching her stomach as her mind whirled. It was one thing to defend her, but to throw one of his friends out so publicly, to break with someone he had surely known for years—

Teddy appeared in the doorway, his brow thunderous, his eyes flashing. 'There.'

No one spoke. The man had a power, a presence, clearly a position in the group that meant no one was going to argue with him.

Sylvia hardly knew what to do. Should she leave? Was she—

'I hope we are not tarred with the same brush as Stafford, Miss Bryant,' said the Duke of Warchester stiffly. When Sylvia turned to him, he looked just as aggrieved as Teddy. 'He does not speak for us.'

'I should think not,' said Mrs Lyndon swiftly. 'Now, come sit with me, Miss Bryant—we've given up on a formal dinner. Simply not possible with this numerous rabble—'

'Far more fun this way!' interjected her husband, their host. 'Trays of food and help yourself.'

Sylvia settled herself gingerly next to Mrs Lyndon and tried not to notice the marked difference between her arm and her companion's. Pine next to mahogany.

The evening rushed by in a medley of noise and chatter and laughter and food—very good food, though she was unable to eat a great deal of it. At no point did Teddy leave her side. His presence there wasn't entirely necessary, but Sylvia found the knowledge that she could at any time reach out, if needed, and touch him, to be intensely calming.

And then it was time to leave.

'I'll be in trouble with the Pike if I don't get Miss Bryant home soon,' Teddy said to his friends, grinning as the gathering made motions to encourage them to stay.

'A pike?'

'Never had you down as a man afraid of a fish, Featherstonehaugh!'

'No, really, we must go,' said Teddy with a laugh, gently but firmly guiding Sylvia towards to the door. 'Until next time—thank you, Lyndon. An excellent dinner without a dinner, as always.'

Sylvia breathed in the cool night air as they stepped outside, the door closing behind them. Only then did the grip of tension between her shoulder blades start to lessen.

'I asked the coachman to wait a few streets away. It won't take long to walk there,' Teddy said quietly, his joviality gone, the character his friends knew melting away as he became her Teddy again. 'Are you quite well?'

Sylvia did what she always did. She smiled. 'Oh, I'm used to it. I am sorry though. I never intended for you and your friend to fall out over—'

'He is no friend of mine,' Teddy snarled, a sudden look of vicious anger overcoming him. 'To speak like that to anyone…but a woman, my guest, my…my Sylvia.'

His fierce eyes had softened the moment they met hers, and there was an ache between her thighs as she saw the determination in his gaze.

He would do it. He would cut off someone he knew, one of the few people he knew, it seemed, because of one comment. For her.

His Sylvia.

That wasn't what he meant, she tried to remind herself, but the voice was being drowned out by thoughts of kisses. Of kissing Teddy.

Perhaps he was thinking the same thing. Somehow, her hands were entwined with his and he had tugged her closer, so close that there were but inches between them. Sylvia's eyes darted unwillingly to his lips. She knew now what those lips could do, what pleasure he would entice from her, and she wanted to—

'Have you ever experienced pleasure, Sylvia?'

Sylvia's eyes widened. 'I… I have.'

Teddy's eyes were sparkling with something both mischievous and wicked. 'You know what I mean. I don't mean the delight in a fresh orange or the enjoyment of the opera.'

Conversations about…about that should not be had on the pavement of a dark street! And yet, in the gentle quiet of the evening, Sylvia found, to her surprise, that truths could be spilled with less embarrassment than would be felt in the soaring sun.

'N… No,' she said softly, trying hard to meet his

look. 'No, I…you mean sensual pleasure, don't you? Erotic pleasure.'

Teddy nodded.

Sylvia swallowed hard. 'I felt something when…when you kissed me.'

'But you haven't felt that before?'

How could he ask her such things? With her breasts pressed against his chest, his hands on her, Sylvia could feel the ache between her legs, did not know why he was teasing her like this—

'This is supposed to be a trick,' Sylvia breathed just as Teddy lowered his lips towards hers.

He halted. His breath blossomed across her lips. 'A trick?'

'This…this false engagement,' she managed to say, she knew not how. 'It's a trick, to allow us more freedom.'

Teddy's chuckle was wry as he, with what appeared to be a great effort, pulled back. His eyes sparkled as he pulled a hand through his hair ruefully as he said softly, 'Who's the fool being tricked, then?'

Chapter Twelve

Pacing had always worked before, and it was discon-certing indeed to discover it could not rid him of these nerves.

Teddy inhaled deeply, the crisp bright heat of the air scalding his throat. He turned on his heel and strode back across the front of the Wallflower Academy.

Back and forth, back and forth…

He just had to do it. That was all. He had to go in there and tell her that this couldn't continue. That there was no possibility of him continuing with this charade. That it, in fact, had gone too far.

Or not far enough.

Teddy pushed aside the thought as best he could, but it was a challenge. Because that was the problem, wasn't it? He wanted more. More than Sylvia could give him. More than was appropriate.

More than he could offer.

'This…this false engagement. It's a trick, to allow us more freedom.'

'Who's the fool being tricked, then?'

A jagged exhale tore at his lungs, but it was all Teddy could manage. Yes, this plan, this supposed engagement had gone on too long. Weeks. And yes, he enjoyed it, and yes, he was starting to find himself daydreaming about her...

The two of them. Himself and Sylvia in their own home. Hosting their own dinners. Laughing and talking on into the evening and then discovering that it was far more enjoyable to use their mouths for other—

Teddy tightened his hands into fists. 'Get a hold of yourself, man!'

The low murmur was for his own benefit, but it did not appear to do much good. It certainly did not assist him in putting aside the daydream of Sylvia as his wife.

Wife. She would never consent to it. She did not wish to be married, and he had nothing to offer her, not now. Even if he could...happiness was not found in the arms of a man. Her mother had proven that.

This was the right decision. He needed to go in there and—

'I cannot help but notice that you're doing a good bit of pacing there, son,' came a quiet voice.

Teddy whirled around, gravel flying out around his boots. Matthews, the footman, was standing in the open doorway of the Wallflower Academy, arms folded and a grin on his face.

Oh, hell. Well, he should have expected that some-one would be watching.

'I like a good pace,' he said defensively before he could think of a proper retort. Teddy tried not to groan.

'So I see,' said Matthews slowly. 'You're not wishing to come in, then?'

He'd borrowed Warchester's horse to come all this way in the heat of the day because he knew he had to have this conversation. He could not put it off any longer.

He had to tell Sylvia the deal was off.

'Where is Sylvia? Miss Bryant, I mean,' Teddy amended hastily.

Judging by the broadening smile on the footman's face, the man was much amused by his evident discomfort. 'You'll find her in lessons.'

'Lessons?' repeated Teddy blankly.

The woman was three and twenty, he was certain she had told him that. She wasn't teaching here, was she? He could not conceive of a lesson that Sylvia would be taking.

Matthews' face was a picture of mirth. 'You don't know much about this Wallflower Academy here, do you?'

No, he didn't, as Teddy was starting to discover. It was not a topic Sylvia liked to speak about, and he had learned swiftly that what Sylvia did not wish to talk about did not get discussed.

'Miss Pike has them on a tight leash,' Matthews said conspiratorially, lowering his voice so Teddy was forced to step closer, right onto the steps up to the front door.

'A rigid schedule every day, lessons to teach them deportment and elegance—'

The idea of Sylvia needing lessons on elegance was almost laughable. Why, Teddy had never met a woman with such natural grace.

He shifted slightly on his feet.

Dammit man, don't think of her like that. You don't want to tent your breeches.

'—and there are them formal dinners, and afternoon teas for Society—'

'It sounds like my school teaching etiquette,' Teddy muttered.

Matthews' eyes fixed him with such a piercing look he found he could not look away. 'Sounds more like a prison, if you ask me.'

Teddy's jaw dropped. Well, he had clearly gained the footman's trust by helping him clear up after the Pike's momentary lapse. Matthews would surely not have said such a thing to just anyone.

A prison. A cage—that was what Sylvia had called it in an unguarded moment. He had not quite understood her then, taking her words as an exuberant description of just how frustrated she was by living here, out of the way of London and its excitements.

'Wednesday, half past eleven?' Matthews nodded as he examined his pocket watch. 'Yes, she'll be in the dining room.'

'The dining room?' echoed Teddy, brow furrowing. 'At this time in the—'

'Lessons in table etiquette, appropriate conversational topics, the art of the napkin, apposite portion sizes and permissible vegetables,' Matthews rattled off as though he had taken the class himself.

It was all Teddy could do not to stare. 'I... I beg your... Permissible vegetables?'

'You see, there are some vegetables inappropriate for young ladies to consume in public,' said the footman with raised eyebrows, indicating that he was of quite a different mind. 'Spinach likely to be caught in teeth... garlic decreases the likelihood of a proposal and...well. Large root vegetables.' The footman grinned. 'Miss Pike is very particular in her ways.'

Teddy gave this some thought and swallowed hard. 'Yes,' he said finally. 'Yes, I can see how—'

'And so them wallflowers have to spend a few hours every Wednesday learning about it all,' said Matthews with a wink. 'That's where you'll find her. Off you go.'

A nod of his head indicated a corridor which swept around to the right before Matthews wandered off through a door to the left. Teddy was left alone in the hall, wondering what on earth the footman was trying to suggest.

Teddy swallowed. His affections were getting involved and that had never been the plan. Admittedly, it had been Sylvia's plan, but still, they were using each other as cover. At least, they had been.

Now, whenever he even thought of the bright-eyed, dark-skinned woman, he wanted to rip all his clothes off. No, rip all her clothes off. It had been all he could do last week, when he had seen Sylvia step down that very staircase in that mouth-watering blue silk gown, not to tear it off with his teeth.

Teddy cleared his throat in the empty hall. He'd done it again. Lost track of his thoughts because they meandered too close to Sylvia.

Too close, and not close enough.

Right, dining room. Come on, man.

'I do not want to marry. I will not escape one cage and place myself into another.'

Sylvia's words from the printer's echoed in Teddy's mind as he walked along the corridor, hoping to find the dining room. She had always made her opinion on such matters quite clear, and it was foolish of him to hope that things could be different.

She was not going to marry. From the sound of it, she thought falling in love itself was rather ridiculous—or rather, made one vulnerable.

Which made it all the more awkward that his feelings towards her were starting to become…inappropriate.

Teddy realised he could hear voices. That was, one clear voice and a general muttering.

'…quite clear from the moment you—Miss Smith, are you paying attention?'

That was the Pike… Miss Pike. Dammit. Teddy's footsteps quickened until the recurrence of Miss Pike's voice quite loudly and clearly from a door to his left that was slightly ajar, which made him halt.

'…absolutely essential that you are paying attention. I won't have you embarrassing yourselves, or me, the next time you need to eat snails! Right. So, you elegantly lift the fork, like this…'

A clatter of cutlery and a flicker of sunlight shimmering off metal. Teddy stepped closer to the ajar door, hoping to goodness Miss Pike would not notice him.

It was difficult to gain his bearings, but from what he could make out through such a small sliver, there were about six young ladies sitting around the dining table with Miss Pike at the head. She had her back to him, and was attempting to demonstrate how to eat snails.

And there she was.

Teddy's pulse throbbed like a drumbeat in his ears. It was most unfortunate that his body responded to her like this. Not that his mind was entirely untouched either. Wild thoughts rushed through his head at the sight of Sylvia rolling her eyes and muttering something to her companion, her blonde friend, who smiled and flushed with equal measure.

Sylvia grinned then looked back at Miss Pike…her gaze sliding off the proprietress of the Wallflower Academy and meeting Teddy's.

He almost lurched back, the connection was so physical. How did she do it—make it feel as if she had wrapped her hands around his heart and squeezed, just for a moment?

Teddy caught his breath and smiled, and was rewarded by an answering grin.

This was getting out of hand. He had to tell her, had to slow down the pace of this...whatever it was. And the only way he could do that was—

'Achoo!'

It was not a very convincing sneeze. Even from outside the dining room, with only a few inches to peer through, Teddy could see that Sylvia's pretend sneeze was a tad pathetic.

It appeared Miss Pike thought so too. 'Please, Miss Bryant, behave your—'

'I do believe my stomach is sensitive to snails, Miss Pike,' said Sylvia brightly. 'May I be excused?'

Teddy stifled a laugh as he watched the proprietress tilt her head.

'There are no snails here, Miss Bryant. Please attend to your—'

'And yet here I am—*achoo!*—being most disobligingly—*achoo!*—affected, Miss Pike,' said Sylvia tremulously, holding her hands to her nose. 'I really do—*achoo!*—think it best if I—*achoo!*—leave—*achoo!*—the—'

'Oh, leave us then, Miss Bryant,' Miss Pike said sharply. 'You are more trouble than you're worth.'

Teddy continued to attempt to stifle his mirth as he hurriedly stepped back from the door. She really was most ridiculous.

Sylvia was having more difficulty than he was in hiding her laughter. She burst into giggles as she shut the door, leaning against it and grinning. 'What are you doing here?'

'Bless you,' Teddy said with a grin.

She giggled. 'Goodness, I never thought I would have to sit through another lesson on how to use a snail fork, but here I am. I must have gone through that lesson about a thousand times.'

Her smile had faded but there was still a merriment in her and Teddy loved it.

Not her. Obviously. That would be ridiculous. But seeing her happy; that was worth a great deal.

'I hope you won't get into any serious trouble, though,' he said quietly, not quite sure why he was lowering his voice. 'I can't imagine Miss Pike will be pleased.'

Sylvia snorted. 'Oh, how much more trouble can I be in? What's she going to do, cut down on my rations? There's no way to punish me here. I've been here too long.'

The edge was back. Teddy knew it well, could see it in her eyes and hear it in her tone, and his heart twisted. To think that a woman like Sylvia Bryant was hidden away here in a school for wallflowers. Wallflowers!

That was the trouble, wasn't it? He cared for her, truly.

'And I like you. You...you're a very nice person.'

It had all been a clever ruse when they were two people who did not know each other, but that had changed. And she was absolutely gorgeous, which did not help. Or did. Too much.

'You look very serious,' Sylvia said, her face growing grave. 'What is it? You've found him?'

'Him?' Teddy said blankly, his mind only able to absorb the fact that he was talking to Sylvia, and they were alone.

A frowning Sylvia. 'Your father, Teddy. The man you're looking for. The truth of your past and what it means for your future.'

Ah. 'Oh, yes,' Teddy said weakly. 'Him.'

Strange, how swiftly one's priorities could change, how quickly one could forget something like that. Because he had. All morning his thoughts had been on Sylvia, not his father.

Teddy's jaw tightened. And that had to change. He had to find his father. He had to know the truth of who he was. Only then could he start to plan his future.

And he could not do that when permanently distracted by such beauty.

So. He had to say that. But in a better way.

'No,' he said awkwardly. 'No, I haven't found him yet. To tell the truth, I believe I have reached a dead end. There seems to be no other place to look, and—'

'Did you contact the bank?'

Teddy sighed. 'I went to the bank—they said a solicitor's firm paid my allowance, but advised me against bothering them.'

'Bothering them?' Sylvia repeated. 'Is it not their job to answer letters and so forth?'

'Yes, that is why I wrote to them,' Teddy said with

a laugh. 'They said that they would advise me in due course. That was three weeks ago. I never took to law at university so I do not know the precise length of time that "due course" is supposed to run.'

Sylvia shifted on her feet and his attention was caught by the curve of her hip. Parts of him braced in a way they absolutely should not do in public.

'Sylvia—' he began stiffly.

'Teddy,' she quipped back, mischief dancing in her eyes. 'What is this all about? You are awfully sober. It isn't like you. And I know you.'

Teddy's shoulders slumped. She did. And he wanted her to know him even better, but he had to put aside that instinct and consider what was best for her.

He had nothing to offer her. His investments wouldn't mature for another eight years. It was a long time for someone to wait.

'Look,' Teddy said as decidedly as he could manage. 'We both knew this day would come.'

Sylvia looked up blankly. 'Wednesday?'

'No, I mean…' Dash it all, it wasn't supposed to be this difficult. He'd wanted to keep helping, perhaps even accompany her to Antigua, but he couldn't—he couldn't take this any longer. The duchess charade had to come to an end. 'I mean the day we realise that this has to stop.'

She was still staring as though attempting to decipher a code. 'Stop?'

'Yes, stop. After all, it has been great fun, and merry and all that—'

'Merry?' Sylvia was not laughing, not quite, but she had a confused enjoyment on her face. 'Are you quite well, Teddy?'

Teddy. Goodness, there were times when he wished he had never invited her to call him that. The intense intimacy was sometimes too much.

Focusing hard on his feet and trying to puff out his chest, as though that would help, Teddy decided to look at a point just past Sylvia's left ear. 'Yes, quite well, I thank you. And it can't continue. The engagement has to—'

'Hush!'

'Argh!' He had not intended to cry out. The sound was involuntary—really, Teddy thought as his pulse raced, anyone would have made that noise if someone had placed one hand over their mouth and the other was used to jerk that person in a sudden rush over to the other side of a corridor.

He had thought, for a moment, that Sylvia was going to inadvertently—or purposely—slam him into the wall. As it happened, she opened what appeared to be a linen cupboard and thrust him in there, closing the door behind them, leaving them in almost pitch blackness.

Teddy managed to gather his breath. 'Why on earth did you—'

'I can't have you bandying about words like "ending" and "engagement" right outside a room in which the Pike is seated. Are you quite mad?' came Sylvia's furious voice. 'What were you thinking?'

About how desperately I want to kiss you, and how the only honourable thing is to make sure I can't, was what Teddy could have said. It would have been true, but somehow it didn't seem the right sort of thing to tell a woman in a pitch-black linen cupboard.

With each passing moment, however, his eyes were starting to adjust. As Sylvia started to talk again, he could see her more clearly, her eyes fixed on his.

'I don't understand—don't you like the plan?'

'It's a great plan,' Teddy said wretchedly. 'It's just—'

'And you're not enjoying it? Pretending to be my betrothed, I mean,' asked Sylvia seriously.

Oh, hell. This room was too small, Teddy thought desperately. He could barely move without touching her, which in his dreams was wonderful, but was truly far too difficult when faced with the reality of her.

'I did not say that,' he said quietly.

A quiet sound. Perhaps the shuffling of feet. Sylvia was closer to him now, so close that if Teddy breathed in deeply, his shirt would brush up against her breasts.

He fought the urge.

'What are you trying to say, Teddy?' she said softly.

Everything. Nothing. He could spill out his soul to this woman but it would not be enough. Restraining himself, pulling away was the only thing he should do.

This couldn't continue.

'You have that look on your face again.'

Teddy blinked. 'What look?'

'That…that look.' If he wasn't mistaken, Sylvia was flushing in the darkness of the linen cupboard. 'That look you had when you kissed me. That look you had after the Lyndons' dinner. That—that look.'

Oh, hell. He had a look?

'You are so beautiful,' he said, his voice a low growl, quite inexplicably.

Sylvia said nothing and all Teddy could hear was the thrum of his pulse. All he could breathe in was that rosewater scent that in his mind was Sylvia, reminding him of her radiant skin and teasing smile whenever he walked past a rosebush.

And then she said something he could not have predicted.

'You can kiss me, you know. If you want.'

Teddy lurched backwards so hastily his shoulder banged against the linen shelves. What appeared to be pillowcases rained down around him as he attempted to regain his equilibrium.

He must have misheard. Surely, he could not have heard her say… She didn't…

'Well, we both know this isn't ending in marriage,' Sylvia said softly. Her hand was on his arm. His arm. What was he supposed to do with… 'I'll never marry. I don't see why I can't experience a little enjoyment with you. A little pleasure. Like you said before.'

Teddy groaned and then he was kissing her. Who moved into whose arms, he did not know. He certainly had not consciously pulled Sylvia into his embrace but the instant her lips touched his, her palms splayed against his chest, then gripping his waistcoat to pull him closer, there was no possibility he would let her go.

Oh, she tasted wonderful—of freedom and power—and she smelled of roses, and as her lips parted and welcomed him in, Teddy groaned with the pain of restraint.

He could give her so much. But he couldn't—he mustn't.

'I'll never marry. I don't see why I can't experience a little enjoyment with you. A little pleasure.'

'Will you let me?' he managed to pant.

Sylvia's head had fallen back slightly as Teddy trailed kisses down her throat, and when his lips reached the delicate mounds of her breasts, she whimpered and quivered in his arms. 'Let you? Let you what?'

'Pleasure you.' He had never asked a woman if he could please her in a linen cupboard before, but Teddy thought wildly that there could be a first time for everything. Why not?

Silence. He straightened, finding to his surprise that his eyes had adjusted so well that he could see Sylvia quite clearly now.

Her cheeks were pinking but she did not look away. 'You…you can do that? Here?'

Teddy bit his lip to prevent himself from moaning aloud. 'If you think you can be quiet.'

'And it won't change anything between us? You'll still… I mean, we can keep pretending to be engaged?

We can keep searching for your father, and planning my escape?' Sylvia's voice was urgent.

Yes, yes, yes.

That was what he wanted to say. He would give her anything she wanted in this moment, anything at all.

Try as he might, he could not say no to this woman. 'Of…of course. You'll always have my respect, Sylvia. We can keep up the pretence a while longer.'

'Then…then yes. You may… I mean, if you don't mind—'

Teddy did not permit her to continue. Her consent freely given, the longing in her voice painfully audible, he crushed his lips on hers and revelled in the way she clung to him.

Oh, yes. She wanted it.

He would have to be careful. Hand slightly shaking as he started to pull up her skirts, Teddy was determined to give her the most incredible experience. He would take his time. He would be gentle with her.

Until he wasn't.

Sylvia's breathing was slow but growing more rapid as Teddy's fingers gently skimmed her knee, the inside of her thigh, and then—

'Oh!'

Teddy kissed her hastily, stilling his fingers, resting his hand against her curls. Only when Sylvia ceased mewling her surprise did he cease the kiss. 'You must be quiet. Anyone could hear.'

She glanced at the door for a moment, then back to him. 'I can be quiet.'

It was all he could do not to smile. Oh, she had no idea what he was about to do to her. She might find it a little difficult to stay quiet then.

Speaking of difficult, it was becoming a challenge keeping his fingers absolutely still against the inviting warmth of her curls. Slowly, delicately, Teddy brushed his thumb against her.

He felt, as well as heard, the impact.

A quiver rushed through Sylvia's body and she gasped. 'That was—'

'You want more?' Teddy murmured, pressing a kiss to her neck and trying desperately to control himself. He'd been hard the moment she'd asked him to pleasure her, but now—

'More?'

Another kiss, and his thumb brushed along her slit again. Another kiss, and Teddy slowly, very slowly, slipped his index finger past the curls and into the wet inviting folds of her secret place.

This time it was he who needed to hush. God, she felt wonderful—and what was even more wonderful was the way she shifted her feet slightly to welcome him in, how she moaned in appreciation as his thumb found her nub and his fingers started to stroke, how her panting blossomed against his neck.

Teddy bit his tongue and tried to concentrate. She

had asked for pleasure, and by God, he was going to give it to her.

'Oh, that feels…that feels—'

'Do you like it?' Teddy could not help but ask.

Sylvia's eyes met his. 'Like it? Such pleasure. Such sensations, oh…oh, Teddy!'

And that was when he kissed her. Teddy could not help it; this gift she was giving him, the chance to give her the first taste of erotic pleasure, it was more than anything he could have dreamed.

His passionate kisses swallowed her stifled whimpers and his fingers began to coordinate a rhythm. The damp between her thighs increased as she twisted in his arms, moaning from his sensual touch, and Teddy almost grinned as his thumb slowly joined with his fingers, circling unhurriedly around the nub that he knew he must attend to if she was to reach her peak.

And somehow the fact that they had to stay quiet was heightening everything, and if he wasn't careful Teddy was going to come undone in his breeches, and then—

Sylvia cried out in his mouth, her fingers tightening around his neck as her entire body spasmed, and Teddy could have wept as he felt her quiver, shuddering as her pleasure roared through her.

He waited. Pressing soothing kisses against her lips, the corner of her mouth, her forehead, her eyes as her eyelashes fluttered, her breathing rapid yet starting to slow, he held her as she recovered from the sudden discovery of such pleasure.

When her breathing appeared to be almost regular again, Teddy whispered, 'I hope that was everything you wanted.'

Sylvia's eyes snapped open. 'You have no idea.'

Their muffled laughter mingled and it was all he could do not to get a very good idea by letting his own body go.

But no. He would restrain himself. He would be controlled—

'Why was it you wanted to end this, by the way?'

Teddy stiffened. 'I beg your pardon?'

'You wanted to end the engagement,' Sylvia said, face still flushed but brilliance and concentration now back in her eyes. 'Why?'

Teddy opened his mouth but no sound came out. She was…and he was…

'No reason,' he said quietly, mouth dry as the lie emerged. 'No reason at all.'

Chapter Thirteen

'Daphne?'

Sylvia poked her head into the music room. She had to be here; she was starting to run out of places to look. Where could a woman hide in a place like this, anyway?

As it was turning out, somewhere that Sylvia had not yet found. She had looked in the library, the drawing room, the ornamental gardens in the shade, where a few wallflowers had sought relief from the sun, and yet nowhere was Daphne to be found.

It was most irritating.

'Daphne?' Sylvia repeated, as though by echoing herself she could find her missing friend.

The music room remained resolutely empty, save for the impressive pianoforte and the harp covered by a silk sheet in the corner.

Sylvia bit her lip. She had woken up that morning with one decision in mind: she had to talk to Daphne.

About all of it.

This secrecy had gone on long enough. Hiding what

she and Teddy were up to; it was not feasible. Besides, she needed advice. Things had…changed.

'Oh, that feels…that feels—'

'Do you like it?'

Heat sparked across her cheeks. Not that she regretted what had happened—after all, they hadn't done anything wrong. Not really. Not as far as she was concerned.

'Like it? Such pleasure. Such sensations, oh…oh, Teddy!'

Try as she might, Sylvia could not prevent the prickling heat from spreading down her neck until she felt like a walking, talking fireball.

Keeping their fake engagement a secret had been all very well before all these feelings and emotions and experiences had got involved. Before she knew what it was to care for the man. Before she knew what it was to experience such pleasure.

And now…

Sylvia turned away from the music room and strode down the corridor, trying desperately to think where Daphne could be. She wasn't in her bedchamber and she'd slipped away from breakfast before Sylvia could accost her. But she hadn't left the Wallflower Academy, had she?

It was unthinkable. Daphne, not at the Wallflower Academy?

'Daphne, where are you?' Sylvia muttered under her breath as she poked her head into the morning room and saw only a pair of wallflowers reading in silence, wearing shawls around their shoulders. In this heat!

She needed Daphne. Everyone went to Daphne with their troubles, and her advice—or at the very least, her ability to listen without interrupting, a skill Sylvia had never mastered—was greatly sought-after.

And if Sylvia had ever needed her friend's advice, it was now.

'Oh, this is ridiculous!' Sylvia threw her hands up in the air, frustration overspilling. 'Where is she?'

How irritatingly typical that the one time she needed her friend's immediate and undivided attention, she was nowhere to be found!

A trio of wallflowers, all shy ladies who had never spoken to Sylvia despite her attempts to make conversation, skittered past her, eyes averted.

Sylvia rolled her own. What, did they think that by spending more than ten seconds in her company, they would suddenly transform into hellions like herself? They probably dreaded being sent to the Pike's room, too…

The Pike's room.

Filled with purpose, Sylvia picked up her skirts and ran. Her lungs were tight by the time she reached Miss Pike's study door.

Was it possible…

Her suspicions were confirmed the moment she stepped closer. The door was not completely closed, a common habit of the Pike's, and so through the small gap between door and frame slipped a conversation Sylvia was most definitely not supposed to hear.

'...any idea whether they have set a date?'

'N-No, Miss Pike.'

There was a heavy sigh from someone in the room— the Pike, probably—and the sound of someone moving about. Pacing?

'I just thought she would have made good, that's all.'

The Pike sounded irritated, but also greatly tired. Sylvia frowned, closing her eyes in concentration. Who could the proprietress be so unhappy with? Set a date? A date for—

'I have to assume Sylvia has talked to you about him. Her future husband.'

'No, Miss Pike.'

'Well, why not, Daphne!' It was not a question from Miss Pike's lips, more an exclamation. 'Honestly, I thought the woman had finally found a husband, a chance for her to get away from this place, as she so desperately wants. So what is she waiting for? Why have they not selected a date for their wedding?'

Sylvia's eyes snapped open.

It was not an unreasonable question. After all, if they truly wished to be married, it would have happened by now. A date would have been selected. They would be on their way to matrimony.

As it was...

'Daphne Smith, I hope you are telling me the truth.' The Pike's voice was sharp now, and Sylvia could just imagine the stern look the older woman was giving her friend. 'If I find out you have been deceiving me—'

'I would not do that, Miss Pike,' came Daphne's quiet yet unruffled voice.

Sylvia tried to smile through the confusion. That was her Daphne. Perhaps it was a good thing she had not told her friend the truth of the matter after all. She had never expected the Pike to put her in such an awkward position, but clearly the proprietress of the Wallflower Academy was far more concerned about Sylvia's wedding than she'd thought.

Her wedding.

Swallowing hard, Sylvia tried to put aside the memories of just what she and Teddy—or Mr Featherstonehaugh, that was how she should think of him—had shared in the linen cupboard.

'I'll never marry. I don't see why I can't experience a little enjoyment with you. A little pleasure. Like you said before.'

'…on and on this engagement goes. I have a reputation to keep! My wallflowers must get married!'

But he never would, would he? He would never offer marriage. She would have hated the thought mere months ago but now…now she had spent such time with Teddy, laughed with him, adventured over London with him, found pleasure together…

Sylvia thought back to their conversations. He was so convinced he had nothing to offer a wife, a conviction that was partly true, but at the same time he was an impressive man with a good heart. That was surely better than any amount of future profit from investments.

'Well, I suppose, if it all falls apart, she can just stay here,' came the Pike's voice with a heavy sigh. 'Though Lord knows she doesn't want to be here.'

It was difficult not to feel guilty at such words. True, Sylvia did not particularly want to be at the Wallflower Academy, and had hardly made a great secret of it.

But she had a home here. The more time she spent with Teddy, the more she grew to know him, the more Sylvia realised there were many children who had never known the sense of a home. Not in any way.

She was better off than so many. Perhaps she should—

'Well, that will be all, Miss Smith.'

Sylvia flattened herself against the wall as the door swung fully open, but thankfully it was only her friend who stepped through it. Her eyes widened at the sight of Sylvia but thankfully her sense caught up with her mouth before she could say a word.

Grabbing Daphne's hand and pulling her rapidly along the corridor, Sylvia did not speak until the two of them had slipped into an empty bedchamber, one set out for the guests of wallflowers. Guests who never came.

Sylvia slammed the door shut, leaned against it and fixed her friend with a look. Daphne's shoulders slumped.

'Thank you.'

Daphne looked up, evidently startled. Goodness, was she often so ungrateful? 'I beg your par—'

'Thank you, for putting up with that interrogation from the Pike,' Sylvia said, sighing heavily as she continued to lean against the door. 'It could not have been pleasant.'

'It wasn't.' Daphne stepped towards the unmade bed, dropping onto it with a look of complete defeat. 'But you are my friend. If Miss Pike wishes to know why your engagement is not progressing, she can ask you.'

Sylvia bit her lip.

That was the trouble with Daphne. Or rather, that was the wonderful thing about being Daphne's friend. She was shy, a true wallflower. Precisely how she had become so shy, Sylvia did not know. Her friend had been that way since Sylvia had arrived, and she saw no reason to attempt to change her.

Still. It made it a mite challenging to draw anything out of her.

'I truly am sorry you were put in that position,' Sylvia said quietly, stepping across the room and pulling a bedside chair around so she could sit and face her friend. 'I will speak to the Pike.'

A flicker of a smile passed over Daphne's lips. 'I don't think it's the Pike that you need to speak to.'

Sylvia frowned. 'It isn't?'

'No.' Daphne looked up and met her eyes. 'It's that gentleman of yours.'

Stomach lurching horribly, and hoping to goodness her friend had not overheard a certain something occurring in the linen cupboard, Sylvia attempted to keep her expression as calm as possible. 'I don't know what you—'

'Does he know?' Daphne interrupted, which was most unlike her.

Sylvia blinked. 'Know?'

'About…about your parentage. About being illegitimate.' Daphne's voice became almost a whisper.

Ah. Right.

It was the one topic Daphne had always been reticent to speak of. Sylvia had always known; that was one of the joys and challenges of the Wallflower Academy— gossip did not settle for long, jumping from wallflower to wallflower.

Daphne Smith—'Smith'.

Her father seemed a jovial sort. Sylvia had met him twice, Lord Norbury, and his new wife, Rilla's mother-in-law. It had all got complicated at Rilla's wedding when the news had been announced.

Daphne, it seemed, had not been told.

Sylvia watched the flickering tension on her friend's face, the downcast eyes, the worry puckering her forehead…

'I just thought… I wondered, I suppose, if he had proposed marriage to you but then… I mean, upon discovering your parentage…' Daphne's voice faded away and she made a great effort to meet Sylvia's eyes before dropping her attention to her lap.

Oh. Oh, was that the current theory?

Well, it was as good a theory as any, Sylvia thought

dispassionately. Perhaps if Daphne knew that Teddy bore the same societal shame about his parentage she would be less concerned.

But that was Teddy's truth to tell. Not hers.

'He has not concerned himself with that,' Sylvia said, as gently as she could manage. 'He…it does not worry him.'

Well, that was true. It wasn't the entire truth, but it was true.

When had she started to become so au fait with lying?

Daphne's head jerked up. 'It does not?'

'It does not,' said Sylvia, trying to smile briskly. 'Please, you do not have to worry about—'

'I will always worry about you, Sylvia,' said Daphne, in a tone which was far more fierce than she had expected. 'You're my friend.'

Her hands reached out and clasped Sylvia's.

And quite unexpectedly, entirely against her will, Sylvia discovered her eyes were—full of tears.

Dashing away the tears most determinedly, Sylvia pulled away from her friend and rose. 'We should probably go downstairs. The Pike will be looking for me, I suppose.'

'Indeed.' Daphne nodded briskly, as though the emotional moment had never happened. 'And I wish to continue reading yesterday's newspapers— You know, they still haven't found the Duke's heir and—'

'Sylvia?'

Sylvia almost fell over, she stepped backwards so hurriedly, her legs bashing into the chair.

It was Teddy.

Teddy. Standing in the doorway of a bedchamber. Teddy—here?

'Oh, hello,' he said cheerfully. 'Miss Smith, is it not?'

Daphne's face went a delicate shade of puce and without saying a word, she strode across the bedchamber, pushed past Teddy and almost ran down the corridor. Sylvia heard the thundering of her footsteps fade into the distance.

Well, that would do it. If the Pike heard a wallflower, any wallflower, making so much noise—

'What are you doing in here?' Teddy asked quietly, stepping fully into the room.

What was she doing in here? *Attempting to persuade my well-meaning friend that you haven't decided to break off our engagement because I am illegitimate.*

Perhaps not the best thing to say.

The trouble was, Sylvia's confident tongue had for some reason decided to abandon her. All she could do, seemingly, was stare and say nothing.

What was wrong with her?

'I'm…talking,' she said lamely.

Teddy's smile was teasing. 'To yourself?'

'With Daphne—I mean, she's gone now,' Sylvia said awkwardly. Why was she suddenly so conscious of her own skin? Why was it prickling like that—and why did she want to throw herself into his arms and—

Well. She knew the answer to that question.

'Oh, that feels...that feels—'

'Do you like it?'

'I wanted to see you,' Teddy said suddenly.

'You did?' Sylvia asked without thinking, her cheeks burning.

He wanted to see her. What did that mean?

Oh, this was getting ridiculous!

'Yes.' He said nothing more but just looked at her, the weight of his gaze somehow more than she could bear.

'Well, you have seen me,' Sylvia said, trying not to laugh. 'Will that be all?'

Teddy's smile disappeared. 'Do you want me to go?'

Somehow, everything had gone wrong. The cordial friendship they had found, the casual intimacy, their ability to even talk to each other, had disappeared. And Sylvia knew why.

'I'll never marry. I don't see why I can't experience a little enjoyment with you. A little pleasure.'

What a foolish thing to say. What a foolish thing to have done. She had found perhaps a kindred spirit in Teddy, someone who understood in part how it was to find herself frustrated by the hand life had dealt her— and what had she done?

Ruined it. Made it so awkward the poor man did not even know how to talk to her any more. It was ridiculous. It was unfair.

And it was all her own fault.

'I—no, I don't want you to go. Unless you want to

go. Or need to go—I am sure you have calls on your time,' Sylvia said, hating how her voice babbled into the silence.

His smile had returned, though it was uncertain. 'I am not really one for numerous appointments.'

Silence fell between them again.

Sylvia shifted from one foot to the other. Why was he here? Before the linen cupboard experience, for that was what she would be calling it from now on in the privacy of her own mind, she could have just asked him, Teddy would have told her, and that would have been the end to it.

And now…now, there was a barrier between them woven of unspoken words and shame and confusion, and she could see no way to break it down.

'I just…after I last saw you, I have been doing some thinking. Thinking about what we should, and…and we shouldn't do,' Teddy said, his voice dropping to a low rumble.

Sylvia swallowed hard. 'I see.'

It was so obvious. He regretted what had happened.

Thinking about what they should and they shouldn't do? Evidently, Teddy wished he had not touched her like that, not brought her to pleasure, not kissed her so passionately and lost all control.

He regretted it. One of the most powerful and precious moments of her life, and he regretted it.

It was perhaps a good thing she had already forced tears away mere moments before Teddy had arrived at the spare bedchamber. It was therefore nothing for Sylvia to push aside the rising pain and prickling tears.

He regretted the intimacy—he had certainly not spoken of it well, nor initiated a repeat. Well, that was fine. She would give him precisely what he wanted.

'We do not need to speak of it,' Sylvia said airily, holding her head as high as she could manage. 'It will never happen again.'

A flicker of some strong emotion crossed Teddy's face. Relief? Pain? It was gone so quickly that Sylvia could not grasp it, but it had to be relief, did it not?

'Never again,' he repeated warily, as though ensuring he had not misheard.

His instant comprehension shook Sylvia to the core. Had she been so unwise as to give herself, that innocent part of herself, to Teddy? He appeared so thankful that he would never have to touch her again. Was she so repellent? Was it so awful for him?

'Yes, never again,' she said smartly, as though they were discussing the weather. 'There. I suppose that is what you came here to talk to me about?'

Teddy nodded, his head a swift jerk. 'Yes. Yes, of course.'

And there it was. She had been foolish enough to encourage him to do something that had filled him with remorse, and he had been foolish enough to give in to her demand.

Well, Sylvia would just have to learn to live with it. It was mortifying, to be sure, but perhaps after this they could move past it. Perhaps Teddy would never mention it again and they could pretend it had never happened.

And then Teddy smiled, and a piercing joy arced through Sylvia with such force that she thought she would fall over. 'Do you have time for a walk in the gardens? I would appreciate your opinion on a newspaper article I found, about the St Kilda's Orphanage for Waifs and Strays.'

That was when she knew.

This heat wasn't desire. At least, it was desire, but it was desire for something greater than an erotic encounter in a linen cupboard.

It was for Teddy. For him—the man, the friend, the person who could make her smile with just a look. The man who had grown up in a world of unkindness and chosen to be kind. The man who had no idea who he was, yet was more centred, more grounded, more sure of himself than any other person she had ever met.

How could she have been so imprudent as to allow herself to fall in love?

'Sylvia?'

'What? Garden,' she said hastily, hating her folly the moment the words were out of her mouth. 'I mean, yes. I have time.'

What would she do when this pretend engagement had to come to an end? How could she leave England, leave Teddy behind, knowing she would never see him again—and not have her heart break?

Chapter Fourteen

One of the benefits of lodging in a very small room was that when someone pounded on your door it took only four strides to reach it.

'What on earth are you doing here?' Teddy asked with a raised eyebrow as the Duke of Warchester strode into his room.

'I could ask you the same question,' Warchester replied, nose scrunched up as he took in the diminutive space. 'How on earth do you live like this?'

It was all Teddy could do not to smile.

Yes, in the eyes of a duke, this place probably was not impressive. A single room: a fire at one end upon which he made tea, a small table that just about seated one, and a bed that was perfectly sized for two. Not that he had ever thought to bring Sylvia here.

His investment in his future had left him short of funds in the present. There had been few places in London which would accept him as a lodger without any visible means of support. This was one of them. He'd considered seeking employment but something held him back. Some…some sense of something about to happen.

It was foolishness, he knew. Idiocy.

'You should have grown up in an orphanage,' Teddy said easily, closing the door behind his friend. 'This is paradise in comparison.' And it was, at least, tidy. He had always been fastidious. The place was immaculately clean, his clothes carefully folded in the dresser, and the only thing without a home were the letters, as yet unopened, from that morning's post. He really must get to them—it was perhaps too early to hope to receive an answer from Antigua, but maybe—

'I wouldn't let a tenant live like this,' Warchester said grimly, peering at the damp patch on the wall and reaching out a hesitant finger. 'What precisely is that green—'

'I wouldn't, if I were you.'

'No, quite right,' said his friend with an artificial laugh. 'Look, I came to apologise,' he went on heavily, dropping onto the bed.

'Apologise?' Teddy moved across the small room in just a few steps, leaned against his table, and immediately straightened as he heard the creak of unhappy wood. 'What on earth for—what's happened?'

Perhaps his friend had returned to the Wallflower Academy for further racing tips and had accidentally revealed to Miss Pike that the man she had thought was the Duke of Featherstonehaugh was in fact an imposter. Perhaps he had gone back to the Wallflower Academy and run into Sylvia, and the two of them had fallen passionately and inexplicably in love, and—

Teddy just about managed to halt himself there. That was ridiculous. People didn't fall in love like that. Probably.

'Nothing's happened—at least, nothing you don't know about. Hell, I won't repeat his words, but I will apologise for them,' said Warchester with a glower. 'Stafford. What he said to Miss Bryant.'

Stafford.

Teddy's scowl creased his forehead. He had managed to ignore the man mostly, only returning to the memory of that moment in the early hours of the morning, when his frustration over his idiotic conversation with Sylvia was echoing in his mind.

'I have to say, I did not realise the woman meant that much to you,' Warchester was continuing, evidently unaware that Teddy's thoughts were mostly elsewhere. 'I mean, throwing him out of Lyndon's house! Most men of my acquaintance barely tolerate their wives, let alone consider defending them!'

His guffawing laughter rang out awkwardly around the room. Teddy did not join in his merriment. Warchester stopped almost immediately.

'Because you do care about her, don't you?' his friend said slowly. 'Hell, man. What are you going to do about that? I presumed…well, given your circumstances, a long engagement of course, but what will you do about—'

'Absolutely nothing,' Teddy said sharply. 'There's nothing to do.'

'But—'

'Oh, you think I should invite her here?' he shot back darkly. 'You think Miss Bryant deserves to live in a single room with a leaking roof and a landlord who helps himself to your post when he thinks you're not looking?'

'You should read your post,' his friend pointed out.

Teddy threw up his hands. 'I've been a tad distracted!'

Warchester bit his lip. 'If you love her—'

'I did not say that,' Teddy said curtly.

Because he couldn't. He wouldn't allow himself to, not after her delicate rebuke of his talents as a lover just two days ago.

She did not want him to touch her again. Was that not evidence enough that there was no attraction between them—at least, not from her side? If he had pleased her, truly pleased her...

'He had no right to say what he said, no matter what Miss Bryant is to you,' said Warchester unexpectedly. 'I had not thought him to be that sort of rogue.'

'He's more than a rogue, he's a blackguard, and I never wish to see him again. The very idea that he said...and Sylvia, she had to listen to...but he should not speak that way about anyone,' Teddy said, his gruff voice trailing into nonsense.

His friend appeared to understand. At least, he did not attempt to correct him, which was understanding enough.

'Miss Bryant is not injured by it?'

Teddy tried not to remember the hurt on her face, or worse, the look of resignation, the way she said that she was used to it.

'Miss Bryant is made of stronger stuff.'

'Good.' Warchester looked at him more closely now, for the first time since he had entered the room. 'What are you wearing? Your own good jacket?'

'Oh, you don't like it?' Teddy didn't know why he asked. It wasn't Warchester's approval he wished to gain.

His friend snorted. 'You look a little uncomfortable, man, that's all. You have an engagement this evening?'

Stomach lurching, Teddy tried to ensure his expression demonstrated a level of nonchalance he did not feel. 'Something like that.'

An engagement.

He should never have permitted Sylvia to convince him into this pretend engagement. He should never have allowed her to become such a vital part of his life. He should never have—

No. He could not regret it, not any of it. Even if tonight was the last time they kept up the sham, it had all been worth it. Just being in her life was a gift.

'I'm attending the Duke of Knaresby's ball,' Teddy said aloud, realising he had allowed the conversation to drift into silence. Sylvia had been clear that her friend Gwen had invited both of them, and he would not let her down if she needed their pretence to continue.

Warchester raised an eyebrow. 'Another duke, eh? You'll be tired of us soon.'

Teddy snorted. 'Soon? I'm tired of you dukes already.'

His friend grinned and waggled a finger as he rose. 'You blighter. Being a duke isn't all that exciting. Well, I'll leave you to your ball—but for goodness' sake, open some of that post. You never know—the answer to who you are could be in there!'

Chortling with amusement at his own joke, he clapped Teddy on the back then left, closing the door behind him.

Teddy sighed heavily as he stared around the empty room.

He couldn't bring Sylvia here. She deserved far better, much more than he could ever offer her. And besides, she didn't want him. Despite the glory of what they had shared, what he had thought they had shared, Sylvia evidently did not agree.

He smiled ruefully as he recalled what he had just told his friend. Yes, he had been distracted. Far too distracted, as it turned out. And that pile of post was getting ridiculous.

Glancing at his battered pocket watch and seeing he had perhaps twenty minutes before he needed to depart to attend the Knaresby ball, Teddy strode over to the tottering pile of letters and pulled one out at random.

Which was a mistake.

The tower had been delicately balanced and removing a letter from the middle caused the whole thing to cascade down in a flurry of paper. White squares fluttered all over the floor.

He should have seen that coming. Dropping to his knees and cursing vaguely under his breath, Teddy started to pull together the scattered letters.

And halted.

The letter currently in his right hand felt different to the others—heavier, a more costly paper. There was a seal on the back too, one he did not recognise.

Dropping back to sit on the floor, he absentmindedly tore open the letter, giving little thought to the envelope, which he allowed to fall to the floor, and started to read.

His eyes widened.

Dear Theodore Featherstonehaugh,
We are delighted to inform you that after a great deal of research and confirmation of the records, and by surreptitiously viewing your person, we can inform you that your father, Theodore Ignatius Charles Burrell, eleventh Duke of Camrose, has died. His wife predeceased him last year. You are his sole heir.

Over the last thirty years we have made payments to a Mr Theodore Featherstonehaugh and have given little thought to your connection to our late client, but his will and testament made clear both your existence and his wish for you to be legitimised. The Camrose estate, comprising no less than forty thousand acres, the manor estate of New Hall, the Scottish estate of Ormskirk, the London townhouse in Mayfair, stocks and investments to the sum of—

Teddy dropped the letter onto his lap.

No. No, he was dreaming. Or hallucinating. Or he had merely misunderstood—they must be seeking the heir of this duke he had heard about. But then why were they writing to him?

Trying to take deep, calming breaths, Teddy picked up the letter again and returned to the second paragraph, which, most disobligingly, appeared to be more of the same.

The Camrose estate, comprising no less than forty thousand acres, the manor estate of New Hall, the Scottish estate of Ormskirk, the London townhouse in Mayfair, stocks and investments to the sum of two hundred and thirty thousand pounds—delivering an income of eleven thousand a year—passes to you in its entirety.

Please come to the offices of Henderson, Henderson, and Tyrell at your earliest convenience. The funds will then be transferred to you immediately, and preparations can begin for your acceptance at Court.

We remain your humble servants,

Henderson, Henderson, and Tyrell

Teddy swallowed. No. No. It couldn't be true.

Despite his thundering heart and rushing pulse, his gaze flickered back to the first paragraph. To one particular section.

Theodore Ignatius Charles Burrell, eleventh Duke of Camrose, has died. His wife predeceased him last year. You are his sole heir.

Theodore. He had his father's name. Why he had not thought to search for a Theodore he did not know. It had never occurred to him that, despite everything that had happened, despite the pain of abandonment and the loss of his mother, his father had, all along, given him something precious.

His name.

And then the realisation of what the letter truly meant rocked him, a physical lurch that made Teddy hunch over and grab his knees as though that would cease the shock.

He was the twelfth Duke of Camrose.

No. No, he couldn't—

But there it was, in black and white.

Oh, dear God. There he had been, wondering whether he was a gentleman or the son of a tradesman, or a vagabond, or a criminal…

And he was a duke.

A duke?

Everything Teddy knew about himself had changed. The alteration felt like an earthquake within him, a terrible comprehension that the solid ground upon which he had been standing was in fact nothing but quagmire.

'The Duke of Camrose,' Teddy whispered to himself in the empty room.

It did not feel real. It certainly would not feel natural to be addressed in such a manner. How on earth was he supposed to grow accustomed to someone like Sylvia calling him…

Sylvia.

Teddy rose hastily to his feet—so hastily his head swam for a moment. *Sylvia.*

'You are a duke—how delightful. I shall add you to my collection.'

His astonished laughter filled the empty room. Dear God—he could never have known, all those weeks ago, that what she said was in fact true. He was a duke. He was a *duke*.

…an income of eleven thousand a year—passes to you in its entirety.

And that meant he had a decision to make.

'Mr Featherstonehaugh!'

Teddy started, unable to untie his tongue to say anything. That did not matter. His landlord had never seen much point in privacy and so strode into his tenant's room without waiting for an answer.

'Mr Featherstonehaugh, there is a woman for you!'

Teddy stared. 'A…a woman?'

Surely, she could not have… Sylvia would not have…

'Says she's a Miss Bryant and you're to take her to

a ball!' His landlord examined him with a curious eye. 'I did not know you had a lady friend.'

Stomach twisting, the letter from Henderson, Henderson, and Tyrell still in his hand, Teddy stared at the man.

A lady friend.

Sylvia.

The Duke of Camrose.

'Well?' snapped his landlord, a frown furrowing his brow. 'Do you have a lady friend, or don't you?'

'You know, I think I do,' Teddy said vaguely, folding the letter and slipping it absentmindedly into his pocket. He could hardly leave it here. One never knew which of his letters the man would take. 'Thank you, sir.'

His landlord snorted.

He probably kept talking. Teddy was not sure. He had marched past him, almost hurtling by the time he reached the stairs, his pulse racing as his eyes desperately sought the image of—

'You know, it's a good thing I remembered where you said you had taken lodgings,' Sylvia said blithely, waiting outside without seemingly a care in the world. 'It's not the nicest part of London, is it?'

Teddy did his best to repress the urge to pull her into his arms and kiss her so passionately she would have to fall in love with him.

A great deal had changed. And he had to think about it, had to meet these Henderson, Henderson, and Tyrell gentlemen and see whether this nonsense was actually true.

And if it was…

He had thought to tell her immediately, to reveal all—to tell her he was not Theodore Featherstonehaugh but Theodore Burrell, Duke of Camrose, and he was rich, and a gentleman, and could marry her—

And then he had seen her.

Teddy's face went slack. Dear God, but she was beautiful.

Not just beautiful. Stunning. He felt stunned, as though he no longer had any control over his body.

Sylvia was wearing a deep rich red silk gown. The shimmering colour was exquisite, but it was the way she had paired it with gold jewellery—earbobs of dropped gold, a bracelet that caressed her skin, a pendant that dropped invitingly between her breasts—that made speech impossible.

And her face—her smile, eyes bright, intelligence in the curve of her smile…

She was Sylvia. And perhaps, if he had not dreamt the contents of the letter that was pressing against him in his pocket, she would be his.

'Teddy?' Sylvia's face had fallen. 'I did not mean to offend—I mean, it's a pleasant enough part of London, I suppose—'

'What are you doing here?' Teddy blurted out.

It was the wrong thing to say. Her smile faltered, the confidence he knew so well bruised.

'We're going to Gwen's ball together.'

'No, I mean—I thought I was supposed to meet

you, in the Wallflower Academy carriage, outside the Knaresbys' home,' Teddy amended hastily. 'Sylvia, your reputation—you shouldn't be seen here, coming to a man's lodgings!'

His pulse was throbbing in his ears and his breathing was rapid and he could not pretend it was due to the exertion of rushing down three flights of stairs. He was a duke. A duke!

…your father, Theodore Ignatius Charles Burrell, eleventh Duke of Camrose, has died. His wife predeceased him last year. You are his sole heir.

Nothing was going to be the same again.

'Oh, I see what you mean,' said Sylvia, a wicked grin tilting her lips. 'I escaped.'

'You…you escaped?' Teddy's voice halted as his mind attempted to catch up with him.

She'd escaped?

Sylvia's joyful laugh tore at his heart. That was the purpose of their fake engagement, was it not—so Sylvia could prepare to escape. Escape England, leave him behind.

His mouth was inexplicably dry.

'Now, I've told Gwen you're a duke and not to ask too many questions, which in hindsight was a mistake,' Sylvia said cheerfully as she slipped her arm through his without a second thought and started walking. 'I advise that we avoid them and dance as much as possible instead. You have no idea how few opportunities I have at the Wallflower Academy to dance, it's truly…'

What it truly was, Teddy did not know. He could not concentrate on Sylvia's words. Not when so many things were whirling through his mind.

She had thought he was a duke. He'd told her he wasn't. She'd told her friends, the Pike, everyone at the Wallflower Academy that he was a duke. His friends knew he wasn't.

And yet he was.

His stomach had still not settled after reading that letter. The eleventh Duke of Camrose—Theodore. His father. Could it be true? Was it possible that his search for his father, for who he was, was over?

'You're very quiet, you know.'

Teddy blinked. Sylvia was looking up at him with no irritation, no malice, but a kind curiosity that was so typical of her.

He tried to smile. 'Just…just thinking.'

Sylvia snorted. 'Sounds dangerous, if you ask me. Come on, Featherstonehaugh—we have a ball to attend.'

Chapter Fifteen

'*S*ounds *dangerous, if you ask me. Come on, Feath-erstonehaugh—we have a ball to attend.*'

It was a foolish thing to say, Sylvia could not help but think in hindsight, yet the words had just slipped from her lips.

There had been a lot of that this evening, and not because she had sampled much of the sparkling wine that had been on offer. She had never gained a taste for it, and had avoided it more and more as she watched some of the older attendees at the ball start to giggle in corners.

No, she did not need wine to lift her spirits. She was here with Teddy.

He was grinning a little inanely as they stood chatting with an elderly couple who had declared that the younger two reminded them of themselves.

'—just like when we were engaged,' the lady was saying fondly. She pinched Teddy's cheek, but he did not appear to notice. 'So charming, so lost in love!'

'I beg your pardon?' Teddy said distractedly.

Sylvia tried not to giggle, she really did. But there was something flowing through her, some sort of exuberance she simply could not stifle.

'And you, my dear, absolutely glowing,' the elderly gentleman said, inclining his head towards Sylvia. 'I can quite see why you have fallen in love with her, young man.'

It was all she could do not to flicker her gaze to Teddy, and in fact, within a heartbeat, Sylvia had done so. The strange thing was, he appeared to have once again lost the train of conversation. His eyes were unfocused, looking in the distance at something Sylvia could not fathom.

The gentleman chuckled. 'I remember those days.'

He was tapped sharply on the arm by his wife. 'Reginald!'

'Not that those days have passed, of course,' he added hastily, a wry smile on his face that Sylvia returned. 'I hope you both enjoy the ball.'

'Thank you.' Sylvia spoke as graciously as she could. Teddy appeared to have completely lost focus and forgotten he was having a conversation.

The elderly couple departed, leaving the pair of them alone, and Sylvia fairly fizzed with excitement. She was not like the other ladies at the Wallflower Academy. She did not enjoy the solitude and silence of that old building, she did not long for emptiness and quiet, she was not delighted by sombre and solo entertainment.

No, this was what she loved. There was a buzz of excitement near the door as a woman wearing a head-dress covered in feathers walked in, and an argument in a corner to her left, where two young men were either debating politics or arguing over a lover, or both. There was smoke issuing from the card room, where cheers bellowed, and a woman already sobbing into the shoulder of her mama as a disgruntled but mostly relieved young man walked away.

Sylvia grinned, pressing her gloved hands together. Oh, this was life! This was what she missed when she was caged in the Wallflower Academy. There was nothing like it.

'Enjoying yourself?' she asked Teddy, nudging him in the arm.

Teddy blinked, gazing around him as though he had completely forgotten where he was. 'What? A ball?'

She could not help but laugh as she rolled her eyes. 'You really are distracted this evening, aren't you, Your Grace?'

Sylvia had presumed her teasing nickname would jolt the man back to his senses.

Apparently not.

'Not distracted, no, not distract…' Teddy heaved a sigh. 'Not tracking, no.'

It was most odd. Losing his train of thought was not like the man she had grown to…well, love. Not that she was ever going to admit to as much. He would soon be off, the moment he found his father. And so would she, Sylvia reminded herself. She had her own adventures waiting.

'You are so beautiful, you know.'

Heat burned across her cheeks as Sylvia's head jerked up to see Teddy staring almost in amazement, as though he had never seen her before.

'What did you say?'

'You are beautiful. More beautiful than I think you realise,' Teddy said vaguely. He raised a hand as though he had no concept of decorum in public, and brushed her cheek with the back of his fingers. 'So stunning.'

Sylvia swallowed hard as she tried not to notice the searing heat in her neck. What was wrong with the man? If she did not know any better, she would have suggested he had drunk too much brandy—but she had not seen him accept a single glass since entering the ballroom.

Had he perhaps quaffed too much before they had met this evening?

'You are acting most strangely,' she murmured under her breath, glancing about to ensure they were not overheard.

And then, in a moment, clarity returned to Teddy's gaze as his eyes regained sharpness. His grin was teasing, his air joyful, and Sylvia's stomach gave that most inconvenient little twist whenever she caught his eye.

Oh, she was in dangerous territory here…

'Perhaps I am, or perhaps you and I are just not suited for Society,' Teddy said cheerfully, giving a laugh as he continued. 'Perhaps Society is not suited for us. Perhaps we should change it.'

'Change it?' Sylvia repeated in astonishment.

He shrugged, that casual handsomeness so obvious in a ballroom full of inadequate men. 'Why not? You and me. We can do anything.'

A tendril of desire crept around Sylvia's heart before she had the good sense to dispel it.

No, she could not fool herself into thinking that he meant… It was not to be. She was not the sort of woman that sort of thing happened to.

Besides, Sylvia attempted to remind herself, Teddy had nothing to offer her. No home, no income, no true name. And she…she still hated the idea of matrimony.

Did she not?

'What a wonderful day this is,' Teddy said dreamily.

Sylvia placed a hand on his arm. This had gone far enough. 'Teddy, are you quite well?'

'Well? I'm more than well,' he said with a beaming smile.

He did not appear inebriated. That was, Sylvia hastily amended in the solitude of her mind as they were gently pushed by a flurry of couples stepping forward to form a set as the musicians started to play, he appeared inebriated, but there was no smell of spirits on his breath.

He was just…well. If she did not know any better, she would have said he was giddy.

'Teddy—' Sylvia attempted in a low voice, grateful that the rising music could hide their conversation. 'Teddy, why are you being…being like this?'

Her hand was still clasping his arm and his other hand came to cover her fingers. Sylvia gasped, not just at the heat which seared through both his gloves and hers, but at the intimacy. And in public, too!

You are supposed to be engaged to be married, a small voice reminded her. *Yes, it's all a pretence, but only you know that…*

'Because,' Teddy said simply, his eyes searching hers and not letting go. 'Because.'

Sylvia narrowed her eyes. This was getting ridiculous—she would hardly recommend that everyone should be shy and retiring, but Teddy was acting in a most odd manner, and she was not going to have any more of it.

'Come on,' she said grimly.

It was not difficult to pull him along with her through the crowd at the ball. It was not much of a hardship, in fact, to weave her fingers through his own and feel the deep-rooted connection that sparked up whenever they did this—

Focus, Sylvia!

The room was inordinately hot. She only noticed when she and Teddy stepped out of the ballroom and into a corridor that appeared, thankfully, to be deserted.

Then and only then did Sylvia round on the man that she adored, but was more than a little confused by. 'Teddy Featherstonehaugh!'

He grinned. 'Something like that.'

'Look, this has gone on long enough,' Sylvia said firmly, as though mere certainty could force a person to behave. 'Something is going on and I don't know what it is, but I know you're hiding something.'

A hunted expression flickered across Teddy's face. 'I am?'

'You are,' Sylvia repeated, attempting to keep a stern look on her face, when all she wanted to do was throw herself into his arms and kiss—

Perhaps it would be a good idea to break off this false engagement. It was not a thought that Sylvia particularly liked, but if she could not be trusted around him…

'Tell me the truth,' Sylvia said hastily, more to drown out her own ridiculous thoughts than anything else. 'Just…just tell me, Teddy. What is going on?'

He stared with those serious eyes of his, and Sylvia's pulse skipped a beat—as though it knew, as though it could predict—

'I'm in love with you,' Teddy said in a rush.

Sylvia waited a moment for what he'd said to seep into her brain. Her hands clasped each other, her gloves warm, tension in her wrists. He could not have said—no. Absolutely not. She had been dreaming.

But he was watching her, the throb of his pulse in his jaw, and not saying anything. His focus was trained on her, as though attempting to decipher her silence.

Sylvia swallowed, her mouth dry. 'I… I do apologise. I don't think… I cannot have heard you properly. Did you say—'

'I'm… Sylvia, I'm so in love with you,' Teddy said, his voice cracking. 'I've never felt… I never thought it was possible to—'

He continued. Or at least, Sylvia was almost certain he continued. Her ears were pounding so loudly with her own pulse that it was difficult to hear anything else.

She reached out a hand to the nearest wall and found it to be both reassuringly solid and most useful. Her legs had gone weak and the floor appeared to be spinning.

'Look, I can't not say it any more,' Teddy was saying, an ardent smile tilting his lips. 'I've felt it for weeks and not saying it feels tantamount to lying, and I can't. I won't do that to you.'

The shock was starting to dissipate now, leaving in its wake nothing but joy.

He…he loved her?

'—and I am not expecting you to say anything,' Teddy was continuing, eagerly filling the silence of the corridor as Sylvia stood there, stunned. 'I know this is a surprise…'

He loved her. Teddy was in love with her.

A twisting joyous enthusiasm spread through her. He loved her. Though nothing could ever come of this declaration, Sylvia found, to her great astonishment, that it cheered her no end to realise that he was the only man she wanted to declare such a thing.

And before Sylvia really knew what she was doing,

before she could restrain herself, before she could consider that someone would come down the corridor at any moment and find them, she had launched herself into Teddy's arms.

He appeared ready and waiting. At least, he caught her instantly and drew her close, and Sylvia was pressing an eager kiss on his lips before she could stop herself.

It was heaven. Nothing else felt like clinging to Teddy's neck, his strong arms around her, the rush of certainty that this was where she belonged mingling with the sudden pleasure of his lips on hers.

They did not remain there for long. In his eagerness Teddy pushed her to the side and Sylvia gasped in his mouth as her back touched the wall.

'Sylvia,' he muttered, more a growl than speech.

Somehow it only heightened her need for him. That dull ache between her thighs that Sylvia now knew would lead to such delights was throbbing, a desperate need to have him touching her overwhelming her, and she did not bother to hold back her ardour as her palms splayed against the vast expense of Teddy's chest.

'Sylvia,' he moaned.

He was kissing her, kissing down her neck and towards her décolletage, and the fluttering press of his warm lips was causing a cascade of need that made Sylvia's eyelashes flutter.

She wanted him—she needed this. She wanted him

closer—closer than these foolish clothes would permit and—

'Sylvia!'

This time Teddy's voice was filled with astonishment. Sylvia pulled back to discover why.

Ah.

'You're attempting to undress me!' He spoke with shock bordering on delight.

Try as she might, Sylvia could not prevent herself from flushing. 'Maybe I am.'

'I would never ask more of you, not more than I thought you could give me, at any rate,' Teddy said in a hurried, almost frantic tone. 'I may not have been born a gentleman, but—'

All this talking, Sylvia could not help but think as she strained against the pinning force of Teddy Featherstonehaugh, and felt with delight the very physical evidence of his arousal in his breeches. All this talking and not enough kissing.

Not enough… She wanted more.

'More,' Sylvia breathed.

Teddy's throat bobbed. 'More?'

'I want more,' she murmured, hardly knowing what she was asking for but knowing that she needed it. She needed him.

And he loved her. Sylvia knew there would never be another opportunity for a man like Teddy—or any man, for that matter—to fall in love with her. This was it. He was it. And she did not want anyone else.

If she were to live the rest of her life on the run from the Wallflower Academy, her frustrations at her father, never trusting, always holding the world at arm's length...well, then.

Why not experience what it was to be loved?

'I would give you so much more,' Teddy was saying as the sounds from the ballroom transformed from music to applause for the musicians. 'If...you would give me yourself...'

Sylvia hesitated, but only for a moment.

Marriage was something she feared, not craved. Even if she had wanted it, the world of the Wallflower Academy was hardly conducive to making her a match. The only match she now wanted was with a man who had neither a fortune nor the skills to create one.

But one night—perhaps more, if she was fortunate—with Teddy?

Perhaps she could even become his mistress.

That was what her mother had become, and look where she had ended up, yes, but this was different. Her father had promised marriage, he had lied, he had taken advantage of her mother's trust.

Teddy would never do that. Teddy had offered her nothing, and she had not promised him anything, not even her heart. Not out loud.

Sylvia swallowed. She was the one in control.

'Yes,' she breathed.

Teddy blinked. 'Yes?'

Laughing breathlessly and hardly knowing how she

had the bravery to say such a thing, Sylvia leaned forward and claimed his lips once more. They were hers: for this evening, perhaps for longer, perhaps for ever.

That didn't matter, not in this moment. What mattered was that they were together now.

Teddy matched her kiss with eagerness of his own and the thrill of being so desired roared through Sylvia. This was scandalous—this was indecent—yet she had absolutely no hesitation.

She wanted him. He wanted her. They entirely understood each other.

One of Teddy's hands had caressed down her arm and was now cupping her buttocks through her silk dress. The other was in her hair, pins pouring down her shoulders as he disturbed them.

'Teddy!' Sylvia whispered against his throat, pressing a kiss where his pulse jumped.

He moaned and delight filled her at the idea that she was making it just as difficult for him to think.

This was wonderful, the promise of more making her skin tingle, and the fact that they could be discovered at any moment—

Ah. Yes. That was not a good idea.

'Come on,' Sylvia said in a whisper, pulling away from Teddy and slipping her hand in his.

The look of abject disappointment was flattering. 'You…you don't want to? You've changed your mind—'

'I don't want my first time to be against a wall, Your

Grace,' teased Sylvia as she pulled him along the cor-ridor. Somewhere here…yes, there.

It did not take them long to creep up the staircase. Their footsteps were light and the noise from the ball-room below loudly echoed through the place. Gwen would never know, Sylvia thought with a flicker of ex-citement, that two of her guests had gone upstairs to… well. Borrow a bedchamber.

From what she suspected of Gwen's courtship, she could hardly take the moral high ground.

The first door they tried, attempting to muffle their laughter as Teddy kissed Sylvia's neck, was locked. The second, however, opened into what was clearly a guest-room—and the bed was made. The door closed, the key turned in the lock—

'Teddy!' gasped Sylvia as he pulled her down onto the bed.

There was something truly enticing about this. She could never have predicted just how intimate it was to be lying here on the coverlet with Teddy's arms around her, his lips pressing scalding kisses down her neck be-fore skimming across her décolletage, her whole body fizzing with pleasure, the need within her building—

'You taste wonderful,' Teddy murmured, one of his hands on her hips as he tipped her onto her back.

Sylvia would have flushed if she was not already burning. 'I don't know what you mean.'

'Trust me, you do,' he said quietly, leaning over her

on his elbow. 'You know, I have half a mind to make sure.'

Make sure? What on earth could he possibly mean?

Pushing herself up on her own elbows as Teddy moved away, Sylvia was about to ask what on earth he meant by such an odd statement—and then gasped.

Oh. He meant…that?

Slowly, without taking his serious eyes from hers, Teddy was lifting up the skirts of her gown and nestling himself between her knees, which he had parted with a caress. Then he was kneeling lower, and lower, his breath warm on her thighs, and—

'Teddy!' gasped Sylvia, falling back, her arms no longer strong enough to hold her.

It was an underreaction, considering what he was doing. Her eyelids fluttering shut and her hands grasping the bedlinen either side of her, Sylvia was helpless as Teddy's mouth pressed hot kisses on her curls.

His tongue slid inside her.

Sylvia whimpered, the pleasure too much, and he halted immediately.

'I can stop,' he breathed against her wet folds.

'Don't you dare,' Sylvia moaned, tangling her fingers into his hair to pull him closer.

Teddy chuckled against her as he resumed his ministrations and she could do nothing but lie there and accept the waves of building pleasure that coursed through her. The rhythm of his tongue, the impressive way it seemed to know precisely how to please her, to coax aching peaks of bliss through her whole body, which was twitching and quivering with the intensity of it—

'Oh, Teddy, yes,' she murmured, her words beyond her control, needing him to know just how wonderful this felt.

His tongue flicked across her nub and Sylvia's back arched against the bed.

She knew where this was going, he had shown her the way before and she was desperate to tread that path again. He was going to—she was going to—

'Teddy!' Sylvia cried as her body sparked into ecstasy.

The pleasure was unlike anything she had ever known. Far more intense than when he had brought her to climax with his fingers, this was an intimacy beyond that, his mouth on her curls, his tongue within her, lashing unrelentingly as her core spasmed with excruciating pleasure.

When the ripples had started to fade, Sylvia opened her eyes. She could not recall closing them.

Teddy was leaning over her with a wide smile. 'God, I could do that to you all day.'

'Careful, or I shall hold you to that,' Sylvia breathed. 'My word, that…that was—'

'I almost came apart in my breeches hearing you, tasting you,' Teddy said quietly, his fingers moving to unbutton the clothing he spoke of. 'I want you, Sylvia— but you don't have to—'

'I want you, Teddy,' Sylvia said quietly.

I love you. That was what she wanted to say.

But no—she had no claim on him, and would not allow herself to admit it. The word love from her lips would merely complicate what should be a most uncomplicated moment between them.

No talk of love, then. Just love in action.

'I've… I've got something that will prevent…'

Sylvia's cheeks burned. 'Oh. Oh, good.'

Yes, it was good there would be no child. They both knew the unintended consequences of a child born out of—

Sylvia gasped as Teddy's manhood slipped from his now unbuttoned breeches. It was…well. She was no engineer, but she had to assume that the mechanics of this were not going to work with him so…so…

'Trust me.' How he had read her mind, she did not know.

It did not matter. She did trust him; she trusted him beyond anyone else in the world. And she wanted to share this with him, as technically challenging as it appeared.

Teddy slipped something over his jutting manhood then lowered himself down between her legs, brushing a kiss against her lips. 'Ready?'

Ready? Would she ever be ready for such an intimacy, for such a vulnerable moment with a man she…? Oh, she loved him. She could admit it here, in the privacy of her own mind.

Sylvia gazed up at the man who had unknowingly claimed her affections. 'Ready.'

She had presumed pain, and there was a certain amount of discomfort—but it was swiftly replaced by a burgeoning sense of delight. Oh, this was wonderful... the way her body welcomed him in, as though knowing precisely what she wanted.

Teddy groaned, his eyes closed as he sank deeper within her, sheathing himself to the hilt. 'God, you feel incredible.'

'You don't feel too bad your—oh!' Sylvia's gasp was prompted by his sudden movement. Just when she thought they could not be closer together, Teddy had withdrawn—almost withdrawn—and plunged back into her.

A tremor of pleasure roared through her body, somehow tingling at her breasts and her mouth.

'How does anyone not do this every day?' Sylvia gasped, clutching at Teddy's shoulders as he started to build a rhythm, not unlike the merciless rhythm his tongue had used to pleasure her mere moments ago. 'How does anyone get anything else done?'

'I don't know,' Teddy said breathlessly as he rocked into her again, a flicker of wickedness in his eyes. 'How will we?'

And Sylvia laughed, and he laughed, and he rained kisses down on her face before claiming her lips as his hips rocked her closer and closer to a new pleasure—and when she reached it Sylvia could do nothing but hold on and cry out as sensual decadence roared through her body and she could have wept as she came undone in his arms.

Teddy cried out her name as his hips frantically jerked. 'Sylvia—Sylvia!'

He collapsed into her arms and she was ready for him. Clutching him to her, their chests rising and falling in agitated movements as they attempted to catch their breath, Sylvia knew what they had just shared was something she could never describe to another.

Perfect unity. Pleasurable contentment. A pairing beyond words.

Teddy nuzzled her neck. 'Tell me when you're ready to go again.'

His whisper made Sylvia chuckle, the brushing of her nipples against his chest sparking desire anew. 'Oh, I will.'

Chapter Sixteen

It was, perhaps, not the locale Teddy would have chosen. But at the same time, they had already arranged to meet there. The pretence of their engagement had to be maintained.

But not for long.

Teddy had arrived fifty-three minutes early. He hadn't intended to. He'd dressed slowly, attempting to think through what he was going to say. He was interrupted at least every five minutes by memories of the most delightful—

'I can stop.'

'Don't you dare...'

After he had breakfasted—a delicious pie from a street seller—and strode along, glorifying in the morning sun and wondering why everyone wasn't astonishingly happy, Teddy had arrived at the modiste with almost an hour to spare.

He could hardly go in. That would be ridiculous. So he had waited at first patiently, then impatiently, outside, trying to concoct the perfect sentence for the woman he knew he loved.

Sylvia, I have to tell you—

Sylvia, I wanted to tell you last night but everything got away from me—

Sylvia, I have the best possible news. I'm...

Teddy cleared his throat as he caught sight of a beautiful woman with dark skin further down the road. Was it—yes, it was her. His Sylvia. The woman he would be spending the rest of his life with. The woman he could not live without.

She looked a little puffed when she stopped before him. 'I'm so sorry—I thought the driver knew where he was going, but he just went round and round in circles and eventually he just—'

'Sylvia—' Teddy said, smiling as something molten shifted in him. 'Sylvia, it is quite all right. You are not—'

'—and I told him to let me down and I could find my own way, but he insisted on—' she continued rapidly, not quite catching his eye.

His smile broadened. She was shy. His Sylvia, shy?

Well, they had shared something so earthshattering, he was hardly certain how he could show his face in Society again.

'—left with plenty of time and I am mortified to be late. I just don't understand how—'

'Sylvia—' Teddy interrupted, taking her hand in his. Her speech immediately halted. Sylvia looked down

at her hand in his and her cheeks reddened. The hustle
and bustle of London continued around them, pedestri-
ans passing them by and giving them no second glance.

They could not know. No one did, thought Teddy with
a rush of excitement. No one knew they were passing
the Duke of Camrose and his future Duchess.

All he had to do was tell her.

'Shall we go inside?' Sylvia slipped her hand from
his and glanced up at the shop window. 'I would hate
for people to suppose our…our engagement has ended,
when we still want use out of it.'

Use out of it. Yes, that was where it had all started.
It was hard to remember that now, Teddy thought as he
opened the door for her and they stepped inside. It had
all started completely differently, in a way that felt a
million miles away from where they were now.

For indeed their engagement was going to end—but
not how she might expect.

'Oh, goodness,' Sylvia breathed, eyes widening as
Teddy followed her into the shop.

He wasn't quite sure what she was gazing at in such
wonder. Yes, there were numerous bolts of silks and
muslins and cottons lining one wall in a dazzling display of colour and pattern. On the other side were a
great number of hats, a cabinet of buttons and fripperies and, along the middle of the shop, a table upon
which lay a variety of shoes, buckles, reticules, parasols, shawls and a few other things that Teddy could
not definitely name.

It all seemed a bit much, to his eyes.

'I should fake an engagement more often,' Sylvia breathed with the hint of a grin in his direction before she started to pore over the different reticules.

Teddy's grin faltered, just for a moment.

She surely did not mean it like that—as though she had done this sort of thing before.

She hadn't done this sort of thing before, had she?

They had never talked about that sort of thing. Strange. Teddy had been so eager to talk of each other, to learn about Sylvia the woman, that he had never considered that Sylvia might have loved before.

Well, they had plenty of time for all that—a lifetime. His spirits soared as Sylvia elegantly stepped about the shop. It was just the two of them here; the modiste must be in the back somewhere, fitting some lady.

He couldn't wait. He should, but he couldn't. He had to tell her.

Now.

'Sylvia—' Teddy said softly.

When she turned to him, there was fear in her eyes, a panic he had never seen before. 'You don't have to say it. I know.'

Teddy blinked. She…she knew?

How could she know? He had only discovered the truth himself yesterday.

'That's…that's not possible,' he said slowly.

'I could see the truth in your eyes as you left. I mean, it's entirely natural—at least, I presume it is. I haven't much experience in…in that sort of thing.' Her voice became a whisper and her gaze flickered away.

Teddy's mind was working so hard, he was almost surprised she could not hear it. Sylvia's nervous fingers had picked up a ribbon and she was fiddling with it as she spoke.

Sylvia, nervous?

'Entirely natural?' Teddy repeated, still at a loss. He glanced at the counter. No sign of the modiste. 'Sylvia, I'm trying to tell you—'

'And though you regret what happened, you should know that I don't!' Sylvia's voice was defiant now, even though her eyes were still focused on the ribbon she was working into knots. 'It was the most…the most wonderful, the most special—'

'Yes, it was—Sylvia, look at me,' said Teddy urgently.

His heart twisted painfully as she finally met his eyes. The fear there, the hurt… What was she expecting? A blasé reunion today as though last night had never happened? A pretence that they did not mean the world to each other? The expectation, God forbid, that it would never be repeated?

'Last night was wonderful,' he said in a low voice, even though they were the only people in the modiste's shop. 'It was special—you are special, Sylvia. None of that has changed.'

There was no mistaking the relief on her face. 'It was just… I thought—'

'Why don't you let me tell you my news?' Teddy interrupted, unable to help himself. The excitement was building, causing a ball of twisting heat within him, and he just had to get it out. 'I have something to tell you.'

The ribbon was forgotten. 'You found your father.'

Perhaps his expression revealed his surprise, for Sylvia grinned as Teddy spluttered, 'B-But how…how did you—'

'That could be the only news you had to tell me in person. Anything else could have been sent in a note,' she pointed out fairly. 'So…so I take it that it is good news? You look…happy.'

Happy.

Yes, he was. Teddy had never known such happiness, though it was not the finding of his father which had done that. It was her. Sylvia. She gave him a joy that nothing else in the world could offer.

And now he could offer her the world.

'I am happy,' he said aloud, realising perhaps too late that he hadn't said anything in a while. His fingers reached out for hers but faltered. She clung to the ribbon.

Teddy swallowed. How did one exactly go about declaring that one was a duke?

'You are a duke—how delightful. I shall add you to my collection.'

A smile pulled at the corners of his lips. Well, she had thought him a duke before. There was no reason she could not think him a duke again.

'I have discovered my father… I mean, his solicitors sent me a letter,' Teddy amended hastily.

Sylvia nodded slowly. 'I did wonder. I am glad to have been of some help. Is…is he a good man?'

Teddy blinked. The question had not even occurred to him. His mind had been filled with titles, riches, an estate far grander than he could ever have imagined.

A good man?

'I don't know,' he said slowly. 'He died. A few months ago.'

'That would explain the ending of the allowance,' said Sylvia, her smile tight. 'But you know his name now. You know who he was. You know who you are.'

Her last sentence was halfway between a question and a statement, and she turned from him as she said it and started to meander along the wall of the modiste's that held so many bonnets.

Teddy watched her. He had to tell her—but only now did he wonder whether this was the right place to do so. After all, it was a little public, even if the place was currently devoid of other patrons.

Was that why there was this tightness in his chest, this strange sense of foreboding, of expectation?

Expecting joy…was he not?

'I'm a duke,' Teddy said in a rush before he could marshal his words into some semblance of coherence.

Sylvia twisted on her heel, blinking with a furrowed brow. 'I beg your pardon?'

'I…' Why on earth was this so difficult? 'I'm a duke.'

And suddenly, there was the Sylvia he knew. Her smile was accompanied by that luscious laughter that filled the shop and filled him, dripping warm honey into his soul. 'You trickster, Teddy. But honestly, can you believe that I thought that of you when we first met?'

Her snort of laughter only served to endear her to him more, but Teddy could not concentrate on that. He had to explain.

'I know, but…but I really am a duke,' he said gently, stepping towards her.

He needed to be close. Wanted to be close, so that when Sylvia rushed into his arms—

Sylvia's laughter died away and her smile faded, though a quizzical expression remained. 'Don't jest, Teddy.'

'I'm not jesting—'

'Come now, tell me the truth about your father. Was he rich? Has he left you a great fortune?' Sylvia quipped, picking up a most astonishingly exuberant bonnet. 'Will you be able to afford to buy me a bonnet or two?'

'Or three,' Teddy managed, his throat constricting momentarily.

…delivering an income of eleven thousand a year…

Sylvia's eyes danced with delight. 'Excellent! You may equip me for my adventures. I have almost decided on touring the other Caribbean islands before seeking my mother in Antigua. I shall need—'

'Sylvia—'

He had not intended to do it. That was the danger of

being around a woman like Sylvia. He wanted to touch her, to feel her skin brushing up against his, hold the heat of her.

Sylvia looked down at his hand, which had captured her left, and smiled wanly. 'I don't suppose you wish to visit Antigua, do you? Now that you are a rich man, I mean. You could come with me.'

And the fear that had somehow lingered within Teddy's chest was chased away by the obvious desire in her eyes.

She wanted him.

What she did not know was that he was already hers.

'Antigua sounds wonderful,' Teddy said, his voice somehow strangled. 'The Duke of Camrose has never been there.'

Sylvia's nose scrunched. 'And what care we with a duke? Come on, now, tell me all about your father. Why did he—'

'I'm trying to tell you, Sylvia, and I know it is difficult to hear but you must.' Teddy had not expected his tone to be so sharp. She had to listen to him. She had to understand. 'I am not jesting when I say that my father was the Duke of Camrose—the eleventh. That makes me the twelfth, there are no other heirs to—'

'Do not jest with me.' She pulled her hand from his, the fierce and resolute expression he knew so well returning. Sylvia glanced up at the bonnets. 'Now, are you going to help me choose a bonnet for my travels or—'

'I am not jesting with you. I tell you nothing but the

truth, always,' Teddy said firmly, suddenly wondering how on earth one could prove one was a duke. He would have to ask Henderson, Henderson, and Tyrell. 'Hand on my heart, Sylvia—'

'You cannot be a duke,' she said dismissively, moving past the bonnets to peer at the parasols. 'I suppose I shall need—'

'And why on earth not?' A flicker of irritation had seeped into his words now, despite Teddy's best efforts.

Sylvia did not look at him as she picked up a parasol. 'You...you just can't be, that's why.'

Well, he had known it would be a difficult entrance into Society and the *ton*, but Teddy had not thought— of all people not to believe him, to take him seriously as a duke, he had not thought... Sylvia.

She was still not looking at him. Why wasn't she looking at him?

'Here,' Teddy said, struck with fresh inspiration.

His hand dived into his pocket and pulled out the letter from the solicitors. She'd have to believe this, and then they could enjoy planning their honeymoon.

Sylvia barely glanced at the paper. 'What is it?'

'Just read it, will you?'

Precisely how she managed to take the letter from him without looking at him, Teddy did not know. He was too occupied with watching her expression as her attention flickered down the letter.

It was, perhaps, not so joyful as he had expected. It was certainly not as celebratory as he had hoped. Instead, the merriment and teasing so often found in Sylvia's expression faded with every passing second.

The damned clock in here was too loud.

Only when Teddy broke his concentration from Sylvia's face to glare at the offending timepiece did he realise that there was no clock in the modiste's. That thump, thump, thump appeared to be his own pulse in his ears.

There was no other sound in the shop.

Sylvia folded the letter. 'I see.'

'Isn't it wonderful?' Teddy did not attempt to restrain his eagerness. 'I could never have dreamed—I mean, what man doesn't hope that riches will one day—? And I want to marry you, Sylvia, I want to marry you and make you a duchess and—'

'I hereby declare our fake engagement to be at an end,' Sylvia said stiffly. 'You are released.'

And Teddy laughed.

He could not help it. This discovery was far more than he had ever expected: a father who not only had truly existed, but who had bestowed upon him the chance to live a life the like of which he had never imagined.

And he could do it all with Sylvia by his side.

Of course their fake engagement was at an end. It had to end, to be replaced with a real one. They were going to be so happy—

'I imagine you have a great deal of calls on your time, and I would not wish to inconvenience you,' Sylvia said, that strange coldness remaining. 'Good day.'

Good...good day?

'What do you mean?' Teddy asked the question before he had a chance to think. 'Sylvia, I—'

'As I said, you must be very busy now. An estate—multiple estates, by the looks of it.' She nodded towards the letter now back in Teddy's hands. 'I would not wish to keep you.'

'Keep me?' Teddy repeated, completely bewildered.

Something had changed. The very temperature in the modiste's had altered and it was all because of Sylvia. She had withdrawn from him somehow, created distance with a subtlety he had never thought possible.

Somehow, she had stepped several miles away in the space of a few feet.

'You are a duke now, you do not have time for it doesn't matter. I just thought...but obviously not, not now,' said Sylvia, turning as though to leave.

Leave? Time for—what had she thought?

Thoughts whirled around Teddy's mind so rapidly that he could barely catch any of them.

Sylvia stepped smartly towards the door to the street. She wasn't truly leaving?

'Sylvia—'

His fingers closed on empty air. She was too quick for him, half walking, half running through the door. The bell jangled and the momentary roar of the street intruded on the idyllic calm of the modiste's. She was gone.

Teddy did not need to tell his feet to move, they

lurched forward of their own accord. He had to be with Sylvia.

By the time he caught up with her, Sylvia was pacing furiously along the street about fifty feet from the modiste's.

'Sylvia, where are you going—?'

'It is none of your concern,' she said furiously, not even looking at him. 'Good day.'

'Good day?' Teddy did not understand it. There he had been, about to lay his heart on a platter and offer it up to the woman he loved, and now she was...well, as far as he could make out, ending their entire connection for no reason at all. 'Is that all you can say to me?'

'Thank you for your assistance in planning my escape from the Wallflower Academy,' Sylvia said smartly, still refusing to meet his gaze as she darted down a street to the right.

So unexpected was the movement that Teddy almost fell over in his attempt to change direction.

He was forced to half run after her, all the while a great frustration growing in his chest. What was going on? Why wouldn't Sylvia just stay put for five seconds together so he could tell her—

'I won't do it!' She spoke with tears in her eyes— tears he was desperate to wipe away. 'I won't do it, Teddy! I won't step into a different cage!'

Cage? He had made no mention of cages—there were none on his estates as far as he knew—what on earth was she—?

'Marrying you would be worse than the Wallflower Academy,' Sylvia said defiantly as Teddy fought to keep up with her. 'Your old friend, the one you threw out, he won't be the only one thinking that you deserve better, deserve someone they expect—deserve someone born to be a noblewoman, not someone born the wrong side of the blanket and abandoned by her father! A duchess, me? More expectations, less freedom. I won't do it!'

'But I would never—'

'You might not, but it's the world I fear!' Sylvia blurted out the words and could not stop more pouring from her mouth. 'Marrying you, marrying a duke— an actual duke! I could not be more central to Society, more visible, and they will just be waiting for me to fail, waiting to laugh, waiting to deride—'

'It wouldn't be like that—'

'You don't know.' She spoke with such finality that, for a moment, he thought she had finished, but, 'You don't know what it is to be stared at, to be watched, to be wondered at. There's never been anyone like me in the nobility—a duchess, can you imagine? The world staring, watching, waiting for you to fail—'

'Slow down, Sylvia, I need to tell you—'

'I don't want to hear it,' she snapped in response. 'Go away, Your Grace.'

Your Grace.

The nickname had been a prank. It had all been a jest. A laugh. Something that she said to irritate him, and something he allowed himself to be irritated by.

And now…

His stomach jolted as Sylvia wove her way through the crowd. He was barely able to keep up with her. 'Sylvia, wait! Sylvia!'

It was too late. As though he were trapped in a nightmare, Teddy attempted to reach Sylvia just as she stepped into what could only be the Wallflower Academy carriage.

'Sylvia!'

She had stormed away from him the moment she had believed him about his father. She had refused to slow down, Teddy thought with a twisting pain, and now…now the Wallflower Academy carriage was pulling away, and his hopes with it.

Despite his pleas for her to return and talk, she had gone.

Teddy stood there on the pavement, the busy Londoners thronging around him. His lungs were tight, his breathing ragged, and there was a dull emptiness where but moments ago his heart had been.

How…how could this have gone so wrong?

Chapter Seventeen

Sylvia allowed her hand to slowly drift along the black and white keys of the pianoforte. The discordant sound rang out in the music room, but as she was the only inhabitant she was not particularly concerned.

Plink. Plink. Plink.

The instinct to return to the Wallflower Academy was not one she could entirely explain, but it had been home for longer than anywhere else. Oh, Gwen and Rilla would have taken her in—but their pity, it was not to be borne. Miss Pike had simply raised an eyebrow and informed her that she was late for afternoon tea.

Her mind unfocused, her thoughts drifting just as vaguely as her hand across the keyboard, Sylvia tried not to allow intruding thoughts of—

'Slow down, Sylvia, I need to tell you—'

'I don't want to hear it.'

Yes. Thoughts like that.

Sylvia swallowed, her throat rasping like sandpaper. Why hadn't she—why had he—the half-asked questions rattled around her mind and made it impossible to think. Or rather, impossible to think of anything else.

And all this time, he had been a duke.

Watching her fingers trail over the keys in a disconsolate medley of random notes, Sylvia tried to think back to the day she had met Teddy. Theodore. Theodore Featherstonehaugh.

He had been handsome, and magnetic in a way she had never experienced before. And he had been aloof, and unwilling to help her escape. It was no wonder she had thought him a duke, and yet when he had proven to be naught but a man, Sylvia could admit it now, if only to herself, it had been so much easier to talk to him.

And now he wanted to marry her and all sorts of nonsense.

Sylvia heaved a sigh, hating her solitude but resolutely certain she could not explain the situation to another soul.

What would she say? I fell in love with a man who was pretending to be a duke, and gave him my heart and soul and body, and now it appears he is a duke and wishes to marry me.

It didn't sound quite like the sob story Sylvia often overheard from weeping wallflowers in corners being comforted. Usually being comforted by—

'There you are,' came a quiet voice as the door to the corridor clicked shut.

Sylvia did not need to look up to know who it was. She groaned. 'Not you again.'

She felt immediately guilty as she looked up and saw the pained expression on Daphne's face.

'There's no need to be like that,' the wallflower said quietly, her cheeks crimson.

Sylvia was not quite sure what made her say it. She wanted to tell herself that it was because of the great panic she had experienced with Teddy. That she had trusted him, opened herself to him, explained to him just how marriage would be like a prison...

The anguish within her was real, but it did not excuse the words that slipped from her mouth to her aghast friend, falling from her lips before she could stop them. 'Don't you get tired of the Pike sending you on errands to find out what's wrong with people?'

The words snapped into the air, caustic and cruel, and Sylvia immediately raised her hand to her mouth in horror.

Had she—had she truly said that?

She must have done. Daphne's cheeks were not pink now, but a deathly white, something Sylvia had not seen on her friend before. The other woman's eyes were filling with tears and her hands had met before her, fingers twisting in silent pain.

Sylvia cleared her throat as she lowered her hands back onto the pianoforte. A terrible cacophony of notes sounded. Once their din had faded, she said quietly, 'Daphne, I—'

Her friend suddenly erupted. 'Just because I seem to

be the only actual wallflower in this whole place, that doesn't mean I don't have feelings, Sylvia!'

Sylvia's shock must have shown on her face. Daphne's face reddened again, but there was a defiance in her gaze that remained, despite the evident temptation to flee the room.

Instead, she merely stood there, staring at Sylvia, who stared back in utter amazement.

And shame. A great deal of shame was rising in her lungs, threatening to drown her. It was appalling, how she had spoken to her friend. No amount of broken-heartedness could excuse it. Was this truly who she was? Someone who teased others to feel better about herself?

With great difficulty, for her throat appeared to be made of stone, Sylvia managed to say, 'I... I am so sorry, Daphne. I...there is no excuse. I am sorry.'

For a moment, she was afraid her friend was not going to reply. Daphne remained impassive, her cheeks flushed and her fingers now worrying her thumb.

'Thank you,' Daphne said stiffly. Then there was an unexpected quirk of her lips. 'The fact that Miss Pike did send me here to ask you about your wedding, and whether or not you have decided on the music to play as you enter the church...that is neither here nor there.'

Sylvia stared, almost unable to believe her ears. She certainly could not feel her fingers any more. Daphne, ribbing her?

The two friends burst into overly loud laughter almost at the same time. Sylvia would not like to say who started to giggle first, but after mere seconds the two of them were clutching their sides as the nervous tension dissipated.

'Besides, I am worried about you,' Daphne added, stepping forward and dropping into the chair their music teacher always sat in when teaching the pianoforte, just behind the instrument's stool. 'You've been awfully quiet for two days. Half the wallflowers are starting to worry that you're sickening.'

Sylvia rolled her eyes. 'What, because there must be something medically wrong with me if I am not loud?'

'Yes,' Daphne said, in what appeared to be a serious tone. 'The other half are taking bets as to whether this is a prank on Miss Pike in some way.'

Despite herself, Sylvia smiled. 'Well, that would certainly be like me, wouldn't it?'

But she could see where this conversation was going, and she did not like it. Half turning back to the pianoforte, Sylvia tried to pick out a tune. It had never been a particularly easy skill for her to gain, and eventually the Pike had agreed that Sylvia's singing voice was more than sufficient to count as musical talent. The unpleasant pianoforte lessons had ceased.

Still, she should be able to remember something, shouldn't she? How about *Three Blind Mice*?

Sylvia attempted to find the tune on the black and white keys. Three Blind—

'Sylvia,' said Daphne quietly.

Sylvia's fingers slipped on the keys. 'I do not want to talk about it.'

'That much is obvious,' said her friend, her tone still quiet. 'But you can't go on like this.'

A lurch in her stomach tightened the knot that had resided there since she had stormed away from Teddy. Sylvia had done her best to ignore it, attempting to weep it away in the privacy of her own bedchamber, eat it away at the dining table, and think it away in those moments when she was alone—a rarity at the Wallflower Academy.

Nothing had worked.

But talking it away certainly wasn't going to help either, Sylvia was sure of it. She was most definite that the gossip would swiftly rush through the Wallflower Academy. And if the Pike found out...

Oh, goodness, if the Pike found out the whole engagement had been a ruse, a cover to help Sylvia escape this place...

'The engagement is at an end, then?'

Sylvia's hands crushed the pianoforte keys they were on and Daphne winced at the unpleasant sound they made together.

'Ah,' her friend said quietly. 'I am sorry he decided to break it off—'

'It is not as simple as that,' Sylvia cut in, hating that she was speaking about it but somehow finding that the stinging sensation in her chest lessened when she did so. 'It was... I broke it off.'

'You did? You—you decided not to marry a duke?'

And that astonishment, right there, was why Sylvia had not wanted to talk about it with anyone. How could anyone else understand? They looked at Teddy and saw—no, they looked at a duke and presumed that anyone in their right mind would want to marry him.

And she did.

No, she didn't, Sylvia reminded herself sternly. She would have married him in an instant if he had been just a gentleman. Just a man who loved her.

But he wasn't just a man. He was a duke. He had responsibilities. He would need a wife by his side, yes, but one Society would accept. His life would be one of restrictions and expectations and—

'Sylvia?'

Sylvia blinked. Daphne was waving a hand before her eyes, attempting to gain her attention again.

'You wandered off there for a moment,' her friend said in her gentle voice. 'You were about to tell me why you're not going to marry a duke.'

Shoulders slumping, Sylvia could see there was no possibility of escaping this conversation. Well, she could launch herself off the piano stool and manage to avoid Daphne today, but what about tonight at dinner? Or tomorrow? Or the next day, or the next day, or the next…?

It was a mite bleak to think about, a never-ending series of days at the Wallflower Academy, during which she would be accosted by her friend to talk about Teddy.

Well, she'd just have to explain it now. Curtly, and shortly, and forbidding any follow-up questions.

Sylvia tried to smile. 'I don't want to marry a duke. I don't want to be a duchess and be trapped in a different kind of prison. There you go, that's that. Have you read any interesting—'

'That is most definitely not it,' Daphne said quietly, her ears reddening. 'Do you think me an idiot, Sylvia? You have been engaged to a duke for weeks! Why the sudden change of heart?'

Ah. Yes, she should have known her secrecy at the beginning of this debacle would come round to haunt her.

'He…he did not do something to you, did he?' Daphne's eyes were wide with sudden fear.

'No! No, Teddy would never hurt me,' Sylvia said hastily. The very idea that someone could think ill of Teddy pained her like a knife into her shoulder blade.

Perhaps, however, she should not have been so swift to defend him. Her friend was now staring with raised eyebrows, as though attempting to work out why she had rushed to his defence with such determination.

'Sylvia. What are you not telling me about your duke?'

Sylvia sighed. Oh, this was going to be a mighty untangle. 'He isn't a duke. At least, he is now. He wasn't then.'

Daphne nodded slowly, then shook her head. 'No, you're going to have to actually explain that one for me.'

The groan that escaped Sylvia's throat was entirely selfish. How had she managed to get into such a muddle?

Because you thought you were going to be so clever, a nasty little voice at the back of her mind muttered. *You thought you could lie to Daphne—yes, let's call it what it is, a lie—and that made you feel smug and superior. And then you could disappear off and never see her again and...*

How strange. Sylvia had never considered that. By keeping the plan a secret from her only friend still remaining at the Wallflower Academy, she would have just disappeared in the night, never to see Daphne again.

Goodness, she was remarkably selfish. How had she never noticed that before?

A nudge in her side. Sylvia looked up and saw Daphne's patient, kind face waiting for her to speak.

Right. How was she going to explain this?

'Teddy wasn't a duke when I met him,' Sylvia said, surprised at how awkward it was to explain this. 'I mean, I thought he was a duke because he was sitting in the carriage of the Duke of Warchester, but that was his friend.'

As she had expected, Daphne's eyes had grown wide. 'But—but you told Miss Pike, you told all of us—'

'It was convenient. If he was a duke and we were engaged...well, I could go out into Society. I could go to

London without the Pike growing suspicious,' explained Sylvia uneasily. 'I… I could plan my escape.'

Understanding dawned swiftly in her friend's expression. 'You and your escape plan.'

'And it was fun to pretend to be engaged to a duke!' Sylvia protested, hoping to draw her friend away from the escape plan. 'It was fun spending time with Teddy. More than fun. But…but two days ago I discovered the truth.'

Sylvia swallowed hard, as though, in doing so, she could force away the memories of the look on Teddy's face as she had told him in no uncertain terms that she had no wish to marry him.

It was the truth. It was a lie. It was a tangled muddle of complicated red-hot emotions that she did not feel she could unravel.

'The truth is that the lie was the truth all along,' Sylvia said simply. 'Teddy was a duke; he just did not know his true parentage. And all the fears…all the worry, all the dread that I have about being caged, being trapped to live by the expectations of others, watching them wait for me to fail…they all flooded back. I panicked. I couldn't… I cannot be his wife. His duchess.'

Daphne sat in silence, just looking at her. Sylvia had half hoped her friend would interrupt, contribute something, stop all these vulnerabilities spilling from her.

As it was, her friend just…sat there.

Sylvia cleared her throat. 'Teddy is a duke. A real one, I mean. He deserves to be with someone with…

with good connections, and a fortune, perhaps a title of her own, a perfect English rose. Not someone like me.'

'But it sounds,' Daphne said slowly, 'like he wants you.'

The simple statement caused a flood of hope to cascade through her, but Sylvia immediately pushed it aside. It was a pleasant thought to indulge in, yes, but it was not the truth. It couldn't be. It was far too good to be true.

'Teddy only discovered that he was a duke the day before he told me,' Sylvia said quietly, her gaze falling to her hands on the pianoforte keyboard. 'It's a reaction—he hasn't thought it all through. He has no idea what his responsibilities will be. No idea what managing an estate will entail, the people who are his obligation now. He'll sit in the House of Lords! He will be someone in Society, Daphne, unlike anything we can imagine.'

'We can imagine.'

Sylvia blinked. It was so unlike her friend to be so… well, combative was not the right word. But it was not far off.

Perhaps Daphne guessed her thoughts, for her cheeks coloured and she said, a little defensively, 'Well, we can. Gwen married a duke. She's a duchess.'

'That's different,' Sylvia said curtly. She was going to make her say it, wasn't she?

'I don't see how it's—'

'Because I look different, Daphne!' Sylvia had not intended to shout the words, but they had certainly come out far louder than they should in a calm conversation. 'Every time I step in a room, people look at me and try to guess where I come from. As though I cannot just be known for me, for who I am. No one takes the time, the patience, to befriend me. They just assume, then they move on.'

Daphne's cheeks were scarlet now. 'That…anyone who knows you wouldn't—'

'But that's my point, don't you see? And I won't… I will not step into a life where I have to do that at court, and with countless tenants and servants, never allowed to wear what I want or go where I please. I won't do it!' There were tears stinging in the corner of Sylvia's eyes but she would not let them fall—she wouldn't. 'What do you want me to do, step from one cage into another? I want to travel, and explore, and adventure, be my own person!'

'You could do all that with Teddy—'

'No.' Sylvia's voice had lowered now, defeat audible in her tone. 'No, I couldn't, and you know that. He's a duke now, a real one. He…he could change. He'll have to stay here, and I need to go. I have to go, Daphne.'

Silence fell like a shroud onto the music room. There was pain in the base of Sylvia's skull, a dull headache she suspected would become a full-blown megrim by the evening.

And she missed him. Oh, the ache in her where Teddy's presence had once been; it was a visceral agony she would never fill. Sylvia knew she would go through the rest of her life hoping to find a way to end the pain, but she never would.

Then Daphne nodded, leaned back in her chair and gave a sigh. 'Well, as you don't love him—'

'What makes you think I don't love him?' Sylvia had not expected to confess such a thing, but she could not allow the misunderstanding to continue. 'I love him so much I am willing to let him go— How could you think I... I...?'

Daphne was smiling.

Sylvia considered swearing, but she wasn't certain her friend could cope with hearing a curse from her lips. 'You are too clever by half, you know.'

'Always underestimated, never beaten,' Daphne said sweetly as Sylvia groaned and dropped her head on the pianoforte, creating a dissonance of sound.

'What on earth am I going to do?' Sylvia whispered to the complaining keys. 'What am I going to do?'

Chapter Eighteen

Teddy blinked. He hadn't drunk two glasses of brandy, had he?

He blinked again. The two cut glasses, half full of brandy and glittering in the candlelight, swam in his vision then swung together to become one. But only when he concentrated.

Ah. He might have—he'd definitely had a little too much to drink.

'Top you up, there?' asked Warchester genially.

Teddy sighed. 'Definitely.'

Getting drunk had not been the plan. Not that he was drunk. Sozzled, perhaps. A tad pickled. At least two sheets to the wind. But not so drunk that he couldn't… that he wasn't…that the thinking engine in his head was not doing the thinking.

Blast.

'Perhaps not,' Teddy said regretfully, placing his hand over his glass just as his friend went to pour more of the delicious amber liquid into it. 'I don't want to—need to walk home to...to home.'

Warchester snorted as he sloshed a generous amount of the smuggled brandy into his own glass and settled back in his armchair. 'Nonsense, you can bed down in the guestroom here. Besides, you're a duke now. You can't be going about the place on foot. We'll have to hire you a carriage. Buy you one. Buy you several. The estate probably owns a few, now I come to think about it.'

The estate.

Just for a moment, Teddy's vision swam again—that, or the floor of his friend's library decided to take a gentle stroll to the left.

The estate—his estate. He was a duke. Yes, that was why he was drinking here with Warchester. Had been for hours. Because if one was going to accept the idea that one had gained a title and lost the only woman one could ever love, one had better do it with a drink inside one. Several drinks.

'You don't have to look so morose, you know.'

Teddy looked up at his friend, who was examining him closely. 'I don't?'

Warchester shrugged. 'Most men would kill to inherit such a title.'

It was difficult not to snort. He was only trying to be kind. He probably even meant it.

After all, he had been delighted when Teddy had turned up on his doorstep a few hours ago, the summer heat suddenly gone and a chill in the air, to inform him that he was now the Duke of Camrose. Teddy was not sure what he had expected, but it hadn't been the handshaking and champagne-popping reception he had received.

That was where he had gone wrong, he thought muzzily, trying twice to take hold of his brandy glass and missing each time before giving up. Champagne. If they'd stayed on the champagne, perhaps he wouldn't feel so…feel so…

Squiggly.

Squiggly? There had to be a better word for the way the carpet kept undulating and the chandelier kept sway-ing.

'Come on, man, I'll ring for pie,' said Warchester with a grin, leaning over to the bell-pull.

Teddy was not quite sure what he had said. Pie could not be right. How would a pie help him win Sylvia back?

'Pie can't help me now.'

'Oh, yes, it can,' said his friend with a snort. 'You just haven't tried the pies my cook makes.'

And, irritating as it was, Teddy would have to admit, twenty minutes later, that Warchester had a point. The pies brought up on silver trays were hearty: solid meat in a delicious sauce, paired with potatoes, carrots and peas within a substantial pie crust that had a salty tang to its aftertaste. And they were huge, at least the size of his fists combined.

After the first mouthful, Teddy realised how hungry he was. After the fifth mouthful, he realised he had never tasted anything so good in his entire life. By the time the pie was almost gone, he realised the appetising meat, copious sauce and impressive pastry had sobered him up faster than he could have imagined.

'Pie,' he said thickly, swallowing his final mouthful.

Warchester grinned. 'A remedy for almost anything. Trust me. I'll have my cook give yours the recipe.'

Teddy snorted without thinking. 'I don't have a—'

'But you will, won't you?' His friend's eyes glittered. 'You probably have a couple already, awaiting your menus.'

Despite the delectable pie, Teddy's stomach turned. 'I don't have—'

'You do now. Or at least the title does, and while you possess it, you possess everything the estate does,' Warchester said seriously. 'You've got a lot to learn, Camrose, but you'll pick it up quickly enough.'

Camrose. The name caused a ripple of disconcerting disquiet to flood through Teddy. It was a title he had never heard of a few weeks ago. Now it was his name. Teddy, Featherstonehaugh—they were gone. He was Camrose and would be for the rest of his life.

His lonely life, now Sylvia had left him.

'I won't do it, Teddy! I won't step into a different cage!'

Something must have shown in his face for his friend sighed, wiped his mouth with a napkin and threw it down onto the tray. 'Right, I'm ready to hear the sorry tale.'

'What sorry tale?' Teddy had not intended to be so defensive, but it was too late to recall the aggressive tone with which he had spoken.

'Whatever it is you are not telling me,' Warchester said seriously. 'I don't mean about the title and your father and all that—interesting as it is, I don't believe that's why I have you knocking on my door on the night of the Graycott ball.'

Horror rushed through Teddy. 'The Graycott ball—tonight? But—' He glanced at the longcase clock in the corner of Warchester's library. It showed they had been talking and drinking—mostly drinking—for hours. It was near midnight. 'But we'll be late!'

'Late? My dear fellow, there is absolutely no point in attending now, it would take us almost twenty minutes to get there as it is, and you're hardly dressed for such an occasion.'

Teddy was not sure if his friend was commiserating or laughing at him. 'I had utterly forgotten. I suppose they will be offended—'

'The only offence will be that they did not have the pleasure of launching the new Duke of Camrose into Society,' said Warchester with a shrug. 'It's a snub, nothing more. They will not risk the displeasure of one of the most important men in the country, not now the papers have got hold of the story. Did you read that piece published yesterday?'

The floor started to do that undulating thing again. Teddy gripped the arms of his chair.

One of the most important men in the country.

That could not be him, could it? Surely not. Yet the Duchy was large, and certainly very wealthy. And now that was him. The Duke was him. He was it.

Oh, hell.

'So, what is the reason for forgetting what promised to be a very good party, and drinking two bottles of my best brandy?' Warchester asked cheerfully. 'It's not a woman, is it?'

Teddy had never been particularly good at controlling his features.

'It is about a woman!' his friend crowed. 'Oh, wonderful, I like a bit of gossip. Tell me everything.'

'It's not gossip, it's…'

Love. That was what Teddy wanted to say. And yet just because it was love on his side, that most certainly did not mean she loved him. She had never said so, had she?

Perhaps he should be grateful. If she had wished to flatter him and had said something she did not mean, he would have to remember the way she had first said it, how she had admitted her love for him, along with the sense of betrayal.

'Come on, man, out with it.'

Teddy sighed. 'It's simple. I fell in love with her, she did not fall in love with me, and when I discovered I was a duke she broke off our…our understanding.'

He was not certain Warchester was sober enough to follow. Sometimes he could barely follow it himself. It had felt so real. So genuine. As though they truly were going to spend the rest of their lives together.

Warchester raised an eyebrow. 'Your understanding? You actually offered marriage and—oh, Theodore. I can see the truth in your eyes. You bedded her, then.'

Teddy's jaw tightened. 'Once.'

Once. A perfect coupling. A connection he had never experienced before. Not just a meeting of bodies, though that had been delicious enough, but a meeting of souls. Two people clinging to each other in a world that did not understand them.

'Oh, well, once—'

'It meant something.' Teddy had not intended to interrupt his friend, but he had to correct the misunderstanding. 'Something more... She is—I mean, she was... No, she still is...'

When he met Warchester's eye, it was to see a knowing look. 'Ah. You love her, then.'

Teddy's nod was curt.

'And she does not return your affections?'

Desperate as he was to say that Sylvia loved him, Teddy had no evidence that it was true. She had never said so. The moment he had offered matrimony, beyond the pretence, she had gone.

She hadn't even replied to his letter. The one he had written the moment he had returned to his lodging.

Teddy tried not to cringe as he remembered the first draft. The final version had been polite, calm, enquiring.

The first version had not.

I don't understand—I love you so much. These last few weeks have been so wonderful. I never thought I would meet anyone so clever, so beautiful, so exactly perfect for me—Sylvia, it's as if we have been designed for each other. I don't understand why you have walked away from the happiness we could share for a lifetime—

It had used up a great deal of paper, and had not in the end said very much. Teddy had burnt it.

'I don't understand,' Warchester said, frowning. 'Why did you not tell her you had inherited the Duchy? Surely then—after all, what woman would say no to a duke?'

'This one,' Teddy said heavily. 'I told her. I… I think that is why she rejected me.'

'Marrying you would be worse than the Wallflower Academy. A duchess, me? More expectations, less freedom. I won't do it!'

His friend's frown was severe. 'She is utterly unique.'

'She is unusual, yes,' Teddy said with a brief grin, unable to stop himself from thinking about the way Sylvia could always speak truth into a room, even when no one else wanted it. 'You know, she once—'

'I mean, a duke! And she would become a duchess, what woman doesn't want to be a duchess?' Warchester appeared utterly perplexed. 'The very idea! Did she not know how fortunate she was to have gained your affections?'

Something painful tightened within Teddy. 'I think I was the fortunate one to have gained her attention at all.'

Just a few months ago he hadn't even known Sylvia. She was not a part of his life and he had not realised the gaping hole within it. Once she'd stepped into his world, there was nothing else to compare to her. Nothing else he wanted.

Warchester looked sceptical. 'I think you've got it the wrong way round, old chap.'

But Teddy shook his head. He had to make him see, make him understand. 'No, anyone who is in her presence is the fortunate one. I had weeks of joy with her, hours and hours of wonderful conversations, and laughter, and teasing...'

And kissing. And touching. And when they had finally made love, it had been—

'You really love her, don't you?'

Teddy blinked. His friend's words had not been sharp, or cruel, or even jesting. They had been uttered in a quiet voice that suggested Warchester was finally starting to understand.

His companion sighed. 'Well, I am sorry for you. The loss of someone you love is a terrible thing.'

Teddy's lungs tightened painfully for a moment, making taking a breath almost impossible.

It was a terrible thing. And he was living it.

A sudden noise made Teddy jump.

Warchester had slapped his knee and was looking

more cheerful. 'Well, let's talk about things that are more cheerful. Your title—it is all confirmed?'

'Yes. I went to see the solicitors the day after I received their letter,' said Teddy vaguely.

What did the title matter? The coldness of her voice, the ice in her expression as she'd read the letter. He had never seen her so aloof. So detached. So distant.

'Mighty impressive that they'd take your word for it,' Warchester was saying. 'How on earth did you convince them?'

It was impossible not to smile. 'You make it sound like I conned them.'

'You know what I mean,' said his friend with a nonchalant shrug. 'There must have been a queue of brigands outside their office attempting to claim an estate that size. What made them believe you?'

'They had my name in his will, apparently,' Teddy said with a heavy sigh. Without thinking, he reached out for the glass of brandy and took a sip. Mighty fine stuff it was, too. 'The circumstances of my birth, the years of monthly payments, that sort of thing. And there's this.'

With a casual gesture he flicked a finger up to the birthmark by his eyebrow.

Warchester waited, as though for further details, then said, 'You have…eyebrows?'

'I have a birthmark, you rotter, you can see it clearly,' said Teddy, smiling despite himself. 'I've never given much thought to it. Apparently, the old Duke, my…my father had the same. The exact same.'

His father.

It was strange. After years of looking, weeks spent with Sylvia on the hunt for the true identity of his father, there was neither joy nor satisfaction in knowing the truth.

Because he knew who he was now…and it did not matter. All the certainty that he had been sure he would feel, the grounding, the comfort in knowing where he came from, none of it had arrived.

The ache, the empty feeling that he had always thought was the lack of a father, the lack of a family, had been filled by Sylvia these last few weeks, and Teddy hadn't even noticed. Had not noticed until she had gone.

He had gained a father, a name, a duchy. And he had lost something far more precious.

The woman he loved.

Warchester was nodding. 'Dashed convenient.'

Teddy snorted. 'I didn't paint it on.'

'And I didn't suggest you did!' protested his companion with a laugh, reaching for his brandy. 'I'm just saying, it must speed up the process. When do you take up your seat?'

Teddy blinked.

'Your seat in the House of Lords, you dolt.' Warchester grinned. 'You will have to catch on quicker than that during debates. You are up-to-date with the progress of the Corn Laws, aren't you?'

It said a great deal about the last few days that the

idea that he would have to memorise a litany of dull old laws held little fear for him.

What did it matter, what did anything matter, now he had lost Sylvia?

In a way, he was still reeling from that argument. He still could not believe that, somehow, he had lost her, somehow managed to let her slip through his fingers. For the duration of a few hours, he had held the most precious thing in the world.

Titles, money, prestige, what did it matter?

He had to do something. He had to win her back—and he would. He would not let such a woman slip through his fingers.

'It's hard to believe all the jesting with Sylvia was true,' Teddy said before he could stop himself.

He started as Warchester slammed his glass of brandy onto the console table beside him, sloshing its contents over the rim.

'You did not say that the woman you loved and lost was Sylvia—Sylvia Bryant, the woman you brought to the Lyndons'?' his friend demanded.

Teddy stared. 'Yes, of course it—'

'Why on earth did you not say so? I liked her. Clever woman, very pretty.' Warchester was shaking his head. 'I can't believe you let that one go.'

'I didn't let her go, she walked away!' Teddy said hotly, affronted at the idea that he had done something wrong. What he had done was irrefutable, though he had no wish to admit that. As soon as he had worked out what he had done wrong, he could fix it. Couldn't he?

'Well, what are you going to do?' demanded Warchester.

Hardly able to keep track of the wildly altering emotions of his friend, and suspecting the brandy had something to do with it, pie notwithstanding, Teddy slumped against the back of his chair. 'I don't know.'

'You don't know? I knew this engagement of yours was a ruse, but I didn't know you'd actually lost your heart to her,' said Warchester, shaking his head. 'What are you going to do?'

'What can I do?' Teddy retorted, piqued. 'I have gone to the Wallflower Academy—'

'The where?'

'—I have sent letters, I have racked my brain to think of a way that I could convince her to even have a conversation with me, and I come up with nothing,' Teddy continued. Explaining the Wallflower Academy was an entirely separate conversation. 'What can I do? I would never force her to marry me, and I do not believe anything could force Sylvia to do something she did not want to do.'

A warmth suffused him at the thought. Sylvia Bryant could eat most men for breakfast, and besides, he was at a distinct disadvantage in any debate with her.

He loved her.

'A man like myself cannot offer Sylvia anything,'

Teddy said, his voice breaking slightly as he spoke, the despair pushing through.

And for some reason, Warchester was grinning. 'Perhaps Teddy Featherstonehaugh has nothing to offer her. But what about the Duke of Camrose—what can he offer her?'

Teddy's spirits sank even further. 'She doesn't want to be a duchess, Warchester, that's what I've been trying to tell you. She sees it as…as a cage. A rigid set of rules she does not want to step into.'

They lapsed into silence for a moment, until—

'Well, then,' said Teddy slowly, a smile on his lips. 'Time to break the rules.'

Chapter Nineteen

'You really should—'

'If the word "should" leaves your mouth again, Daphne Smith, I shall throw this book right at your—'

'You know you should!'

The thump against the wall was not nearly as invigorating as Sylvia had expected, which was a shame. The act of throwing it, however, felt marvellous.

Daphne straightened up, frowning. 'Now, is that any way to behave?'

Sylvia's shoulders slumped as she sat on her bed, now devoid of book, which was her primary occupation when her friend had entered her bedchamber. 'I don't want to go.'

She sounded petulant, and she hated that, but she had no other response. That was the trouble with the Pike. She did not ask. She ordered. It made it far more irritating—even if Sylvia had been minded to attend another of the Wallflower Academy's pompous dinners, which any gentry who could be scraped together by the Pike would attend, the manner of the 'invitation' was quite off-putting. A yelled order up the staircase was not the most inviting, after all.

'All the other wallflowers are attending,' Daphne said quietly, appearing slightly nervous that Sylvia might throw something else. 'You may enjoy the distraction.'

'What I would enjoy is being left alone,' Sylvia said darkly, knowing her statement was not entirely true.

Her friend gave her a look that told her in no uncertain terms that she was not fooled.

Sylvia sighed heavily and tilted to her left to lie on her bed. 'I don't want to sit there with a gaggle of inane gentlemen—'

'They may not be inane!'

'—who want to brag about their horses or the size of their—'

'Sylvia!'

'—carriages,' continued Sylvia ruthlessly, though with a grin on her face. 'I don't want to see men chew with their mouths open or slurp their soup—'

'I am sure Miss Pike would only invite gentlemen who know how to behave,' said Daphne a little doubtfully.

Sylvia snorted as she sat up. 'You know that some of the troglodytes we've had dine here have been absolutely awful.'

'Rilla's husband dined here, before they were married,' pointed out Daphne quietly. 'He's an earl, he knows how to—'

'Well, as long as he's an earl, that's acceptable,' snapped Sylvia before she could help herself.

Silence fell between them as she bit her lip. When had she become so…so cruel?

So like her father, a nasty voice muttered in the back of her head.

No, she was not like him—not really. She was upset, Sylvia attempted to tell herself. Though wasn't that what he had said, whenever he had shouted at her? That it was her fault, for upsetting him.

'I am sorry, Daphne,' Sylvia said hesitantly. She seemed to be saying that a lot at the moment. 'I don't want to go to another of the Pike's dinners. What would be the point? I've fallen in love already, and he won't be there.'

Just for a moment her lungs tightened. He wouldn't, would he? Surely the Pike had realised the engagement between them was at an end.

'And then I had to be noble and give him up so that he could find someone better to become his Duchess,' she continued darkly. 'The irony is not lost on me.'

'There's a rumour that there will be a nobleman here this evening,' Daphne said in her soft voice. 'A real peer.'

'I told you, I am not interested,' Sylvia said flatly, reaching to her bedside table and picking up another book. 'And there is nothing that you can say to make me—'

'Miss Pike says if you don't come down and dine with our guests, you won't have dinner at all.'

Fourteen minutes later, Sylvia was stomping along the corridor to the staircase in high dudgeon.

'Blackmail, that's what it is,' she muttered darkly.

'I think it's technically bribery,' said her friend helpfully.

Sylvia glared at Daphne as they reached the head of the stairs, but her gaze swiftly meandered to something that should not be there. A great number of things that should not be there, in fact.

The hall of the Wallflower Academy appeared to have been covered in…roses.

Oh, such roses. Large, resplendent blossoms and tightly curled buds, the scent was overwhelming. Some were in pots, whole rosebushes somehow transplanted to the centre of the Wallflower Academy, while others were festooned in vases. There even appeared to be a bower near the front door, an arch that swept over the two oak doors.

Sylvia's eyes widened. So many roses.

'What on earth?' breathed Daphne as they started to descend the stairs.

Somehow, several wallflowers had managed to step through the cascading flowers in the hall and were giggling, muttering in low voices that nonetheless managed to travel up the staircase.

'Who could it be—'

'No one I know would send me these!'

'Surely not for Miss Pike?'

Sylvia snorted. No, the Pike was not the sort of woman to receive such a ridiculous display of affection.

But now she came to think about it—now she had reached the foot of the staircase and was wondering how she could pick a path through the ridiculous display of roses to the dining room, eat rapidly, then disappear as soon as possible—who at the Wallflower Academy would receive so many roses?

Daphne certainly wouldn't.

It was not a cruel thought. At least, Sylvia did not think so. Daphne had always been the first person to say she would rather die than speak to a gentleman alone.

Sylvia cast her friend a sidelong glance. Daphne looked just as astonished as the other wallflowers, and though her cheeks had pinked, that was likely due to the impending dinner and its required conversation than anything floral.

'What is going on?' came a sharp voice from the other side of the hall.

Sylvia could not help but grin as she saw the Pike struggle past a pair of rosebushes and stagger into the centre of the hall.

'I demand to know the meaning of this!' the Pike said as she tripped over a vase, spilling the water and its roses across the floor. 'Blast—I mean, bother! Come on then, girls, admit it. Who did this?'

All the wallflowers near her stared in shock. Sylvia was certain she was giving voice to their joint confusion as she said, 'Why would we do something like this, Miss Pike?'

'Sylvia Bryant, I knew it was you,' said Miss Pike darkly as she attempted to weave past another rosebush. Her shawl became entangled in the thorns and she eventually abandoned it, leaving the silk to remain pronged on the rosebush as she attempted to stride towards Sylvia. 'This time you have gone too… What on earth?'

What on earth? was right, thought Sylvia as she and the Pike stared at the string quartet that was somehow moving through the plethora of roses, playing music so delightful it was difficult not to be swept away by it.

But this was madness. Who on earth had done this?

Sylvia giggled as she watched the Pike grow red in the face.

'I have guests coming! I have a dinner to host! I don't have time to clear up roses and… What are you doing here, you musicians, you?'

'You know, I have to admit,' Sylvia said conversationally to Daphne, who had tiptoed around the vases like a ballet dancer and reached her side, 'whoever has done this has perhaps outshone even me. Why, I would never have thought of such a scale of foolishness!'

'All we need now is the knight in shining armour,' Daphne said quietly.

Sylvia snorted as the Pike attempted to interrogate the giggling wallflowers in a gaggle on the other side of the hall. 'Don't be ridiculous, there's no knight in—'

The double oak front doors opened in a flurry of rose

petals and the low evening sunlight poured in. The light was so blinding it was impossible to see who was there.

It won't be him, Sylvia tried to remind herself even as her heart beat faster. *It wouldn't be him. It can't be him.*

Teddy stood in the doorway.

Sylvia's jaw dropped.

'Oh, my!' breathed Daphne.

'Ah, His Grace is here—for Sylvia, we must presume, even if he has put us all at great inconvenience,' said the Pike hotly, sleeve caught on a rosebush that wasn't letting go.

'It's not possible,' Sylvia murmured, her fingers numb, her weak legs making her sway for a moment.

'Come on then, everyone, out of here. Out, out…'

It was the Pike's voice, but Sylvia could not concentrate on it. It was all she could do to remain upright. Her eyes had not wavered from Teddy the moment he had appeared in the doorway and he had made no movement towards her.

Why would he? This could not all be for her. Why would he do such…such a thing?

Tears prickled at the corners of her eyes but she did her best to quell them. She was not going to cry. Not as she stood here in the dying sunlight of the day, surrounded by roses, a string quartet playing and Teddy striding towards her, his fierce gaze blazing, unrelenting, pinning her in place—as if the flood of roses had not already done so.

'What are you doing here?'

The words were a mere croak as they escaped from her mouth. She was using all of her strength to remain standing.

Somehow, Daphne had melted away. She was alone, and all she could do was stare at Teddy. He was only a few feet from her, examining her with those serious eyes of his.

'What am I doing here?' he repeated, a slight line appearing between his brows. 'Proposing to you, of course.'

There was tension in her shoulders and a flare of hope in her chest, but both faded swiftly. 'You can't—'

'Turns out, as a duke, I can do almost anything I want,' Teddy interrupted, a wry smile creasing his lips. 'And what I want is you.'

This could not be happening. And yet the scent of the roses, the stunning display of their petals, the strains of the violin behind her…no, Sylvia could not have dreamt all this.

'You're a duke now—you…you can marry anyone,' she began to say, voice cracking.

'You're right. I can,' Teddy said softly. 'Sylvia, I can marry anyone. There is not a single woman in the *ton* who would not gladly accept me as her husband.'

It was all Sylvia could do not to allow the disappointment and pain cross her face. Did he need to taunt her in such a cruel way? Did he have to make it so obvious that he could have anyone he chose?

For some reason, the blighter was still smiling. 'And I want you.'

Sylvia's throat clenched as she tried to speak, the words not coming.

'Sylvia, I am not going to invite you into a life that would just be another cage,' he said seriously, taking a step forward and taking her hand in his.

She considered pulling away, but there were two reasons why she could not. Firstly, because it felt so right to be holding onto a part of Teddy. Perhaps this would be the last time they would ever see each other. It would certainly be the last time she could touch him like this; she might see him at Almack's as he stood surrounded by giggling debutantes attempting to flirt their way into a duchess's coronet.

And the second reason was because she did not want to.

'You deserve the world.'

Sylvia blinked. 'Wh… What did you say?'

Teddy's grin was bold, and yet gentle. Just like him. 'It's not like you to be without words.'

'It's not like me to be standing in a glade of roses with a duke before me, offering me marriage, after I was most clear I could not marry him,' Sylvia said quietly, heart breaking.

Because nothing had changed. He was still a duke, and she was still a woman who wanted her freedom. He offered marriage, a constriction she had always sworn to avoid.

But he was Teddy. And she did not know how she would ever let him go.

'We've both been harmed by the abandonment of our fathers,' Teddy said quietly, squeezing her hand. 'We've both looked at the world and seen that it is unfair, and cruel, and cold. And I cannot imagine… Matrimony for a woman can be naught but restriction.'

Sylvia's chest was constricting painfully, every breath an effort. 'You're right. No amount of roses can change that.'

'But I can.'

Teddy's voice was strong, certain—so certain that, for a moment, she almost believed him. It was a wonderful dream, the idea of being his wife—of loving him and being loved by him for the rest of their lives.

But it was nothing more than that. Just a dream.

'What…what do you mean, you—'

'All this time, you've worried about matrimony,' Teddy said to Sylvia's bewildered silence. 'But my love, I am not going to hedge you in. You can do whatever you—'

'You know perfectly well that I cannot!' Sylvia had not intended to speak, to interrupt whatever pleasant words he was about to say, nor had she intended her voice to be so sharp, so pained. 'A duchess must look a certain way, dance a certain way, dress a certain way—'

'Says who?' Teddy said sharply, his eyes warm. 'You and I were not raised to that life, and I see no laws saying—'

But Sylvia was laughing bitterly now, turning from him. 'You speak as though we can change the world!'

She had forgotten that Teddy still held her hand. He tugged her back to face him, his expression so serious she could not look away.

'Why not change the world?' he said quietly. 'Why not forget the rules of the *ton* so we can be happy?'

He could not be in earnest.

'What will everyone say?'

'What does it matter?' Teddy said dismissively. 'I want you, Sylvia. We can go adventuring together. I've corresponded with my stewards already and they're happy to continue managing the estates just as they have done the last three months. I'll come to the Caribbean with you, we'll visit your mother. We can do whatever we want. And they'll call us eccentric, even wild perhaps—'

'I think they'll call us a great deal more than that,' Sylvia muttered darkly.

'—but I don't care. Not if I have you by my side. Not if I can love you every day of my life,' said Teddy quietly.

Sylvia bit her lip. It was all she had wanted, and more. The freedom to be who she was—the opportunity to travel, to see the world, to be free of the Wallflower Academy and all its rules and routines and to choose her own path in life.

But...

'Marrying me...' she said quietly, and her heart fluttered as she saw the joy brighten in Teddy's eyes. 'Marrying me would end your place in Society—'

'Hang Society—I'm a duke now,' interrupted Teddy with a mischievous grin. 'You think I haven't spent years around dukes and earls and the like at school and then at university without learning a few things? Sylvia, none of them abide by Society's rules. They break them all the time and they get away with it—sometimes they're celebrated. Trust me, I can marry whoever I want, and I want you.'

His words were precisely what she wanted to hear, but she couldn't trust them. How could he believe that? Just face the *ton* without a care for what anyone thought? He would be snubbed! He would receive the Cut Direct, and she could not do that to him.

Sylvia swallowed. 'I am never going to be like them, Teddy. I am never going to mind my manners or think before I speak or—'

'And you think that's what I want?' Teddy's expression was incredulous. 'You think I want a partner in life who will walk two paces behind me and nod mutely at everything I say?'

It was difficult not to smile at that.

'No.'

'I told you I love you, Sylvia Bryant, and I spoke advisedly,' he said softly, taking her other hand in his. 'And I… I have no expectations for you to feel the same, or say the same, but you have to know…'

At some point, the string quartet had gone. It was

only now, in the silence of this moment, that Sylvia noticed. It was a relief, for what she was about to say was not for anyone else's ears but Teddy's.

'I love you so much,' she whispered, cheeks burning at the admission. 'I… Teddy, I haven't known what to do with myself without you. Every day, every hour I'm not with you—'

When he kissed her, it was hard and desperate and Sylvia clung to him—clung to the one man in the world she knew she would love for ever.

As they finally broke apart, Teddy said fiercely, his forehead pressed against hers, 'Don't you ever frighten me like that again, Sylvia Bryant.'

She laughed breathlessly, hardly knowing what to say. 'I don't underst—'

'For almost a week I thought I'd lost you,' he said darkly. 'I thought I would have to go through life without you, and no amount of money or a fancy title could make up for that. I need you.'

Sylvia's hope soared at his words. 'But I don't deserve—'

'You are right—you deserve far better,' Teddy said with a laugh, straightening up. 'But in the meantime, will you have me?'

There was no hesitation this time. 'I suppose I will.'

'You suppose?' Teddy shot back with a laugh.

'Well, then, I will,' Sylvia said, stealing a quick kiss and feeling joy ripple through her whole body as his strong arms clasped her. 'But with one condition.'

The expression of unrestrained excitement quickly disappeared from Teddy's face. 'And what, precisely, is that?'

Chapter Twenty

'I knew I should have been more suspicious of this condition of yours,' Teddy said darkly as his stomach lurched.

Sylvia's laughter was enough to make his stomach lurch a second time, though in a much more enjoyable way. 'I didn't want a lot of fuss.'

'And you thought this was the best alternative?' He couldn't help but smile as the carriage rattled along, his arm around the woman who would soon become his wife. 'If we wanted to begin by offending almost every single person of note in Society, I don't think we could have done much better.'

The gentle tap Sylvia gave him on the arm was enough to rile him. Teddy leaned forward, pressing a passionate kiss on the woman's lips. She responded in kind, her tongue tangling with his own as their breathing quickened, their ardour uninhibited.

It was a good five or six minutes before either of them had enough breath to speak.

'I was certain you would not want everyone staring,' Sylvia said, her lips bruised with the evidence of their sensual appetite. 'Imagine the gossip! The wallflower and the surprise duke, both with a mysterious past, none of their parents present at the wedding... You can just imagine it.'

Teddy could. A flicker of excitement soared through him but he pushed it aside as he tried to focus on the here and now.

'I suppose I shouldn't be surprised that in this, in everything, we are going to be different.'

Not that it mattered. With his arm around Sylvia's waist and her evident joy seeping through every word, he was content. This was what he wanted. This was what he had always wanted, though he had not known it. The loneliness that had crept around his heart as a child had never before been broken through.

Perhaps he had thought, once, that finding his father would end that—but Teddy knew better now. It wasn't riches or a title or prestige which had brought him this happiness. It was her.

'I suppose this wasn't the worst idea in the world,' he said with mock grudging surrender. 'Ouch!'

His future wife did not look concerned at all that she had just jabbed him in the ribs. 'You deserve it.'

'You just wait until the Pike—blast, Miss Pike—hears what we're about to do,' Teddy said with a warning grin. 'She is going to be absolutely furious.'

'She will, won't she?' Sylvia spoke lightly and cheer-

fully, and Teddy could not help but laugh at her uncon-
cern. 'I made sure to leave her an invitation for our
wedding in a week's time, which I am sure she will
appreciate.'

Teddy groaned. 'You didn't.'

'I had it embossed with gold,' said the woman beside
him, her eyes lighting up, 'and I said that His Grace—'

Teddy groaned again.

'—that His Grace would require and expect the attendance of—'

'Well, that's it, we can never go back to the Wallflower Academy,' Teddy said firmly.

Sylvia grinned and his manhood jerked. 'Exactly.'

He would never be bored, that much was certain.

He could not imagine a future without her. His good
fortune was not the sudden discovery that his father had
a rather impressive title, but that his future wife had a
rather impressive soul.

And…and other parts of her.

Try as he might, Teddy could not prevent his eyes
from meandering down the beautiful travelling pelisse
Sylvia was wearing. The swell of her breasts, the curve
of her—

Teddy enjoyed another nudge in the ribs for his trouble.

'You can enjoy me later,' Sylvia said sternly, though
the curve of her lips suggested she was not truly offended. 'Afterwards.'

They sat in silence for a few minutes, the rocking

carriage threatening to lull Teddy to sleep after their long journey. But just when his eyelids were starting to droop, and he was wondering whether he could enjoy a nap before their arrival, a low voice caused his eyes to snap open.

'You…you still have time to change your mind.'

Sylvia looked…diminished, somehow. As though, being left alone with her own thoughts, she had managed to convince herself that she did not deserve him.

Teddy could see the fear in her eyes, but he could not blame her for it. What they were doing, it was utterly against the rules of the *ton*. Some would be scandalised. Others would be horrified.

He was just eager to make her his own.

'I want to be with you,' Teddy said quietly. 'For the rest of my life, I want you by my side. Thoroughly irritating our housekeeper—'

'You never know, I might like her,' Sylvia protested with wide eyes.

'—and surprising everyone we meet—'

'That won't be hard,' muttered the woman beside him.

Teddy halted. It had been a jest, a joke, yet he could see the barely suppressed panic in her expression, rippling beneath the surface.

It was always a wonder to him that Sylvia Bryant did not think herself enough. That there was insecurity there beneath the bravado.

It only made him love her more.

'I can't promise you that life will always be easy. Lord knows, we've both seen the darkness in humanity, but we've come out of it and found each other,' said Teddy quietly, squeezing his hand around Sylvia's waist. She gave a wan smile. 'And I am desperate to marry you.'

'Only so we can—'

'Not for that reason!' Teddy's manhood protested, and he breathed a laugh. 'Well, not only for that reason. But because being your husband is the only title I really want in life.'

Sylvia's wan smile grew and as she opened her mouth to speak, the carriage started to slow. Her gaze snapped out of the window. 'Are we here?'

Teddy's attention followed hers. He had never been to Scotland, so was not quite sure what to expect. Not this luscious, striking countryside that seemed to demand one's attention at every moment. Not this small village, its cottages with smoke floating out of chimneys and flowers blossoming in pots by front doors.

Not the smithy.

Teddy smiled as he turned to his future wife. 'Are you ready to get married?'

He watched her steady herself, watched as she took a deep breath and faced the fear of such a commitment with grace. He was so fortunate that he had somehow gained Sylvia Bryant's heart.

'It was my idea to elope,' Sylvia said boldly. 'Why wouldn't I be ready?'

'Because you are not the tough, uncrackable nut you

claim to be,' Teddy pointed out, trying his best to keep his smile to himself. 'Because you can be brave and afraid, bold and shy, all at the same time. Because you're Sylvia. Because you're mine. Because this is a big day.'

It was a big day, although she did not know it yet. Teddy had attempted to keep a lid on his excitement for days now, but it was a challenge and he wasn't sure how long he could keep the secret.

Just a few more minutes, he told himself. *Just a few more minutes...*

'You are disgustingly supportive, you know,' Sylvia said with a grin. 'Come on then. Let's get married.'

One of the numerous footmen from the townhouse in Mayfair that Teddy had inherited opened the carriage door for them after he tapped on the roof, most awkward at giving the signal. Teddy had worked hard to memorise a few of the names of his servants but there were so many.

'Thank you...' *Oh, blast.* He was almost sure this one was Greddins. Greddins? That didn't sound right.

The footman grinned. 'It's Gardiner, Your Grace.'

Sylvia snorted with laughter as Teddy winced.

Your Grace. Would he ever grow accustomed to that?

'Thank you, Gardiner,' Teddy said hastily as they stepped down from the carriage. 'We'll just go and—'

'Get married,' said Sylvia with a grin, winking at the now flushing Gardiner. 'He's got to make an honest woman of me.'

'Sylvia!'

'Well, you do,' she said blithely, seemingly all concerns cast to the wind. 'Come on, Your Grace.'

'You know I don't like it when you call me that,' Teddy said darkly as he was pulled by the hand towards the smithy, a great deal of smoke billowing from the chimney. 'Even if it is my title now.'

'I think it's your address, not your title,' Sylvia pointed out as they neared the smithy.

Excellent. More things that he had to learn, more things that he could get wrong.

It was going to be a long, hard road, growing accustomed to being a duke. Teddy pulled at his cravat, which had somehow tightened since they had left the carriage. He would have to start wearing more of today's fashions, too. And find a valet. Had he inherited one of those too, up at New Hall?

Well, he'd find out soon enough. When he had his Duchess, he would go to New Hall and survey the place. Which was precisely why they were here...

Teddy blinked. They were standing outside the smithy and there was an all too knowing look on Sylvia's face.

'I'm not the only one who is nervous, I think,' she said softly. 'Are you sure about this, Teddy? We don't have to—'

'I want to,' he said quickly, and was rewarded with a tender smile that made his loins tighten. He very much wanted to.

No other woman had ever made him feel like this. At home.

Reaching out, Teddy turned the door handle and stepped into the smithy. The darkness was blinding and it was hot, something in the air making his eyes water and his throat cough.

'G'morning, m'laird,' said a tall man, leaning over a blazing fire, speaking without turning around. 'Y'ken I need a-payin' afore—'

'Yes, yes, of course,' said Teddy hastily, thrusting a hand into his pocket as Sylvia grinned beside him. 'And…and how much—'

'M'lady.' The blacksmith nodded as he turned and greeted them. 'A guinea, m'laird.'

Teddy could not help it. His jaw dropped. 'A guinea?'

A guinea? Why, that could buy almost anything one wanted in London, and that was with southern prices. He had to assume that up here in the back of beyond—

Sylvia cleared her throat meaningfully. Teddy shook his head slightly, the haze of heat in the room utterly overwhelming, and saw the determinedly set jaw of the blacksmith.

'I heard tell yers a duke,' the man said quietly.

Teddy opened his mouth, realised he had absolutely nothing to say, and then closed it.

A guinea. Well, he was now in possession of an annual income of eleven thousand pounds. What was a guinea?

'A guinea, right,' Teddy said hastily, rummaging through his pocketbook, relieved he had such money on him. 'Here you go, my man.'

He cringed as he said the words, but there was no taking them back.

'Nobility has changed you,' Sylvia whispered solemnly.

'Oh, shut up,' Teddy said with a laugh.

'Well, if that's everything,' she said, stepping away from him towards the anvil. 'I suppose we just stand here and—'

'Y'ken ye shoulda brought yerselves a witness?' said the blacksmith, wiping his hands on his leather apron and making them dirtier than they had been to start with.

Teddy's pulse skipped a beat. This was it. This was the moment.

He watched as Sylvia's face fell, but she rallied almost immediately. 'We can ask Gardiner. Why don't I go and get—'

'Actually,' said Teddy, heart in his mouth as he stepped into her path, blocking her from the door, 'we don't need to ask Gardiner. I… I invited someone.'

Sylvia's response was not what he had expected.

'Oh, honestly, Teddy, the whole point was that we were running away to get married without anyone knowing!' Sylvia fixed him with a stern look. 'It isn't the Pike, is it?'

For the flash of a moment, Teddy considered what the proprietress of the Wallflower Academy would say if invited to the elopement of a duke and one of her charges in Gretna Green.

'No,' he said hastily.

Sylvia sighed. 'Well, I suppose having a stranger at our wedding is acceptable—but I wish you had spoken to me about it first.'

'Yes, well…' *This is it, man!* 'The thing is, I wasn't sure how to tell you.' Teddy smiled. 'They had to come a long way, you see.'

'They aren't the only ones—do you know how many miles it is from London to—'

'They've travelled a great deal further,' Teddy said, cutting across her and trying not to visibly vibrate with excitement. 'I hoped you wouldn't mind. It's your guest.'

Now there was confusion creasing Sylvia's brow. 'My guest? But I don't know anyone—unless you invited Daphne, in which case…'

Teddy shook his head. 'No, I invited someone far more important.'

For some reason, that was the wrong thing to say. 'Poor Daphne, she's always overlooked,' Sylvia said fiercely as a door opened behind her and a tall woman in a white muslin gown stepped in. 'It's most unfair that she…that she…'

Teddy watched with unbridled delight as Sylvia glanced over her shoulder at the newcomer and found she had no words.

The woman smiled, her skin creasing around her nervous eyes, and her hands twisted before her. 'Is…is that you, my Sylvia?'

Sylvia appeared frozen. Teddy was in half a mind

to nudge her. The moment stretched out, second after second, until—

'Mama?' Sylvia breathed. 'No. It can't be.'

'Yes, it can,' Teddy whispered.

She snapped around to glare, expression expectant. 'Explain.'

'Warchester helped. His great-uncle—' He saw the look in her eye and skipped to the end. 'I found your mother weeks ago and when I inherited a stupid amount of money I thought, well, I know what to do with it,' Teddy said in a rush. Dammit, he'd had an impressive speech prepared. None of that seemed to matter now. 'As it turned out, the moment your mother received my letter, she booked a passage and began to journey here. There's so much we can't gain from our pasts—our fathers are gone—'

'Or worthless,' Sylvia muttered.

'—and my mother is gone, but your mother is here. She's here, Sylvia,' Teddy said gently, stepping forward and squeezing her hand. 'There's pain in the past, but there's hope in the future. Whenever you both wish, we can all go to Antigua, you can show me the hibiscus and—'

'He's a chatterer that one,' Elizabeth said with a grin at her daughter. 'I don't know how you put up with him.'

'Neither do I,' breathed Sylvia before rushing forward and throwing her arms around her mother. 'Oh, Mama.'

Teddy studiously looked away and met the gaze of the blacksmith, who was doing the same.

It was a beginning. There would be awkwardness—one could not be parted from one's mother for over a decade and slip straight back into the same routines. There would be hard conversations and difficult revelations, and it would take time.

They had time. They had all the time in the world.

When Sylvia pulled away from her mother, both sets of eyes were sparkling with tears. Then Sylvia stepped away from Elizabeth, approached Teddy and whacked him hard on the arm.

'Ouch!'

'How could you not tell me?' she said with a broken laugh. 'All this time, you had been searching for her!'

'I know how much you like pranks.' Teddy grinned with inexpressible joy. 'I thought it was only right that she was here to witness our marriage.'

'I can hardly believe it. I can hardly believe you, you rotter,' Sylvia said with a laugh. 'And now, if it's all the same to you, I would rather like to be married.'

Pulling her into a sudden embrace, Teddy said gruffly, 'Then let's get married.'

It was not a long, complicated ceremony. It did not need to be.

'Hold yer hands together here,' the blacksmith grunted. 'Did ye want ter make any vows yerselves?'

Teddy looked over the anvil at the woman he loved. 'Vows?'

'Things yer want to say that cannae be found in yon

church ye have in England,' said the blacksmith with a grin.

Right. He probably should have thought of this. In truth, Teddy had just presumed they would have a few words spoken over them and they would be married. He hadn't attended too many weddings and—

'I'll go first,' said Sylvia with a smile.

Teddy's mouth went dry.

'Teddy Featherstonehaugh, I love you. I loved you when I knew you were not a duke, and I've come to find that I'm loving you more with each day since,' Sylvia said simply. 'And I want to keep on loving you, and being loved by you, and that's why I want to marry you. You are not a prison. You are the adventure.'

Teddy attempted to wipe away an escaped tear without making it too obvious. By the knowing smile on his mother-in-law's face, he had not been successful.

'And how am I supposed to follow that?' he said in a weak voice.

Sylvia grinned. 'Now you know why I went first.'

He had to laugh at that. 'You never cease to surprise me, Sylvia. But you know what I'm not surprised by? Your kindness and your gentleness, despite everything you've faced. Your wit and your cheek. I hope I never cease being surprised at how much I love you. My heart was empty for so long, and now you've not only filled it, but made me want to become a man worthy of your love. Even if I have to be a duke at the same time.'

There was a loud sniff. Teddy turned, expecting to

see Elizabeth dabbing at her eyes, but it was the burly blacksmith who was wiping away a tear.

'Tha's right bonny,' he said with a sniff. 'Right. Rings.'

Teddy pulled the two gold bands from his pocket. Sylvia had pointed out that gentlemen did not wear wedding rings. He had pointed out that for most of his life he had been no gentleman. There had been no further discussion.

'With thon rings, and th'power I keep as a smith,' said the man as Teddy and Sylvia pushed the wedding bands on the fourth fingers of their beloved's left hands, 'I declare ye man and wife. Ye may kiss. And the rest.'

Teddy leaned across the anvil and kissed his wife hard, breathing in her rosewater scent, knowing he would never have to leave her side again.

When they pulled apart, Sylvia was grinning. 'Well, it looks like this duchess charade has finally come true.'

Epilogue

Six months later...

Sylvia Bryant hadn't expected there to be anyone actually standing beside the carriage.

'Whoops!' she said in a rush, skirts flying, bonnet clinging to her head for dear life. 'My apologies—did I whack you very hard?'

Teddy rolled his eyes. 'Very hard.'

It was impossible not to laugh as she descended from the carriage. 'Well, I think I have done sufficiently well for myself, irrespective of my whacking power.'

Sylvia breathed in the fresh air, so different from that of London. There had been, as it turned out, far more things to attend to in London than they had thought. Debts and invoices, introductions at St James' and organisation of investments…but now, finally, they had travelled west to the estate that Teddy had never known was his and was now master of. There was a sharp saltiness in the breeze, perhaps because the road they had journeyed along the last hour or so had cradled the sea.

If she listened closely, she could still hear the roaring, crashing waves against the cliffs.

'Dear Lord...' muttered a voice behind her.

Turning, she watched as Teddy Featherstonehaugh, Duke of Camrose, clambered out of the carriage and shielded his eyes from the brilliant sun. He'd decided to keep his mother's name. The *ton* was not happy about it.

But it was his mother's legacy that he wanted to carry forward into his new life, not his father's. She had done everything for her son, and she had never lived to see his rise. He would honour her memory.

Then his eyes widened. 'No.'

'Yes,' said Sylvia with a laugh.

'No,' Teddy repeated, his jaw dropping as he stared past her. 'No, it can't be—the direction must be wrong. The coachman must have—'

'This is it,' Sylvia said cheerfully. 'I befriended the serving maid at that last inn we stopped at—'

'Of course you did,' said her husband, rolling his eyes as he slipped his hand in hers.

'—and she described it perfectly. It's quite famous about these parts, apparently,' continued Sylvia, trying not to laugh again.

Really, the expression on Teddy's face was truly hilarious.

'Apparently so,' breathed Teddy, continuing to stare past her.

Sylvia turned to look at what he was staring at, and her stomach lurched in a most unexpected way.

They stood there in silence for a few minutes. The coachman appeared to recognise their need for mutual solitude, for he returned to his place on the carriage and pulled out a sandwich which looked a little worse for wear. Sylvia turned away from him and back to the sight which had struck her new husband silent, and squeezed his hand.

'It's not so bad,' she said consolingly. 'I suppose we'll get used to it.'

'Get…get used to—Sylvia!'

'I honestly think we could be happy anywhere,' said Sylvia cheerfully, trying not to giggle at the look of outrage on Teddy's face. 'You know, over time, we may come to love it.'

'Love it? Not so bad?' Teddy's face was a picture. 'You have got to be jesting.'

Sylvia turned back to the outrageously huge manor house before them. Four floors, from what she could see, constructed from grey stone that seemed to shimmer in the sunlight, balustrades along the roof, a dome topped with gold, chimneys that spiralled in the Stuart style, half of them with smoke pouring out, an ornamental garden before them edged in gravel, while sunlight glittered off what had to be an orangery to the west side—

'Not so bad,' repeated her husband weakly. 'Not so—Sylvia, it's twice the size of the Wallflower Academy and it's only us who will live in it!'

'I think you have forgotten our numerous servants

and frequently visiting friends,' she scolded, unable to stop herself from laughing. 'No, honestly, those solicitors of yours—'

'They're not mine,' Teddy growled.

'I think you will find that they are the solicitors of the Duke of Camrose, which is who you are,' Sylvia pointed out fairly, merriment tinging every syllable. 'Anyway, they sent me what they called an incomplete list of our servants, and—'

'New Hall,' her husband said weakly.

Sylvia blinked. 'I beg your pardon?'

'They said it was called New Hall,' Teddy repeated, grinning as he glanced at her. 'New Hall! I thought—I don't know, that it would be somewhere small, somewhere modern. Not…not this.'

This. Sylvia turned back to the house and tried to take in its splendour. Even from here, without entering the place, one could almost hear the luxury and wealth whistling by on the wind.

This was the Camrose ducal seat, and it was her new home. Not a cage, not a prison—it would not bind her or restrict her or prevent her from being who she was.

A home.

'I suppose everything is new at some point,' she said lightly. 'Shall we explore?'

Explore was the right word for it. Sylvia made a mental note as they traipsed down a third corridor and peered into rooms awkwardly, like house guests who had forgotten the way to the dining room, to ask the housekeeper for a map of some kind. If she was going to learn to be mistress of this place, the first thing she needed to do was prevent herself getting lost.

'We'll have to send out a search party,' she murmured.

Teddy turned on his heel. 'What did you say?'

'Nothing,' said Sylvia hastily as they opened a door to reveal a library smelling of leather and knowledge. 'It's beautiful in here, isn't it?'

'It is indeed. It's hard to believe that it's all mine,' Teddy said softly, as they stepped into the second drawing room they had found so far. The resplendent wallpaper was the same colour as the rich carpet. 'All mine.'

A shadow passed across his face and he fell silent.

Sylvia swallowed hard, but managed to prevent herself from saying anything. She knew, without him needing to say a word, what he was thinking. Who he was thinking of.

His mother. She had never known such luxury. She had not known the joy and the comfort of living in such opulence. If things had been different...

But then, things would be different, wouldn't they? Teddy would have been raised Theodore Burrell, heir to the Duke of Camrose. He would have been different, perhaps not the kind, thoughtful, passionate man she had fallen in love with. They would never have met.

Perhaps it was better this way. Perhaps both of their stories, painful as they were, were the only stories they would have wanted. Because their journeys had brought them here.

'Thank you.'

Sylvia looked around as they peered into what had to be a sewing room, judging by the furnishings. An entire room, just for sewing? 'Thank me? For what?'

'For your nonsense,' Teddy said dryly.

She could not help but laugh as she gently shoved him in the side as they continued walking. 'Well, I don't call that gratitude!'

'If it hadn't been for your ridiculous idea of pretending to be engaged, then I never would have found my father. I would never have fallen in love with you,' her husband said with a shrug.

'Oh, I don't know. I think you would have fallen in love with me anyway,' Sylvia teased. 'I am irresistible, after all.'

'You're certainly something.'

'Teddy!'

Their mingled laughter echoed through what appeared to be a third drawing room, one with large windows overlooking a splendid lawn that curved around the orangery on one side and a ha-ha on the other.

'You know what I mean,' Teddy added softly. 'Thank you. Without you by my side, I may never have known who I was. What I was.'

'What you are is a good man.' Sylvia had not intended to speak so fiercely, but seeing the momentary uncertainty in her wonderful husband's face was impetus enough. 'I didn't need you to inherit a title or a heap of money—'

'You want me to give it back?'

'—to fall in love with you,' continued Sylvia with a laugh as they stepped past what appeared to be another library. 'This place is a maze!'

'It really does seem far too much,' Teddy agreed, staring around himself in wonder. 'Too much.'

Too much for him. That was what he was thinking, she knew.

Oh, this man. This kind, ridiculous man.

'New Hall,' Sylvia said with a wry smile as they stepped into what appeared to be a study, a desk in the corner covered with papers all written in a spidery hand. 'Strange, to think your father knew all this time, yet never...well. Invited you here. Acknowledged you as his heir. Prepared you for the future he knew you would lead.'

Teddy's determined smile told her far more than his words. It hurt. But it would pass. 'Apparently, he could not bring himself to contact me. Guilt-ridden, after discovering my mother's death, according to his will. He thought I would be happier at a distance. He thought I would not welcome the intrusion, that I would blame him. I wish... I wish it could have been different.'

'We'll be happy here, won't we?'

Her words were bright, exuberant, and Teddy threw her a look. 'You don't have to give me that false smile, you know.'

Sylvia's hands rushed to her mouth. 'It's not—I don't have a—'

'You think I haven't memorised the contours of your face? You think I don't know every one of your expressions, and their meanings, and that I don't love them all?' Teddy's eyes were soft and warm and loving, and her shoulders relaxed. 'That's your false smile, and I don't ever want to see it.'

'False smile indeed,' Sylvia muttered with a shake of her head as they stepped into what could only be a card room. A whole room, for cards? 'What nonsense.'

'I just can't believe how lucky I've been.' Teddy sighed as they left the card room and found what certainly smelled like a smoking room. 'So lucky.'

Sylvia glanced around as they stepped back into a corridor lined with golden frames surrounding impressive landscape paintings, chandeliers glittering near the ceiling, wooden panels lining the corridor.

He was lucky. And she was lucky to have him—a set of coincidences that had brought him to her, or her to him, could never have been conceived and orchestrated.

'You deserve it all,' she said impulsively, taking his hand and wrapping her other hand around his arm. 'A title, a large and beautiful house, an income—'

'A family,' he said, almost as though he had not noticed he had spoken aloud.

Sylvia swallowed.

This was not the time. Or was it? They were home now, weren't they? They could build a home here, a real life, one of joy and exploration and knowing, entirely, who they were.

A place to build a family.

'I mean, obviously, if we are blessed with children—I mean, if we can't, you are more than enough for me. I mean more than I could have hoped for,' Teddy babbled, his cheeks pinking in that delightful way that they did whenever he got his tongue tangled. 'Dammit, Sylvia, you know what I—'

'I know what you mean,' said Sylvia with a wry laugh. 'And…and I don't want to be hasty, but I think…'

Why was her heart pattering so painfully? Why was her skin prickling with goosebumps all over, the words still unsaid?

A line had appeared between Teddy's eyebrows. 'Sylvia?'

For some reason, her courage failed her. It was more than she could have hoped for, more than she could express, this knowledge, and so when it tumbled from her lips it was to the floor, not to the man she loved.

'I think I'm with child—Teddy!'

The squeal was not one of distress, more delight. Before she had been able to finish her sentence, her husband had pulled her into his arms and kissed her most decidedly.

Sylvia melted into the kiss. This was where she belonged; this was home. No impressive manor or fancy series of rooms could replicate the sense of belonging she found right here.

Teddy's tongue delved into her mouth and swept an aching rush of pleasure through her. Sylvia whimpered, her hands clutching his neck as she clung on for dear life.

When the kiss finally ended, she could not help quivering, 'Teddy—'

'Oh, Sylvia, you don't mean it?'

'I haven't yet seen a doctor—Gwen and Rilla will undoubtedly have recommendations—'

'A child?' Teddy whispered, placing a reverential hand on her stomach.

Sylvia blinked away tears. She had known, deep down, how her husband would respond to the news. A child. Part of her, part of him. The combination of two people who loved each other and who had found each other when the world had seemed a cold and empty place.

And soon, within a year, there would be three of them.

The adventures would wait—that was, the adventures abroad would wait. Though a part of her longed for adventure, to escape England, to see a world that she had read about but had never seen, having her mother so close had softened that desire. Perhaps it was not travel she had wanted, but a sense of belonging. She had thought that belonging was in Antigua. Only now did she see that belonging meant the people she cared about.

With each passing day, Sylvia was discovering that the most exciting adventure of all was facing her fears,

Teddy alongside her, and staring them down. She had opened balls and hosted dinners, and lost spectacularly at cards with a countess and a marquess, and…the world had not ended.

It had opened.

'Thank you,' Teddy murmured, his arms strong around her.

Trying not to cry was getting far more difficult the more she fell in love with this man. Most irritating.

'Don't thank me, you put it there.'

He laughed at that, and unless Sylvia was much mistaken, Teddy dashed away a few tears of his own. 'No title or manors or income could ever make me feel luckier than when you stormed into my friend's carriage and demanded that I carry you off.'

Sylvia snorted. 'Now, hang on, that wasn't exactly what I—'

'That's how I remember it,' interrupted Teddy, bringing up his hand to gently caress her cheek. The hand drifted lower, his fingers slowly brushing against her neck, her décolletage, the tops of her breasts…

Her breathing shortened. The tingling between her legs that Teddy could always spark had returned and her knees were shaking, her legs finding it difficult to keep her upright.

'You were saying?'

His teasing tone wasn't enough to make Sylvia laugh, but it was close. 'You rogue, you know I can't concentrate when you're doing that.'

'Fine, I'll—'

'I didn't say stop,' Sylvia breathed as she leaned up to kiss him again.

Their kiss became more passionate. Before she knew it, Teddy had pressed her against the wooden panelling of the corridor, narrowly avoiding knocking over a tall vase on a stand, his jacket and cravat falling to the floor.

'We mustn't,' Sylvia whispered, tendrils of pleasure caressing through her body and making it difficult to speak over a whisper. 'We mustn't do…do this…'

They really shouldn't. Here they were, in the middle of a corridor for goodness' sake! Anyone could find them—anyone could stumble across them and—

'Why not?' Teddy's low voice was more a growl than a whisper and its vibration thrummed something delightful through her. 'You're my wife. This is our house, our home. Where else should we do this?'

Sylvia's eyes widened as she pulled back from Teddy and stared in astonishment.

Because he was right. They were married—they belonged to each other now in a way that no one could take from them. This was their home. He had found his father, and she had found her mother, and they had found each other.

And now…now they would be mother and father to a child of their own.

'You know,' said Teddy slowly, his grin far more wicked, 'we have done a great deal of exploring down here…but we haven't even begun to venture upstairs.'

Her smile matched his own. 'How neglectful of us.'

'It is disgraceful and must be remedied immediately,' said Teddy formally, though laughter managed to seep through his words. 'Will you accompany me, Lady Camrose?'

Something twisted in her stomach—not unpleasant, but most unexpected. 'Lady Camrose—I still haven't got used to that.'

'The Duchess of Camrose,' said the Duke of Camrose. 'It suits you.'

'It would suit anyone,' said Sylvia with a roll of her eyes as she took her husband's hand. 'You know, I think as well as exploring, we should test out the rooms. Make sure they are suitable for a refined couple such as ourselves.'

Teddy kissed her hand as they started along the corridor to where Sylvia hoped was a staircase. There had to be staircases in this place, did there not?

'You are thinking of testing out the bedchambers,' he teased as they turned a corner to discover a lavish staircase.

'I am indeed,' Sylvia said, her mouth going dry.

This man. She could not imagine a time in her life when she would not want to remove his clothes and kiss him all over.

'You know, as the new Duke and Duchess of Camrose, it is our duty to ensure that every bedchamber is up to scratch,' Teddy said solemnly as they started up the stairs. 'Every single one of them. I think we should test them all, just to be on the safe side.'

Sylvia's joy mingled with unbridled delight as they reached the top of the staircase and Teddy pulled her into another embrace, before dropping her into a low dip and kissing her hard on the mouth.

She clung to him, the one man she needed, and gloried in the kiss as her body came alive with desire.

When Teddy pulled back to look at her, Sylvia sighed with happiness. 'You always were impossible.'

And their laughter rang out through New Hall as the two of them ventured along the corridor to find their first bedchamber for a full and thorough testing.

* * * * *

While you're waiting for the next instalment,
make sure to catch up with the previous
books in Emily E K Murdoch's
The Wallflower Academy miniseries

Least Likely to Win a Duke
More Than a Match for the Earl

MILLS & BOON®

Coming next month

HOW TO COURT A RAKE
Bronwyn Scott

Book 1 of **Wed Within a Year**
The brand-new regency trilogy
from Bronwyn Scott

It was a quick waltz and Caine wasted no time getting them up to pace, taking her through turns with a rapidity that left Mary breathless, her cheeks flushed from the exertion and the sheer thrill of waltzing at top speed. 'I've never dared to dance so fast,' she said with a laugh as he guided them through a sharp turn, expertly avoiding another couple.

'You're a good dancer.' She managed to catch her breath long enough to make conversation. Caine had a keen sense of navigation on a crowded floor and an innate confidence in his own skill. She was struck once more by the agility and enjoyment on display when he danced.

'You seem surprised by that.' Caine took them through a corner using a reverse turn as if on cue to illustrate the point.

'Big men aren't usually so gifted with such grace,' she managed to say, still somewhat in awe of the reverse he'd just executed. It was one of the most difficult parts of the dance and he'd managed it effortlessly.

'Aren't we?' He raised a dark brow, his gaze fixed on her, the hint of a sinful smile teasing his lips. 'Are you an expert on big men, Mary?' A low purl of naughtiness rippled through his words and her breath caught for entirely different reasons than the speed of their dance. She didn't understand his reference entirely—no decent girl would—but she understood enough to know his innuendo was wicked. While she wasn't an expert on big men, she suddenly wished she was, especially if that big man was him.

'It's only that you don't dance much. I assumed it was because you didn't enjoy it or lacked skill,' she confessed openly, smartly letting his innuendo go untended. That was a battle of words she hadn't the experience to win. She cocked her head and took in the dark gaze, the smiling lips. 'Surely you see the contradiction. If you love to dance so much, why do you do it so seldom?'

His gaze lingered on her, meltingly warm. 'Perhaps because there are so few partners worthy of my efforts.'

She felt the heat rise in her cheeks yet again at the implied compliment—that *she* was worthy.

Continue reading

HOW TO COURT A RAKE
Bronwyn Scott

Available next month
millsandboon.co.uk

COMING SOON!

We really hope you enjoyed reading this book.
If you're looking for more romance
be sure to head to the shops when
new books are available on

Thursday 27th March

To see which titles are coming soon, please visit
millsandboon.co.uk/nextmonth

MILLS & BOON

Afterglow Books is a trend-led, trope-filled list of books with diverse, authentic and relatable characters, a wide array of voices and representations, plus real world trials and tribulations. Featuring all the tropes you could possibly want (think small-town settings, fake relationships, grumpy vs sunshine, enemies to lovers) and all with a generous dose of spice in every story.

♪ @millsandboonuk
⊙ @millsandboonuk
afterglowbooks.co.uk
#AfterglowBooks

For all the latest book news, exclusive content and giveaways scan the QR code below to sign up to the Afterglow newsletter:

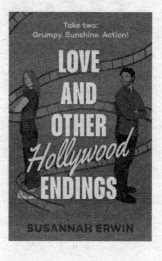

LET'S TALK

Romance

For exclusive extracts, competitions
and special offers, find us online:

f MillsandBoon

X @MillsandBoon

⊙ @MillsandBoonUK

♪ @MillsandBoonUK

Get in touch on 01413 063 232